Wild Horse Springs

Center Point
Large Print

**This Large Print Book carries the
Seal of Approval of N.A.V.H.**

Wild Horse Springs

A Ransom Canyon Romance

Jodi Thomas

CENTER POINT LARGE PRINT
THORNDIKE, MAINE

This Center Point Large Print edition
is published in the year 2017 by arrangement with
Harlequin Books S.A.

The text of this Large Print edition is unabridged.
In other aspects, this book may vary
from the original edition.
Printed in the United States of America
on permanent paper.
Set in 16-point Times New Roman type.

ISBN: 978-1-68324-429-5

Library of Congress Cataloging-in-Publication Data

Names: Thomas, Jodi, author.
Title: Wild horse springs / Jodi Thomas.
Description: Center Point Large Print edition. | Thorndike, Maine : Center Point Large Print, 2017.
Identifiers: LCCN 2017014591 | ISBN 9781683244295
    (hardcover : alk. paper)
Subjects: LCSH: Large type books. | GSAFD: Love stories.
Classification: LCC PS3570.H5643 W547 2017 | DDC 813/.54—dc23
LC record available at https://lccn.loc.gov/2017014591

CHAPTER ONE

Midnight
Friday

DAN BRIGMAN HAD been sheriff for half his life. He knew the county, the people and the potholes for miles around Crossroads, Texas. Now that his daughter, Lauren, was grown, being a lawman filled his time. He'd settled into a comfortable aloneness and counted himself lucky.

When he turned onto the county road on the third Friday in November, featherlight snow circled in the cruiser's headlights as if the beams caught winter's breath dancing in the dark along the silent stretch of highway. The first freeze of the season was whispering across the flatland, but Dan feared a storm would rage in a few hours.

He smiled. He loved this time of year. Most folks complained about the cold, the short days, the colorless landscapes, but he liked coming inside after a long day and warming by the fireplace. He loved napping through football games and craved all the food that came with the season. Green chili enchiladas, Hopkins County Stew, spicy pork ribs simmered all day in a slow cooker.

The sheriff laughed out loud. He was starting to sound like an old man. True, there was a brush of gray along his temples, but inside he felt like he was still young. In twenty years, if he kept getting reelected, he'd retire and have time to fish off his dock at the lake house. If he got bored, he'd drop by his old office to tell the next sheriff how to run the county. He'd never run with the bulls or climbed Everest or seen a foreign country, but he'd had a rich life.

Something bright blinked in his headlights just in front of him.

Dan hit the brakes.

With his beams on high, he climbed out of the cruiser, a flashlight in one hand and the other on the butt of his service weapon. The county road might be silent tonight, but this was 111, the stretch of highway where he'd been ambushed four years ago.

That day flashed through his mind more in sounds than pictures. Bullets pinging against the sides of his cruiser like hailstones. Tires popping as they went flat. Brakes squealing while he fought for control. Glass shattering across the windshield and raining onto the pavement.

Then, when all the noise stilled, all he'd felt was pain.

Three bullets were dug out of his body a few hours later. The six months of recovery seemed endless. Four years of peace since, and yet he could still hear the sounds of that one day. He'd watched his blood snake across the highway like a tiny river and pool into the dirt. He'd counted his heartbeats as if needing to know how many were left.

If it hadn't been for one kid pulling him away from the gunfire, he'd be buried in the Ransom Canyon Cemetery, his grave covered in snow tonight.

Dan pushed the memories aside as he focused the flashlight's beam on a sparkly blue object in the road.

A boot. One tall blue woman's boot stood proud on the center stripe. The kind of fancy boot with rhinestones and stitching in the leather from the ankle up. One like cowgirls wore to dance in until the bar closed. One that would never be worn to work cattle.

Dan relaxed as he stared down at the boot. County Road 111 was mostly traveled by locals, and none of the ranch folks wore fancy footwear like this.

"It's a mystery," he said aloud. Dan was fully aware that he was talking to himself, but then who was around to object?

He picked up the boot and walked back to his car. If someone had tossed it out, which wasn't likely, it probably wouldn't have been standing straight up on the center line. No one would have thrown away just one even if they hated wearing them. A pair like this probably cost five hundred dollars or more.

By the car light he examined his find. Deep blue, like the sky turned just before it rained. The sole was worn. No other scrapes. Whoever wore this never shoved it into a stirrup.

Dan put the boot in the passenger seat and pushed the car into gear. "Well, pretty lady," he said with a laugh. "How about riding along with me tonight?"

Any woman who wore a boot like this one would show it off. She'd have on tight jeans tucked into the top. She'd be outgoing, maybe wild. She'd laugh easy and probably yell when she argued. She'd take big gulps of life.

That kind of woman would never be attracted to him. Dan was as solid as the canyon walls, probably borderline boring if he thought about it, and as his daughter often reminded him, predictable.

Dan never allowed himself to daydream. He was always serious, a man who was his job, not one who just wore the uniform. But tonight, cloudy starless skies made the world seem more fantasy than real, and the rich blue leather sparkled in the dashboard lights.

"I guess I better start looking for Cinderella, because some cowgirl princess has lost her slipper."

He remembered how Lauren was always telling him he needed to go out now and then. Maybe he could text her a picture of the boot and tell her he'd made the first step. Lauren had probably meant he should date one of the church ladies who asked him for favors, such as judging the jams competitions for charity, or invited him to the Wednesday morning breakfast because they "needed more men." His daughter had not meant for him to step out with the kind of woman who'd wear a rhinestone boot.

It was almost one o'clock when the sheriff pulled into the Two Step Saloon's dirt parking lot. The bar was outside the city limits of Crossroads, but Dan swore he could hear the bass beating some nights from his office a few miles away. Most Friday nights he would have already had at least one call from the bartender before now. But since the Nowhere Club opened thirty miles south of Crossroads, business had dropped off along with arrests in Dan's county.

Grabbing the boot, Dan walked into the Two Step. Maybe, if the place wasn't too loud, or the folks too drunk, someone would remember seeing a lady wearing blue boots.

He relaxed. The main room was only half-full and most of the crowd looked far more interested in talking than fighting. Ike Perez, the owner, had put in a big-screen TV. If a game wasn't on, he played reruns. The drunks didn't seem to care. They cheered and bet as if they hadn't seen the game before.

"Evening, Sheriff," the bartender said as she reached for a cup and the coffeepot. "Wondered if you'd make it in tonight."

9

Dan stood at the corner of the bar, his back almost touching the wall. It was the only spot in the room where he could see the whole place. "Evening, Kimmie." The bartender might have been in AA for ten years, but she was still working making drinks. She reminded Dan of an old bull rider who walked among rough stock on the night before a rodeo. Kimmie might not take the ride anymore, but she stayed near the noise and the excitement.

When he set the fancy boot next to his cup, Kimmie winked at him. "If that's your date, I'd say you lost a bit of her on the way in."

Dan shrugged. "Story of my life. I start out with a woman and end up with a boot."

Kimmie crossed her arms and leaned against the railing of the bar that was just right to be boob resting height to her. "It might help, Sheriff, if you didn't wear your gun and uniform on a date. You're one fine-looking man, tall, lean and just enough gray to tell a lady that you probably know what you're doing, but, honey, all that hardware around your waist won't encourage any woman to cuddle up."

Dan took a gulp of the coffee. He never added any comment when Kimmie started telling him how to live his life. She might be in her late thirties, which made her dating age for him, but she'd never be his type.

In truth, Dan had decided he must not have a

type. Near as he could tell, any women he liked usually ran the other way. The first and the noisiest being his wife twenty years ago. When he'd refused to move to Dallas, Margaret packed a bag and left him with their only child. He'd raised Lauren and kept loving his wife for a long while, hoping she'd come back, but she only called monthly to lecture him on all the things he was doing wrong with his job, the town and most of all with raising their daughter.

It took him years to try even talking to a woman other than to ask for her driver's license. And then, none seemed right. Some never stopped talking; others expected him to carry the conversation.

Finally, when he decided to date a little, no woman felt right in his arms on the few occasions he managed to stay around long enough to hug her. Or, worse, she didn't seem that interested in him. At first he'd thought it was because he was divorced and raising his daughter or because of the career he loved, but lately, there just didn't seem to be a woman in the state he wanted to go out with.

Dan got to the point of his current problem. "I found the boot out on 111. Thought you might have seen someone wearing it."

Kimmie shook her head. "I found a cowboy boot under my bed once. Worn and muddy. Never did remember who it belonged to."

Dan didn't want to hear more of the bartender's love life. If she ever got around to writing down just the facts she'd been sober enough to remember, she'd have a shelf full of steamy encounters. Since she'd quit drinking, talking about sex had become her favorite pastime.

"Where's Ike?"

"He went over to check out that new bar. They call it the Nowhere Club like it was something fancy. What kind of name is that for a bar? Someone said they got a real singer over there. Can you imagine someone trying to sing to a bunch of drunks?"

Dan picked up the blue boot. "Maybe I will go check it out sometime."

Kimmie cleared his empty coffee cup and wiped down the bar. "I'll keep my eye out for a woman hobbling around on one boot. If I spot her, I'll send her your way."

"Thanks." Dan left thinking about what the owner of the boot must look like. Tall, he'd guess, to wear this high a boot. And wild as the West Texas wind. His imagination filled in the rest of her through the night when he should have been sleeping.

MONDAY MORNING HE carried the boot into his office and set it on the corner of his desk, still thinking about what kind of woman would own it. It might be nice to meet her when he wasn't in

12

uniform. Maybe, halfway through his life, it was about time he did something unpredictable.

All morning he worked on the paperwork that always piled up over the weekend like leftovers from Sunday dinner.

The blue boot kept crossing his line of vision as if whispering to him.

Pearly, the county secretary, came in a little after eleven with the mail. She spotted the boot. "You thinking of cross-dressing, Sheriff?"

Dan simply stared at her. Pearly hadn't asked a question worth answering in years.

"I have to leave." He stood. "I'll be back in an hour or so."

"Might as well eat lunch while you're out, Sheriff." Pearly started planning his day. "It's already almost lunchtime, and you know when you get back you'll have calls to return, and by the time you're finished it'll be too late to catch a lunch special. Next thing I know, Lauren will be home from Dallas complaining about how thin you look and telling me I should take better care of her father, like she left you in my charge."

"And the point of this discussion, Pearly?"

She puffed up. "Eat!" she shouted as if he needed to be addressed in single syllables.

Dan dug his fingers through hair in need of a cut and put on his Stetson. "Thanks, Mom, I'll remember that." He grabbed the boot and walked past Pearly. Dan hated being mothered, but some women had that gene wired in them.

He was two miles out of town when he glanced at the boot and grinned. "Where you want to go, babe?" he asked as if a woman were beside him.

Funny. Something about the boot riding shotgun made Sheriff Dan Brigman feel reckless.

CHAPTER TWO

Noon
Monday

BRANDI MALONE WATCHED a sheriff walk into the Nowhere Club as she worked in the shadows of the small stage. The place wouldn't be open for hours. She'd planned to rehearse for a while, but now she couldn't do that until the sheriff left. Somehow having someone watch her work out the kinks in her performance seemed like singing to a voyeur.

She liked this time of day in the bar when all was quiet and the air felt almost clean.

Growing up in a big family was noisy, and living close to them as an adult always made her feel like she was being watched. Her two brothers' and sister's families had settled within sight of the house they grew up in. But even when Brandi had moved back in her twenties, Malone Valley wasn't where she'd wanted to be, and when she'd left the second time, she'd sworn, as she had once before, that she'd never return.

The road had been her home for fourteen months. Brandi didn't have a house, an address, or anyone to report in to, and that was just fine with her.

Gig after gig on the road was her living room,

15

and at night she stepped out onto her front porch, which was her stage. Brandi Malone was butterfly free and wanted it that way.

She stood perfectly still, no more than a shadow, and waited for the man in uniform to vanish from her world.

The sheriff disappeared down the hallway to the owner's office. She wasn't curious. Her job was to be onstage for three sets a night. That was all. This was a bar; of course lawmen would drop by now and then. The sheriff was probably only checking the new liquor license, same as another sheriff did last week, or maybe he was looking for an outlaw, though this place didn't seem much like an outlaw bar.

She moved the mic closer to the piano, where she'd lined up her songs for tonight. Though she knew them all by heart, she always kept the sheet music close, just in case her mind wandered.

Brandi didn't worry about much, not where she lived or what she ate, or even what town she was in, but she wanted every performance to be perfect. It had to be. It was all she had left that mattered in her world.

Maybe she wanted, if only for a few minutes, for all those who were sober enough to listen, to forget about their problems and just enjoy. She wanted them to step into the music and dance on the sawdust floor or in their minds. That's what she did. For a few hours, if her songs were just right, she forgot all about the cavernous hole in her heart and swayed to the music. Her thoughts would slow to match the beat those nights, and for a short time she'd drift. She'd breathe deeply and almost believe life was worth living.

"Brandi!" Hank, the owner, yelled. "Sheriff's got something for you."

The tall man in a tan uniform moved toward her, and for a moment she considered running. But he was between her and the door, and the guy's face, framed in the shadows of his hat, looked like he operated strictly by the book.

She had no outstanding bills or fines or tickets. She hadn't committed a crime. There was no reason the law wanted her, so the sheriff must have questions about the bar, or maybe her old van parked outside . . .

Brandi stood and waited as the sheriff neared. She was stronger than she'd been months ago. She didn't have to run from questions.

When she'd first hit the road, she hated strangers asking where she was from or anything about her family. She didn't want to talk about anything but her music. Nothing else mattered. Nothing else existed.

Only, when this stranger in a uniform raised his eyes to look up at her standing on the small stage, he smiled as if he was happy to see her. "Morning, ma'am," he said.

She didn't miss that the lawman's eyes ran the

length of her body before he reached her face. Could he have been checking her out? Surely not. Not if he called her ma'am.

"Morning," she managed to say. "What's the problem?"

"No problem."

He smiled again, and she had the feeling that he was a man who didn't smile often. Brandi relaxed slightly. He had honest blue eyes.

"This wouldn't happen to be yours?" he asked as he lifted a boot. "It kind of looks like something you might wear."

Brandi exploded. "Yes! Someone stole them out of my van two weeks ago. In their hurry, they dropped the left one in the parking lot." She bounced down from the two-foot-high stage. "I loved those boots. I thought I'd lost this one forever, but I couldn't bring myself to toss the other one away."

The sheriff stood as stiff as a mannequin while she hugged him.

"Thank you. Thank you." She reached for the boot.

He pulled it away. "Now wait a minute. I have to have proof." He was smiling again, obviously enjoying himself. "Maybe you need to try it on. The slipper needs to fit. I think it's the law, or maybe just a rule."

She looked down at the tennis shoes she was wearing. "I have to have that boot. I own the match. One boot's no good without its mate."

"I'll need to see the left one first before I hand this one over."

"Follow me." She shifted and straightened as if planning to march, playing along with his game.

Her long legs made it easy to make the step onto the stage. She rushed behind a black curtain and opened an almost invisible door. She hoped the sheriff carrying her boot was following her. Guessing that he was watching her every twist, she slipped quickly into a narrow hallway, then left toward her dressing room.

He was right behind her.

The sheriff was in his forties, maybe five or six years older than her, and definitely interesting. She'd always liked talking to men with honest eyes. They were rare.

Brandi grinned as she tried to guess what the sheriff might be like out of uniform. He was that kind of handsome most women didn't notice. There was something so solid about him he seemed hard, except maybe for his mouth. The man had kissable lips, she decided, but she'd bet he'd never had an irresponsible thought.

And he wasn't for her. Forget that "attracted at first sight" thing. She no longer acted on impulses. Brandi had not only sworn off men, she'd sworn off family and friends, as well. For months she had simply drifted in the emptiness and the music, telling herself there was no future or past, just now. If she worked hard on just getting through one day at a time, she could survive and almost forget that her reason for living had gone.

Fourteen months and counting. Now wasn't the time to break her streak even to make one friend or take a lover. The very thought of having a lover after all these years made her smile. If she ever did take another lover, he would have blue eyes like the sheriff's. True blue.

She opened the door to a small room that doubled as her dressing room and the paper storage for the bar and bathrooms.

The sheriff followed her in.

"Leave the door open," she ordered.

"Of course," he answered, as if it were a rule he already knew.

He seemed to take up half the space in her small quarters as she tossed clothes around looking for the other boot.

"I'm not very organized," she admitted.

"I've seen squirrels better at it." He crossed his arms and waited.

"The boot is here somewhere." She was loaded down with clothes and still saw no sign of it. "Maybe it would be easier to try on the one you have." She plopped down on the room's only chair and tugged off her tennis shoe. The leggings she wore were warm and fit like second skin. "If it fits, I get to keep it, right?"

To her shock, he knelt on one knee and helped her with the boot. His hand slid along her calf as he pushed her foot gently into the leather.

Brandi couldn't move. His hand glided ahead of the boot until his fingers rested just above her knee. She could feel the warmth of him through the material as he pressed gently into her flesh as if he was testing to see if she were real.

"It fits perfect," he said. "I guess I've found Cinderella."

"Thanks for bringing it back. I'm really grateful, Sheriff."

"You're more than welcome. Just part of the job." He stood and offered his hand. "Dan Brigman."

She took his hand and stood, noticing he was only a few inches taller than her as she balanced on the one boot. "Can I buy you a drink, Sheriff, to say thank you?"

"No, thanks."

He hadn't turned loose of her fingers, and she wondered if she should ask for her hand back. When she looked down, she spotted the blue toe of her other blue cowboy boot and squealed as she jerked her hand away from him. She dropped to the floor so she could crawl under the card table that served as her dressing table.

He tried to step out of the way, but her bottom bumped into him several times before she backed out from under the flimsy table. Then she hopped around trying to tug on the second boot while accidentally bumping into him again.

He gripped her waist and steadied her as she finally got the boot on.

When she straightened, he let go of her, but one hand rose to brush her hair from her face.

"You have a mass of long hair, pretty lady. It seems to fly around you like a midnight cloud. I've got a daughter who has hair as long as yours, but hers is straight and the color of sunshine."

"Sorry." She shook her head back. "My hair's always had a mind of its own. I not only kicked you while I was trying to pull on the boot, you probably got a mouthful of curls."

"I'll survive." He laughed.

"Sure you won't take that drink? I feel like I owe you one, Sheriff."

"No, but I might let you buy me lunch. The best Mexican food place for a hundred miles around is right across the street."

Brandi wasn't looking to be picked up, and she couldn't tell if the sheriff was trying to start something. If so, he was so far out of practice with this switch from a drink to lunch thing. She needed to cut this off quick. "Wouldn't you rather go home and have lunch with your family?" The last thing she needed was to get involved with a married man.

He hesitated but didn't back away like a man who'd been trying to flirt might. "My wife left me twenty years ago, and my daughter is grown and now lives in Dallas. If you don't want to come along, I'm still planning on eating Mexican food. Pearly, my secretary, told me to eat lunch before I came back, and she's not an easy woman to cross."

Brandi felt like a fool. The sheriff wasn't using a line on her. If he thought he was, it came pretty close to the worst one she'd ever heard. He'd given her the facts of his life as small-town people did. As people who have nothing to hide did.

"My name's Brandi Malone."

"I guessed that. Saw it on the board out front." He backed a few steps to the door. "It was nice to meet you, Miss Malone. Maybe I'll come hear you sing sometime."

"Do that," she said, noticing neither bothered with goodbye.

After he disappeared, she decided that the sheriff was shy. She'd embarrassed him by insinuating that he was trying to flirt, or maybe he felt like he'd dumped too much information on a total stranger.

She dug through her pile of clothes and pulled on her leather jacket with fringe. It wasn't warm enough for today's weather, but she didn't have time to find another coat.

Five minutes later she stepped out of the Nowhere and walked across the street. One car,

23

the sheriff's cruiser, was in the café's parking lot. The lunch run was long past being over. She wasn't surprised he'd kept to his word.

Brandi was shivering when she made it to the table in the back where he sat alone. "This place still open?" she asked.

He looked up from his cell phone. She caught the surprise in his eyes before he glanced away.

"I'm buying your lunch, Sheriff. You have a problem with that?"

"No." He stood and moved his hat off the empty chair. "You think you could call me Dan? I don't think of myself as on duty while I'm eating."

She slowly slipped into the place across from him and stared at the menu. Most men, including her father, were liars or manipulators. But this one had something about him that said he could be trusted, at least as long as lunch, anyway. All she had to figure out was if Sheriff Dan Brigman was what he seemed. Not that she planned to stay around long, but at least if those honest eyes were true, she might start to believe in people again.

It might be fun to eat a meal with someone for a change. She could pretend to be happy, and interested and normal.

She glanced at the menu for a few seconds more, then ordered the lunch special when the waitress appeared. The girl looked tired, or maybe bored, and wasn't overly concerned with the last two customers in the place.

When the waitress went back through the kitchen door before it stopped swinging from her arrival, Brandi was suddenly aware that she was alone with the sheriff.

"You look exactly like the woman I pictured would be wearing that boot," he said, as if trying to start a conversation.

"How's that?"

"Wild and free. Beautiful." He glanced down, twirling a chip in the tiny bowl of hot sauce.

There was that shy smile again, she thought. Another hint that the sheriff might be one of the real people in this world of marionettes. "You don't mind if I'm wild, do you? I'd think a thing like that might make a sheriff nervous."

"Nope. I don't mind. You're the kind of beautiful that could haunt a man's dreams, Brandi Malone. Being wild just adds spice to perfection."

No one had said such a nice thing to her in years. He seemed to be seeing her as she wanted to be. *Wild and free,* she almost whispered aloud.

To prove him right, Brandi leaned over and kissed him on the mouth.

When she pulled away she whispered, "You taste like salsa, Sheriff."

He just stared, and she swore she could be hypnotized by those steel-blue eyes.

Brandi ate one of his chips dipped in the hot sauce, then took a drink of his iced tea. He just kept watching her. No one had accused her of being wild and free for years, and she loved it. She loved the version of herself she saw in his eyes.

She glanced around the empty café. The lone waitress was probably in the back warming up the last two specials. "Aren't you going to say something about me kissing you?"

He leaned back and spoke so low even if people had been at the next table they wouldn't have heard. "I wouldn't mind if you decided to do that again."

Before she could decide, the waitress swung through the kitchen door with two plates of enchiladas.

"Maybe later." She grinned like the wild woman he thought she was. "If I'm still around and you're still available." After all, how much harm could one more kiss do?

As they ate, the sheriff asked her where she was from and how she ended up at the Nowhere Club.

She avoided answering and asked him how long it had been since he'd been kissed.

Unlike her, Dan answered directly. "Three years ago on New Year's Eve."

Brandi nodded. "The midnight kiss. Open-mouthed or closed?"

When he didn't answer, she knew. Closed, she decided. She would have sworn the handsome sheriff was blushing.

"You're right about me, Sheriff. But I'm drifting more than free. I live out of a suitcase and travel whenever and wherever I like. I'm not looking for a man to tame me or tie me down or tell me he loves me. I make no promises, but if you'd like to share a meal or something now and then, I might be interested." Brandi couldn't believe she was stepping out of her comfort zone to even think of getting together with him. But one kiss with him was like one taste of salsa on a salty chip. She wanted another.

Dan took a long drink of his iced tea.

She knew she'd shocked him, but if she was going to spend a while with a man for the first time in years, she wanted all the cards on the table. And, she decided, she wanted to be remembered as being someone's unforgettable encounter, no matter how brief. She'd like to be the one woman, the one memory that would always make Dan Brigman smile.

He ate, and she picked at her food.

Finally, he broke the silence. "What time is your last set over tonight?"

"Eleven. Why?"

"I'll pick you up for a late supper."

"If you can find a place around here still open, I'll be hungry."

He left a twenty on the table and stood.

"I . . ." She'd told him she'd pick up the check, and she planned to.

"It's not happening," he answered, as if he knew what she was about to say.

She followed, already wondering if she'd done the right thing to join him here. She hated bossy men, but then maybe there was some kind of rule that sheriffs can't accept gifts, even a lunch.

She'd been just fine staying away from men. She liked being alone. She hated strings and planned to live the rest of her life without getting attached to anyone. So why had she hinted at another promise? Another meeting? Why had she offered to spend time with him before she knew what kind of man he really was? Maybe honest blue eyes lied? She hadn't been around enough to know.

Brandi mentally slapped herself. She was overthinking this. Just go with it. She was wild, remember.

Maybe it was enough that he had kissable lips and he made her feel young like she had ten years ago when she'd first been on the road. She'd been twenty-five then and loving the gypsy life of a singer.

When they stepped out of the restaurant into the little tin windbreaker foyer, the sheriff turned and helped her with her coat. The plastic window in the entryway door looked like it was shivering as wind howled over the cloudy day.

He lifted part of her curly hair, caught under her collar. "Before we step out I want to give you something back."

Before she had time to say a word, he pushed

her against the rattling, icy tin wall and kissed her full out. Openmouthed.

Her sheriff might be quiet, but he definitely wasn't shy.

Brandi forgot all about being cold. For the first time in longer than she could remember, she felt alive. She wrapped her arms around his neck and kissed him back like this one kiss might be the last in her lifetime.

His arms tightened around her. She leaned into him. This wasn't a first-time, hesitant kiss. She could feel him breathing, his heart pounding next to hers. A tiny spark came alive inside her where only dead embers had lain for so long.

When he broke the kiss, he didn't say a word; he just circled his arm around her shoulders and held her tightly as they faced the wind and rushed back across the street.

Just inside the club, the whole world lost all sound. No one around. No music. He held her for a moment as though unable to let her go. Though he hadn't moved, she could feel him pulling away, turning back into the in-control sheriff. His lips pressed against her forehead in a quick peck. "You're unbelievable."

"You, too," she whispered, swearing she could see passion sparkle in his blue eyes.

Then, with a very formal nod, he turned and walked away without a word.

Brandi grinned as she watched him climb into

his cruiser and thought she'd add that Toby Keith song "A Little Less Talk and a Lot More Action" to her last set tonight. If the sheriff wanted someone wild and free, she could make it happen.

In a few weeks she'd drive away from this place. Maybe she'd take a memory of her own with her. But that was all she had room to pack.

A memory. Nothing more.

CHAPTER THREE

RAINY NIGHTS IN DALLAS were never as beautiful as they had been when she was a kid growing up at the lake house just outside Crossroads. There, the old cottonwoods whispered when the wind blew, and the rain tap-dancing on the water twenty feet from her window often lulled her to sleep.

Her hometown seemed a million miles away tonight. She stared out her apartment windows at the solid brick wall of the condo next door. No view.

If her pop wouldn't think she was a failure, she'd load up all she owned in a U-Haul and drive back home. She could be there in five or six hours. She'd cook her father's breakfast and then follow him to the county sheriff's office, where she'd work all day organizing his files. They'd eat lunch at Dorothy's Diner across the street and pretend she was sixteen again with the world waiting on her to grow up, and not twenty-five, waiting for the world to realize she was a failure.

Lauren pulled out her cell, thinking she could call her pop. It was almost nine. He'd probably be finishing up his day, heading home with his supper in a bag, looking forward to eating in front of the TV, which would be tuned to a football game. In an hour he'd be sound asleep in his recliner.

Pop was so predictable. When she was growing up, he cooked the same meals every week. Chili dogs on Monday, pancakes with burned sausage on Tuesday, grilled chicken and baked potatoes on Wednesday, meat loaf or spaghetti on Thursday. They had take-out pizza on Friday and leftovers, if there were any, on Saturday. Sundays they ate out or warmed up cans of soup. Oh, she almost forgot, they usually had hamburgers if he got home late. If she hadn't learned to cook early, he probably would have stuck to that menu until she left for college. She was twelve before she knew appetizers could be something besides potato chips.

Now, their conversations were the same. For her, work was always great, yes, she was making friends, no, she didn't need any money. For him, he'd tell her about the weather, talk about the folks in town who'd ask about her, and say no, he wasn't lonely, he was doing fine.

Lauren shoved her cell back into her pocket. She didn't call. Tonight she wasn't sure she could stand to hear him tell her one more time how proud he was of her.

His Lauren was moving up, honing her skills as a writer. It wouldn't be long until she finished a book and was on the bestseller list, he'd say.

Crossroads just might have to open a bookstore in town with Lauren's first book about to hit any day and Tim O'Grady working on his fourth novel.

She'd heard Pop brag to everyone, and she hadn't said a word. She'd had three jobs in a year, all ending in being laid off. None in publishing. She was not moving up or working on her book. The chance of anyone from Crossroads filling a bookstore shelf was highly unlikely, with her manuscript unfinished and Tim's novels all ebooks.

If the Crossroads Bookstore ever opened, the "local author" shelf would be empty.

Lauren jumped out of her self-pity when her phone buzzed.

Tim O'Grady's name flashed along with his smiling face. She grinned and answered.

"Hello, Hemingway, don't tell me you've just finished another book." Lauren tried to sound happy. He always called to celebrate over the phone when he finished anything. The outline. The edit. The final draft.

She always acted excited, and she suspected he always tried his best to sound sober.

"Hi, L."

For once he actually did sound sober.

"You able to talk? Not on a date or anything?" He paused. When she didn't answer, he added, "And no, before you ask, the book's not finished.

Tonight I'm dealing with real life."

"I'm home." She dropped to the couch. "Alone. What's up? Talk to me." She needed a little bit of home, and talking to the boy she'd grown up next door to might help.

"I don't know what you can do about it, but I need help. We've got a real mess here, and I don't know how to handle it."

"What's happened?" She could feel bad news coming and wished someone would invent an umbrella that could protect her for just one breath so she would be ready.

"Thatcher Jones is in jail." Tim said the words fast, as if he had to get them out of his mouth. "He's eighteen, so no juvie for him. He's locked upstairs at the county offices."

"What! Does Pop know? What happened? Is he okay?"

"Slow down, L." Tim's laugh didn't have much humor in it. "Of course your pop knows. He's the one who arrested him. Which was lucky for the kid. Thatcher's easygoing, but when he gets mad, he blows up. Your pop can handle him."

"Facts, Tim, give me the facts."

"You know that truck stop on the Lubbock Highway? The one where we used to stop because you couldn't make it all the way home from college without a potty break, then you'd complain about how dirty it was?"

"I remember. It has a little grocery store on one

side. Carries two cans of everything, including motor oil."

"Well, I don't know why Thatcher was out there. It's the opposite direction from Charley Collins's place, and he said he was heading home from school. You'd think Charley would be a good influence on him. But I guess some people are just destined to cross with the law."

Lauren rolled her eyes. Charley Collins had been as reckless as they come when he was in high school. His own father disowned him, but Charley was a good man and so was Thatcher. "Tim, stop sounding like a line from a book. Get back to what happened to Thatcher."

She swore she could almost hear Tim nodding. "Right. Thatcher was in the store out at the truck stop with a backpack full of groceries that hadn't been bought. He said he was bringing them back, but old Luther, who owns the place, didn't believe him. Called Thatcher nothing but a lying thief. Said he'd known three generations of his people, and they were all trash."

"What happened next?"

"Thatcher swung. Knocked Luther out, I heard."

Lauren closed her eyes, almost able to see the scene in her mind. "Go on," she whispered into her phone.

"Thatcher was the one who called 911. When the sheriff and medics got there, Luther said he

35

was pressing charges for assault and robbery. The medics took Luther to the clinic to be checked, and your dad took Thatcher to jail."

"No!"

Tim swore. "Believe me, L, your pop wasn't happy about it. He looked like he was thinking of strangling the kid for making him do it."

"When did this happen?"

"A couple hours ago. When I heard the sirens, I drove over to the county offices thinking whatever was happening might give me a plot idea. I could hear Thatcher yelling the minute I walked in the door. He was mad and scared and all wrapped up in nervous energy."

Tim finally paused. When he spoke again, his words came slowly. "We can't let him go to prison, L."

She thought of mentioning that they were not his parents, but in a strange way the whole town was. Thatcher Jones had been over a year behind in school and living on the fringes of right and wrong when Charley Collins at the Lone Heart Ranch took him in. Anyone could see that the kid had a heart bigger than Texas, but he was proud and had a stubborn streak.

"What do we do?" Tim asked in a dull tone, as if he really didn't expect her to answer.

"You're right. We have to fix this. Thatcher saved Pop's life once. He might have been only fourteen or fifteen then, but he ran through gunfire to get Pop to safety. Pop will do his job, he's always played by the book, but he'll help where he can, too." Her logical mind began to put all the pieces she knew together. "Why would Thatcher steal food? I've heard Charley's place is going great."

"He swears he didn't. Says he was just bringing the canned goods back, but he says he doesn't remember who he got them from. Wouldn't even tell the sheriff if it was a man or woman who must have stole them in the first place. Just says he can't say." Tim laughed. "While Luther was out cold, Thatcher put the food back on the shelf, so there is some confusion as to exactly what was taken."

"So there is no evidence of a crime?"

"Right, unless you count the shiner on Luther's face." Tim hesitated. "L, you were in law school once. You'll figure out something."

"I never took the bar, remember. I decided to be a writer. Only that doesn't seem to be working out so well for me. I don't think taking customer complaints at the mall counts as training." She didn't want to go into all the reasons she was failing. Part of her wanted to simply say she was failing to thrive out in the real world.

"Come home." Tim ended the silence, his voice already pulling her. "Thatcher needs you and I miss you."

"I'll see if I can get off by noon tomorrow. I'll be there by five."

"Great." Tim hesitated. "How about staying with me this time? I've completely remodeled my folks' old place on the lake. You'd like it. Plus, your pop knows you're an adult. He'd understand. You could just say we're having an adult sleepover."

"I'll think about it," she answered. Tim had asked before, but she wasn't ready for any commitment between them. Staying over at his place meant sleeping together. "I'll call when I'm close to Crossroads so you can meet me at the county offices." She hung up without saying goodbye, then sat very still thinking of Tim, not Thatcher.

She'd grown up with Tim O'Grady, gone skinny-dipping in the lake with him when they were ten. Spent a thousand hours talking with him. He was her best friend.

A friend with benefits, she thought, though she could count their nights together on her fingers. Of course she loved him, but not in the way he wanted her to love him. When they occasionally slept together, it was more out of a need not to be alone than passion. She hated that she thought of his loving as vanilla, but somehow she wanted more. Everyone said they were right for each other, a match. Only everyone was wrong.

Tim loved her, really loved her, but she couldn't love him back. They never talked about it, but somehow they both knew the truth, and that one silent truth broke both their hearts.

She'd go home. She'd find a way to help Thatcher. But this time she wouldn't sleep with Tim. Even though it felt good for a while. Even though they both understood the silent rules.

She wouldn't sleep with Tim because she couldn't bear the look he'd give her when she had to walk away. Every time. Always.

CHAPTER FOUR

Tuesday

WEAK AFTERNOON SUNLIGHT filtered through the blinds, reminding Dan Brigman another hour had passed without sleep, and the day was only getting worse. He'd barely had time to hug his daughter before she was storming up the steps toward the third floor of the county offices. The tapping rain off and on all afternoon had already given him a headache, and having Lauren show up to interfere with his job wasn't helping.

He'd left the sexy singer yesterday after lunch, looking forward to seeing her again before midnight, but a call came in an hour after he got back to the office that ended that possibility. Since four o'clock yesterday, he'd had to arrest a kid he cared about for assault, then field a dozen calls from people telling him how to do his job. Midnight passed with him sitting up in the third-floor lockup with a teenager who refused to talk about what he'd done. Now, after he'd had no sleep for nearly thirty hours, his daughter arrived, demanding to know if he'd lost his mind.

At this point, Dan wasn't sure his ears still worked. The whole town could take turns telling him how to be sheriff, and he still wouldn't let

Thatcher Jones out until the judge set bail. Once he knew how much it would take, Dan had already decided he'd pay it himself.

His daughter was running through facts he already knew about the crime, so Dan simply followed one step behind as she headed upstairs.

"Now calm down, Lauren," he finally commented when she breathed. "We're doing all we can. The judge says he can bail out if he'll give a statement, but Thatcher isn't cooperating."

"Did you offer him a lawyer?"

Dan huffed. "I did. He said he didn't need a lawyer to tell me that he's not talking. He can do that himself."

She wasn't listening, and he didn't blame her. If they were doing *all they could do,* Thatcher Jones wouldn't still be locked up in the first place. His daughter always thought the world had to be balanced and fair, but it just wasn't.

If it had any fairness at all, he'd be sleeping off a wild memory and not putting in a forty-hour workday.

He almost swore. If the world were fair, he would have picked up that singer, Brandi Malone, last night like he'd planned, and not be stuck babysitting Thatcher. The kid was so wild he probably would have gnawed through the steel bars if he'd been left alone.

Dan unlocked the third-floor door, deciding that Lauren's anger was all his fault. He'd raised her. "We're working on it. We'll figure this out," he said as she stormed past him.

Before he opened the second door to the county lockup, he waited for his daughter to calm. The sound of Tim O'Grady tromping up the stairs echoed through the building. Tim was like the Ransom Canyon County Offices' resident ghost. He came, night or day, if he thought something was happening. He claimed it helped him with his writing, gave him ideas, but since his last two books were postapocalyptic thrillers for hormone-crazed teens, Dan didn't see that his research at the sheriff's office was doing much good. The young writer was interesting, though, and he'd been Lauren's friend since they could both walk, so Dan tolerated O'Grady even if it did irritate him that Lauren called him Hemingway.

Of course, Dan wasn't the least bit surprised that Tim was with her today. He'd probably called her to notify her about Thatcher.

Finally, Lauren turned and faced him. "Why is he in jail, Sheriff? Give me the facts."

Lauren only called him that when she was too angry to remember he was her father.

"He won't talk. No one believes he stole food from Luther's old truck stop, and nobody believes his story about not remembering how he got the backpack full of canned goods obviously from the store."

Thatcher must have heard them because he

42

yelled from twenty feet away, "I ain't telling who I got the stolen groceries from, and that's final. I took them back, isn't that good enough? I'll rot in this place before I talk. And I didn't attack Luther. He insulted me and my whole family. I'm not arguing that my no-name dad and run-off mother were trash, but that don't give him the right to remind me."

Lauren stormed into the next room, which had one cell on either side of a wide-open space in-between. "Stop talking like an idiot, Thatcher. We're trying to get you into Texas Tech this fall, and you'll never make it talking like that."

Dan left the doors open for O'Grady as he leaned against the opposite cell and enjoyed watching his daughter yell at someone besides him for a while.

Tim O'Grady and Lauren might not be more than six or seven years older than Thatcher, but they'd thought of themselves as his substitute parents since they'd all three worked together one summer. Thatcher had been painting the county offices, working off fines. Tim was collecting ideas for his writing. Lauren was organizing her father's office, something she'd done every summer since she was ten.

Thatcher might be four years older than he'd been that summer, but his respect for Lauren was obvious as he stood and gripped the bars. He'd grown a few inches since Lauren had been home, but he was still bone-thin. His hair was as wild as prairie grass, and he was tanned so deep his skin hadn't lightened even if winter was settling in for a long stay.

Part of Dan hoped no one ever changed the kid. He was a blend of Tom Sawyer and Billy the Kid with a little bit of a young Abe Lincoln mixed in. He'd been born two hundred years too late to be understood and damn if the kid cared.

Thatcher smiled suddenly, that easy smile that would melt hearts someday, but Lauren didn't smile back.

He lowered his voice. "Hell, look at me, Lauren. I'm in jail. The chances of any college taking me are not looking too good right now." He bumped his forehead against the bars. "But double damn. I got to make it to Tech for Kristi's sake. If I don't get there and save her, she'll find some brainiac like O'Grady and start hanging out with him. They'll probably marry and have a dozen little redheaded kids with not one of them having a lick of common sense."

Tim finally caught up with the sheriff and Lauren. "What's wrong with red hair? And what makes you think my kids wouldn't have common sense?"

Thatcher sighed. "You superglued your fingers together that summer I met you. You hooked your ear the last time we tried fly-fishing. You—"

"I'm not in jail," Tim interrupted.

Lauren slapped at Thatcher's knuckles and flashed Tim a dirty look. "Shut up, the both of you. We've got to get organized and get you out without some kind of record hanging over you. If we just knew who did steal the food, maybe we could clear this up."

"I already told you I ain't telling. Not even if you torture me."

The sheriff leaned over Lauren's shoulder. "Don't give me any ideas, kid."

Tim swore as he paced the space between the cells. "I've already tried getting him to talk, Sheriff. Nothing works. We always end up back at square one. The kid is tormenting me. Maybe I should file a complaint. I've been here all morning talking to him, and all that's happening is my red hair is falling out."

Thatcher reached out and almost grabbed the front of Tim's sweatshirt. "I'm not a kid, O'Grady. Call me that one more time, and you'll be swallowing teeth. The sheriff's the only one who can call me that. I'm eighteen."

"What are you going to do?" Tim shouted. "Knock me out, too, like you did Luther when he accused you of stealing? At the rate you're going, you'll have to do double time in prison to ever see daylight."

Lauren shook her head. Her long, straight blond hair waving down her back reminded Dan of how Brandi Malone's dark hair had seemed to come alive when she moved. Had it only been noon yesterday when he'd touched those dark curls and thought he'd see her by midnight? It seemed like a lifetime since he'd kissed the singer on the forehead and left the Nowhere Club.

He should have kissed her that last time on the mouth. The way his luck was running right now, Dan might never see his wild beauty again.

Tim's loud lecture drew the sheriff back from his thoughts. O'Grady was overreacting as usual. If he wrote as fast as he talked, he'd have a dozen books out by now.

When Lauren glanced in Dan's direction, he winked at her, silently letting her know that the world was not as dark as she thought it might be.

She finally realized that her father, not just a sheriff, was right beside her. She leaned close to him so he'd hear her over Tim's rant. "Okay, Pop, what do we do now?"

Tim gave up talking and listened for a change.

"I tried talking Luther out of pressing charges," Dan began. "I had no luck. But he used to give you free ice cream even after I'd already said no. Maybe you and Tim should go out to the truck stop and give it a shot. Since the stolen goods were found in the store, that charge won't hold, but the assault might." Dan was too tired to think of any other option.

"But—" Lauren started to argue.

Dan pushed his only option. "Talk to him. It

might not change anything, but who knows, it might help."

"What about Thatcher?"

"I'll be right here." Dan glanced at the kid. "He's not going anywhere for a while. Charley Collins has already talked to him and is out trying to get him a lawyer. The Franklin sisters called to tell me I'd better not even think of feeding him prison food. They're bringing his meals from the bed and breakfast."

"You have prison food?" Lauren smothered a giggle.

Dan shook his head. "That's not the worst of it. I've had half a dozen blankets delivered and threats called in that I'd better not let the boy freeze in a cold cell."

"You let people threaten you?"

"Sure. One was Miss Bees. She has to be ninety, but she considers it her civic duty to call in a threat at least once a month. Another was Vern Wagner. I don't think he knew what he was mad about, but Miss Bees probably told him to call in. A few others just dropped off threats with the blankets."

Lauren tilted her head, looking in the cell. "I don't see any blankets."

"Pearly's examining them now for hacksaws. She learned the word *contraband* from a TV show last year, and now her new word keeps bouncing around in the office." Dan realized he was starting to sound like a Saturday Night Live skit. Big cities had gangs and major crime; he had senior citizens and do-gooders. Some days it seemed to Dan he had the roughest beat.

Lauren put her hand on her father's arm. "Maybe I should come home to help you, Pop? I did study law, even if I did chicken out on taking the bar."

"I thought you did come home to ride shotgun," he said with a smile. "Any chance you and Tim could take the late shift, if Thatcher is still locked up tonight? You two are as close to deputies as I've got right now. Fifth Weathers is down in Austin for training, so I'm shorthanded. I've got something I have to do tonight, and Thatcher is in no danger other than being fed to death or smothered by quilts."

"You got a date?" she teased.

"Yeah, with a wild, hot lady." He told the truth, knowing she wouldn't believe him.

"Sure, Pop." She laughed. "Any way I can help. You look tired. Go home. Go to bed."

"My plan exactly." In his mind, his fingers were already moving into Brandi Malone's mass of midnight hair.

FIVE HOURS LATER, Lauren was curled up next to Tim in the empty cell, watching a zombie movie on his laptop.

Thatcher had borrowed her phone and moved to the far corner of his cell. She guessed he was

48

talking to Kristi, the only girlfriend he'd ever had, but Kristi must have been carrying the conversation because Thatcher hadn't said a word in ten minutes. He just nodded now and then, as if Kristi could see him through the phone.

"This is not what I meant when I suggested spending the night together, L," Tim whispered as he inched his fingers under her sweater.

"Look at the bright side. We're almost alone." Lauren gently shoved his hand away. She gave him a look that silently whispered, *not here, not now.*

"Yeah, but we're both dressed and have a teenage jailbird watching over us." Tim looked more resigned than frustrated. He never pushed, even when they were alone, even when she didn't bother to give a reason for shoving him away.

She shifted out from under his arm. "We've got to do something to help Thatcher. I can't stand just waiting around to see if something happens. This could go bad fast, Tim, and if Thatcher's officially charged, it may be too late."

"What can we do? It's almost midnight."

She didn't look at him when she whispered, "We've got to call Lucas."

Lauren didn't want to chance Tim seeing how she felt about Lucas, so she glanced away. They'd all been friends in high school, which seemed like a lifetime ago. "If we call him tonight, he could be here by eight in the morning."

"Lucas is big time, L. I read an article online that says he's moving up in that fancy firm he stepped into right out of college. A few years from now, I wouldn't be surprised if he runs for office or becomes a judge or a senator or something. He wouldn't drop everything and come back home to maybe help a kid he's probably never met. We might have all been friends years ago, but those days are long gone."

Lauren closed her eyes, fighting back tears. The Lucas she once knew would come, but the Lucas who worked in Houston now hadn't called once to check on her since she graduated college. That Lucas, if he came home at all, didn't call friends from the past when he was in town.

She'd never told anyone, not even Tim, how much she'd loved the young Lucas, the one full of dreams.

Tim would only be hurt if he knew another had been in her heart since she was fifteen. It was better that he didn't know about what had happened between her and Lucas, the promises they'd whispered once, the few stolen moments they'd shared. As her best friend, Tim would be surprised she'd never told him. As her lover, he'd be crushed that she'd held someone else in her dreams all this time.

Lauren stood and walked to the window. Had anything really happened between her and Lucas? she wondered. Had she simply cobbled together a romance from a few kisses and wishes? At fifteen she'd been crazy about the boy who'd saved her from an accident. At eighteen she'd thought they'd be together through college, but he'd pulled away. At twenty-one they'd shared a passionate kiss that had gone nowhere. Maybe the Lucas she knew was more in her imagination than real.

Stick to the facts, she almost whispered aloud. How she felt about Lucas Reyes didn't matter. Thatcher needed help, and Lucas was the most powerful lawyer she knew.

Lauren held her hand out toward Thatcher. "I need to borrow my phone back."

He said a quick goodbye and handed over her cell. "No problem. We were into reruns of the argument anyway."

Lauren felt sorry for him. "Everything all right with you and Kristi?"

Thatcher shrugged. "I don't know. I don't think so. She talked for a while and then got real mad because I asked her for the summary. I told her I was too tired to listen much longer."

He dropped onto his cot, which was padded with several blankets. "I swear I don't understand her. Every time I think I know where I stand with her, the world shifts and I lose my marker."

Lauren knew how he felt.

Walking out into the hallway, she sat on the first step. All the offices were closed now, and the wooden steps descended into darkness below.

Pushing the number that had been Lucas Reyes's cell in college, she waited. If he'd changed his number, she had no way of reaching him. If he said no, she could think of nowhere else to turn.

One ring. Two, three.

She shouldn't have called. Not this late. Not without having thought about what she'd say.

Four, five, six.

"Hello," a deep, sleepy voice said.

"Lucas?" She couldn't believe he was on the line. It had been so long. A thousand days, a million dreams.

"Lauren," he whispered.

For a few moments, they just breathed as if they weren't hundreds of miles apart.

"Is something wrong?" he asked. "Is there some emergency?"

She could hear his voice hardening, becoming more formal, putting a distance between them that couldn't be simply measured in miles. He'd whispered once when they stared up at the stars that she was his sky. Did he remember?

Lauren followed his lead. Talk about the problem at hand, not her own feelings. "I need some legal advice."

"Are you in trouble?"

"No. It's a friend. A kid in Crossroads. I was hoping you could come help." She realized she wasn't the right one to talk to a lawyer about Thatcher's case. He obviously didn't even want help, and her father might be mad that she hadn't waited to see if he could figure things out.

She heard paper shuffling and a click like a lamp being turned on.

The voice that finally came back was cold, a stranger. "Give me the facts."

She suddenly wished she hadn't called. "It's really only an assault charge. I thought you might be able to do something. I shouldn't have bothered you. I'm sorry I woke you."

"Give me the facts, Lauren."

"I shouldn't have called." It dawned on her how Lucas probably made sure their paths never crossed. He'd never called. Never texted. She knew he was still on the other end of the phone waiting for her to make sense.

"Goodbye," she whispered, as she fought not to cry.

Just before she ended the call she heard him say, "I'll be there tomorrow morning."

The phone went dead before she could say no.

CHAPTER FIVE

Tuesday night

THATCHER JONES WALKED to the barred window in his cell and looked out at the snowy streets three flights below. Most folks thought of Crossroads as a wide spot in the road and had little reason to slow down as they passed, but he'd always viewed the tiny place as grand. When you'd grown up out in the Breaks where folk hunted their own meat and some did without electricity, the town felt like big time.

Few people who lived between the city-limit signs knew what it was like to check the house for snakes before you turned in at night, or wash your clothes on a board and hang them out to dry. They'd never had to eat a potato or a can of beans and call it supper. Or to grow up, not only without cell phones and computers, but without TV or microwaves or heat in more than one room.

He'd known that life and felt lucky for it, but Thatcher didn't want to go back. He loved living in his own little place on the Lone Heart Ranch. He'd walk over to the main house for meals, or to work with Charley, or help Lillie, Charley's daughter, with her homework, then the rest of his time was his. Thatcher heard someone say once that the measure of wealth was being in control of time. If so, he was a rich man at eighteen.

Or he had been, before he ended up here in jail.

He knew some of the people on the two floors below worried about how he was surviving being locked up. They didn't understand this was a five-star hotel to him compared to living in the Breaks when he was younger. Great meals, company sitting up with him and being toasty warm. If he hadn't had to give up freedom for the place, he might ask if he could stay awhile.

Crossroads might not have a movie theater or a Starbucks, but the town had stores and a clinic and churches, and, unfortunately, a jail with locked doors. Kristi told him she was ashamed of him because the whole town knew he was there. He guessed she was right. The window's light reflected out on the crossing of the two main highways, so anyone who looked up could see him.

Staring out over the sleeping town, the porch lights shining like tiny stars and the shadow of a half-finished bandstand right in the middle of it all, he tried to figure out where his life had taken a wrong turn. All he was trying to do was help out, and somehow it ended him up here.

He'd seen a frightened little girl no bigger than Lillie, Charley's daughter, had been when he'd met her. The girl had on an old red coat that was way too large for her and was trying her best to lug a big backpack along the muddy side of the road.

"Who wouldn't help?" he murmured to himself. But somehow it had all turned bad, and he couldn't figure out how to get out of trouble without bringing harm to the little red riding hood.

Lauren and Tim took turns lecturing him after the sheriff left last night, but nothing they could say was as bad as what he was yelling at himself inside. He had his future all planned out. He was focused. He'd saved enough for the first year of college, even though Charley Collins had said he'd pay.

Thatcher had Kristi waiting for him to get to Texas Tech. He figured if he got to Tech and studied hard, she'd plan the rest of their lives. Marriage, a couple kids, maybe a farm.

He looked around, hoping Lauren would bring her phone up and he could call Kristi back. Man, she was mad at him. Like this was all his fault.

The sheriff's daughter was still somewhere beyond the doors of his prison, and Tim seemed busy writing notes. He'd mumbled that he had to get inspiration down when it hit. Thatcher had read a few of his books, and apparently inspiration came to "Hemingway" more as a dribble than a solid hit.

Maybe they'd left him alone to think, but Thatcher had given up on that, too. What good was it doing him? He might as well become an outlaw. Too bad it wasn't the Wild West, where a man lived by a code and his Colt. Where right was right and wrong was wrong.

He wished it were that simple now. When he'd stopped to help the little girl, she'd run away from the truck stop, and he knew she'd stolen the food in the old backpack that looked like it weighed as much as she did. It took him ten minutes to get her to trust him enough to talk. He'd taken her to not much of a home, parked way back in a junky trailer park. The run-down model home was in a cluster of others that looked to be in the same shape. She said she lived there, but it didn't look like any kind of place a child would stay. No toys or bikes. Only old loading crates and empty beer cans.

He talked the girl into letting him take the canned goods back, even gave her a twenty to buy food. But as he stood to leave, a man inside spotted him looking in the trailer window and threatened to kill him for trespassing. A few of his drunk buddies spilled out behind him, offering to help with the murder.

Thatcher took off with them yelling what they'd do if they ever saw him again. The leader even threatened to hurt the kid if Thatcher ever spoke to her again.

The worst part of it all for Thatcher was the shame he felt. There might have been five or six of them and only one of him, but he felt like a coward running and leaving her there. She wasn't his kin. He had no right to interfere. But somehow it didn't seem right leaving her there.

Then, when he was thoughtful enough to take the stolen food back, Luther accused him of stealing the cans. Like he'd drive two miles out of town to shoplift beans probably two or three years out-of-date.

Thatcher had had enough and he'd swung, not so much at Luther, but at the whole world.

Now, he stared into the night as if he could find an answer. So much for being a Good Samaritan. He knew how it felt to be hungry. He'd wanted to help. Now one good deed might just screw up his whole life.

He'd told people that he wanted to major in criminal justice. Maybe be like the sheriff. Only that was a pipe dream now.

Word was that there was a real hero living around the Panhandle of Texas. A Texas Ranger who'd survived a gun battle on the border. He'd been dealing with genuine bad guys and not some bum smoking pot in a trailer with his buddies while his little girl had to shoplift to eat. Thatcher wanted to fight for right, but yesterday he'd had his chance and ran.

Why couldn't his life be exciting like the ranger's? It must have been something to be in a real fight against drug runners. Thatcher guessed he already had most of the skills to be a lawman. He was fast, and much stronger than most gave him credit for. He'd been shooting game for food since he was nine.

Only, people with a criminal record didn't become rangers or sheriffs. They didn't become anything Thatcher wanted to be.

Tim must have finished writing his thoughts because he walked to the other side of the cell, the free side, and joined Thatcher.

"I think it's creepy out on nights like this," he said, as if he thought Thatcher would welcome conversation. "Town's growing so much it seems brighter than it used to."

"Tim, stop talking like you were born before electricity. You're twenty-five." Thatcher hated how Tim—and Lauren too—both thought they were so much older than him.

"I know, but the town's growing. There are two whole new blocks of houses behind the church and half a dozen new cabins out by the lake."

Thatcher decided he must be brain-dead, because he started talking to Tim. He pointed toward the building project in the empty space between the two main streets. The city council said it would look like a grand town square when they finished, but the land was cut by roads into a triangle and who ever heard of a town triangle? "Does that look like a bandstand or a gazebo to you?" he asked Tim, hoping to avoid talking about jail for a while.

"Nope." Tim tilted his head one way, then

the other, as if the question would make more sense that way. The framed-out bandstand was covered in snow. "It reminds me of a ten-foot-high white spider now, with legs that stretch out thirty feet."

"You're right." Thatcher wouldn't have been surprised if the monster lifted one of its legs and began to walk. "You think it'll look any better when they get it finished? Folks say there will be grass and benches and maybe even statues."

Tim nodded as if finding a topic to discuss. "Sheriff said the construction companies brought in crews to build it and the new baseball field with under-the-stands locker rooms at the high school. Everyone claims the construction crews have caused more trouble than they're worth. Most of the workers moved into trailers behind the gas station, and word is there's a party out there every night. We got a crime scene waiting to happen out there. The foreman from across the street complained to the sheriff that his crew either shows up drunk or high."

Thatcher almost said he knew that for a fact, but telling Tim anything would be telling him too much. He simply wanted to forget what he saw yesterday when he looked in that trailer window; what was going on in there had nothing to do with the trouble he was in now. He shouldn't have hit Luther.

Thatcher tried to reason it out, but he swore

his fist was flying before his brain had time to think about the consequences.

His momma always told him to stay out of other folks' crimes unless you want to be a part of the next one they commit. She was right. Of course, she also told him she could see him from wherever he was because they shared the same color eyes.

"Mom, if you're watching now, you might want to look away," he mumbled to himself. Tim was too busy talking to notice.

Lauren finally came back and Tim abandoned talking to Thatcher, so he moved over to his bunk and tried to sleep, but questions kept running through his brain. Why'd he get involved yesterday? Why didn't he just mind his own business? If he hadn't tried to help the little girl. If he hadn't followed the kid home. If he hadn't taken the food back, he'd be out at the Lone Heart Ranch eating supper with Charley and his wife and Lillie. He'd be teasing her, calling her Flower and she'd be talking back calling him "That."

Thatcher smiled. Life hadn't given him many breaks, but meeting Charley's family made up for that. Lillie was nine now and thought she knew everything. Only once she'd been small like the kid he'd tried to help yesterday. That thin little girl was vulnerable. She didn't have parents who cared if she ate, and that was the least of their crimes.

CHAPTER SIX

Tuesday night

DAN BRIGMAN CALLED himself every kind of fool as he walked into the Nowhere Club. He'd asked a woman for a date and then stood her up. He hadn't even called last night. She'd been everything he needed right now. Someone fun, easy to get to know, great to kiss. A wild, beautiful lady he could spend some time with and not worry about getting involved. No strings. No complications. She'd made that plain from the first.

She was the dream he'd always wanted and never had.

And, thanks to Thatcher Jones, Dan had blown his one chance. She probably wouldn't bother to speak to him tonight, and all he had was a memory of one great kiss. Maybe the best kiss he'd ever experienced, or ever would.

There was the possibility she hadn't thought it was a date. She'd just said that if he could find a place open, she'd be hungry. Maybe showing up a day late wouldn't matter. Brandi Malone didn't strike him as a woman who made long-term plans.

By the time he'd left the sheriff's office

after one final check of Thatcher and his two babysitters and gone home to clean up, it was almost eight o'clock. If he was lucky, he'd hear her second set, even if she didn't talk to him afterward.

Any plans of taking the lady back to his place had vanished when his daughter showed up this afternoon. The singer he met might be beautiful and wild, but they were both too old for him to even suggest making out in a car. His old Jeep didn't have much of a heater, and he was not taking her out to dinner in the county cruiser.

At least he'd switched into civilian clothes and left his gun belt at home. Of course he did have a small revolver strapped to his calf and his badge was tucked into his coat pocket. A lawman was a lawman; it was not just his job.

He almost turned around halfway to the county line. The weather was getting worse. If he stayed a few hours at the bar, he'd probably be fighting snow going home.

"No," he said aloud as he pushed on the accelerator. He was going. It was about time he made a memory. At the rate he was going, he'd head into old age without having that "once in a lifetime" affair.

Twenty minutes later, Dan climbed out of the Jeep and turned his collar up against the freezing mist. He might as well go in and make a fool of himself. At least he'd have something to regret.

"Evening, Sheriff," the bartender said with a nod as he shouted loud enough for half the drunks to hear. "You coming in undercover tonight?"

"No." Dan smiled as if the question didn't bother him. Dan never went undercover, even though the club was officially in the next county. "I'm just here to have a beer and listen to the music." He glanced at the bartender's nametag. "You got any objections, Sorrel?"

"Nope." Sorrel Douglas shrugged his bony shoulders. "Would suggest you don't order food. Kitchen's backed up. We're getting a lot more folks in here on weeknights since Brandi came. Drunks around here act like they've never seen a real country singer, so they come in early and eat during the first set, then hang around way too late for a weeknight to catch the last set. It'll be closing time before you get anything but nachos."

Dan ordered a drink and found a table in the back just as Brandi Malone stepped onstage. The crowd settled. Even the drunk who'd been drooling on the next table raised his head and grinned.

The sheriff swore the air in the place settled as conversations stopped and people who had been playing pool in the back moved where they could see a woman in knee-high blue boots take the stage. Her skin looked pale in the lights, and her dark curls floated around her like a cape.

Dan held his breath. Even if she never spoke to

him again, it was already worth the drive to just see her.

As he always did, Dan measured the crowd for trouble. Mostly couples, a few small groups of girls-night-out types. A dozen men standing at the bar. Cowboys, oil-field workers, truckers and a few bikers. No one in the place appeared to be looking for trouble, but a few were starting to drool in their beer as they stared at Brandi. She wore a long silk shirt over leggings, and the boots he'd seen before. Her hair wasn't tied back as it had been yesterday. When she looked down at her hands, she curtained most of her face from view, and he wondered if she did it on purpose.

Dan wasn't sure what he expected, but when she began a song, he was lost in her world. He wasn't even sure she could see him in the crowd, but he swore she was singing just for him. Some of the songs were old favorites that anyone who loved country music liked to hear, but others were new, fresh, almost like she was making up the words as she sang.

For once he didn't watch his surroundings. All he did was listen. Her music drifted around him like a gentle hug, and her words spoke straight to his sleeping heart. The crowd grew quiet as if they all knew just how good the lady was.

Dan caught himself holding his breath, waiting for her to look up, but she rarely did. For her it was all about the music, and he realized something no one else seemed to see—she was playing for herself, not the audience.

Finally, the spell was broken when she finished the last song and lowered her guitar. A roar went up from the crowd and Dan stood with everyone else.

She took one quick bow and vanished behind the curtain that covered the backstage door. Hank, the owner of the bar, was there as guard, making sure the men who moved toward the stage didn't make it past the door.

Dan remained in the dark corner without taking one step toward her. Part of him was mourning the wild, crazy woman he'd thought about spending a few nights with. She was so much more. Not just attractive—there was something deep inside her that poured out in her music. She was one of those rare people who were truly gifted.

The lady was obviously hurting so deep down she might never heal. There was a richness to her that had nothing to do with money or diamonds.

"Sheriff?" A voice jerked him back to reality.

He frowned and turned. "What do you want, Sorrel?" The bartender's name matched the color of the few strands of hair left on his head. He reminded Dan of an in-between man. Not tall or short. Not young or old. Not handsome or ugly enough to be noticeable in bar light.

Sorrel Douglas took a step backward as if

surprised the sheriff had taken the time to remember his name. "Miss Malone said she'd like it if you'd come backstage." Sorrel looked like he was trying to piece a puzzle together. "Probably wants advice about this guy who's harassing her. He comes in a couple nights a week, and by the last set he's drunk and thinks he's going to take her home." The bartender's head twitched to the left, but when Dan turned, the big guy who smelled of motor oil at the next table was rushing for the restroom.

Sorrel stopped trying to point with his head. "I know you said you're off duty, but she wants you to come talk to her for a minute. You wouldn't believe the number of losers who want to get their hands on Miss Malone. Last week we had a drunk in a suit say he was going to stand at the bar and cry until she showed up to comfort him. He claimed he'd known they were soul mates after two songs. A few boys have even offered me money if I'd pass them her phone number."

"Right." Dan made up his mind he wasn't leaving until midnight. "I'll be happy to advise her." Maybe it would be best not to mention that he was one of those men Sorrel was talking about. He wanted to know the lady, too.

"You'll have to go behind the bar. Hank makes sure the stage door is locked after she disappears."

Dan pulled his coat off the back of his chair.

67

"Any of those guys make it behind the curtained door?" he asked casually.

"You're the first I've seen." Sorrel laughed as if even the thought of the sheriff going back for any other reason than to answer questions would be ridiculous. "But, it being official business, I guess you don't count."

Dan fought down the urge to thump Sorrel in the back of his bald head as he followed the bartender to the sliding door hidden behind the bar. Why was it bartenders and preachers always thought they could read people?

Once Dan stepped through, Sorrel closed the door, leaving the sheriff in almost complete darkness. He felt his way along the littered hallway that smelled of old grease and mold. This part of the club must have been the original space before Hank built on and tripled the size of the place.

The owner had spent money fixing up the front, brought in a polished bar made of solid mahogany, but he hadn't wasted a dime on even lightbulbs backstage. If it wasn't for the country music whispering through the wall, Dan would swear he'd fallen into a tunnel. Boxes, trash, an old cot, lawn chairs. Finally he saw a beam of light slicing through a slightly open door just beyond the backstage entrance.

Tapping the wood with his fingertips, he slowly pushed the door open.

Brandi Malone was brushing out her beautiful hair in front of a mirror, so he could see both the back and the front of her at once. Her curly hair hung in waves now. She still wore the wine-red silk blouse and tight leggings that she'd worn on stage. For a few minutes he just stared. Women so beautiful didn't walk through his life often, and he wanted to enjoy every second of it.

Finally, she looked up and her gaze met his reflected in the mirror.

Dan had no idea what to do. Apologize? Tell her how great she was on stage? Run like hell before he got involved? If he had any heart left for love, this lady could break it with a feather. She probably shattered a dozen guys' fantasies every night.

Brandi stood and walked to him. He loved watching her move. So graceful, as if the music was still in her.

When she stood a few inches away, he breathed her in as if she were the only fresh air he'd known in years.

Without a word, she leaned against his chest and kissed him.

Dan felt like he'd been frozen for so long that he didn't remember any warmth. Her kiss wasn't a passionate attack, or a friendly embrace. It was pure need, and Dan couldn't have turned away if the building caught fire.

He pulled her close, loving the way the feel

of her ran the length of his body. The slow kiss he returned was long and hot. Dan took all she offered. He hadn't kissed a woman like this in years. Correction, he'd never kissed a woman like this. All out. An overload of every sense. Paradise.

When she moved away enough to laugh, he couldn't stop smiling. He could feel her laughter against his wet lips.

"I missed you, Sheriff," she whispered as her warm mouth brushed over his cheek. "I knew you'd be back. We haven't kissed near enough."

He'd missed her, too, this woman he'd met once, this lady he'd been hoping to find forever. His arm tightened at her waist. "Again," he whispered.

She settled against him and gave him what he'd asked for, letting the fire build, letting him know she was in no hurry.

Dan took his time moving his hands along her back, molding her closer. He'd felt passion in his life, but he'd never been lost to it.

Finally, she straightened to look at him.

He stared into her green eyes as he slowly moved his hands over her hips. "You feel so good," he whispered.

She pressed closer and reached around him to close the door, then returned to study him. "I like you out of uniform, Dan. You look more like a man I might be able to handle."

He thought of saying he'd like her out of everything, but the words wouldn't come. His hands slowly moved up her back and dug into her hair. Handling her was exactly what he wanted.

She winked, as if reading his mind. Opening her mouth slightly, she neared until almost touching his lips. "I'm thinking you're a little rusty when it comes to kissing. How about we start with a little practice?"

She didn't wait for an answer. She kissed him again, taking the lead as before, teaching, demanding, making him feel totally alive for the first time in years.

His life had been about his job and raising his daughter. He'd settled for a comfortable kind of loneliness. Eating meals in front of a ball game. Fishing for hours without really planning his day. Never looking for more than he had.

When she first tried to pull away, he didn't let her go. He couldn't. For once he wanted more from life than just settling.

She gently shoved again.

Then he heard someone bumping down the hallway toward her dressing room. Dan nodded once and stepped to the side.

By the time Sorrel tapped on the door, Brandi was sitting in her chair and Dan tried to look as if he was listening while he leaned against one of the storage shelves with his notepad in his hand.

Sorrel let himself in, seemingly unaware that

he'd interrupted them. "I brought your nachos, Sheriff, and a beer."

"Thanks," Dan answered without looking at the food.

"It's not any trouble. I always bring Miss Malone a sandwich between the last two sets."

Dan flipped his notepad closed and accepted the plate. "I've a few more questions to ask, Brandi." He tried to sound official. "Then, when you have time, Mr. Douglas, I'd like to ask you a few."

"Okay," Sorrel said as he handed Brandi her tray. "But give her time to eat. It's a short break, and tonight the crowd is already asking when she'll be back."

The bartender turned to Brandi. "Now you tell him all about that creep on the back row who's been bothering you. The sheriff needs to know." He turned to Dan. "You wouldn't believe all the losers and nuts that think she's singing just for them. The other night after closing one almost knocked the back door down. He was so drunk he thought he had a date with her. Said she was sending him secret messages in her songs."

Dan nodded. He believed the bartender. After Sorrel left, he set his plate down on the table beside her food. "Much as I'd like to go back to doing what we were doing, I think Sorrel is right." He turned a box of paper towels over and pulled it up as a chair. "How about we eat as you talk?"

She stuck out her lip in a pout, and he almost withdrew his suggestion.

Before saying a word, she brushed his arm when she reached across and took one of his nachos. "It's nothing really. Part of the job. If you're good, the drunks always fall madly in love with you. If you're breathing, some nut's going to hit on you. It's a bar, Sheriff."

She ate while he stared, knowing what he had to do. If she was really in danger, he needed to make sure he was near. This assignment was no hardship at all. "Tell me the facts, Brandi."

"This big guy in his forties comes in almost every Tuesday and Saturday. He drinks Jack and Bud until he passes out, or gets generally obscene and Hank kicks him out. I think he's a trucker because sometimes he looks like he's put in a long day. He smells of motor oil and fresh-cut wood. There's no trouble if he only has a few beers. He leaves early, probably going home to his wife, or he's out of money. But when he settles in for the night, he's like a wild boar by midnight."

She shrugged. "I'm not afraid of him, but I hate that Hank and Sorrel have to deal with him."

Dan brushed her arm when he leaned closer and took half her sandwich. The touch, like hers, had been no accident. There was something very sensual about sharing food. Something lovers did. "And if he had more than a few, is that when he bothers you?"

"No." She smiled, stealing another chip. "He bothers me all the time. Staring at me. Making obscene signs of what he wants to do with me. Telling anyone who will listen that I'm going to go home with him one night.

"When he's drunk, he gets loud and starts saying I'm his girl. That's why Hank started locking the stage door. I step off stage, Hank locks the door from the inside and goes back down the passage to the door by the bar. One night when the trucker tried the door, he pounded so hard they had to throw him out. After that, he's been better, but he waits outside even after we close." Brandi bumped Dan's shoulder with her own. "How can you help?"

"I could talk to him, but unless you want to file a restraining order, there's not much the law can do."

She smiled that sad smile again. Like she was forcing sorrow away. Like her whole life was a lie. "I don't want to think about it right now. I have another set to do. I've been hoping you'd come back to hear my songs."

Dan couldn't let the problem go. "And if he's still here later or waiting in the parking lot?"

"Then I'll sleep here. I'm not driving back to the motel worrying that he might be following." She stood and fluffed her wild hair, painted her lips, pulled on a vest with fringe that tickled her hips.

He watched, fascinated at how she turned into someone else so fast. The hungry eyes he'd seen when he'd kissed her had frozen to porcelain like a doll's stare, unreadable, cold. He didn't know which Brandi was the real one, but both fascinated him.

"I'll stay until you finish and follow you home, just to make sure." He hadn't slept in two days, but Dan knew he wouldn't close his eyes tonight if he thought she was in danger.

She walked past him and opened the door. When she turned back, no smile curved her full lips. "If you follow me home, Sheriff, you're not leaving until dawn."

Every cell in his body wanted to pull her to him, but there was no time. The canned music had stopped. Hank must have unlocked the stage door because his voice blared down the hallway.

Dan stared at her, his words low. "I'm following you home. You'll be safe tonight."

"And warm," she whispered back.

CHAPTER SEVEN

Tuesday night

CODY WINSLOW THUNDERED through the night on a half-wild horse that loved to run. The moon followed them, dancing along the edge of the canyon as they darted over winter buffalo grass that was stiff with frost.

The former Texas Ranger watched the dark outline of the earth where the land cracked open wide enough for a river to run at its base.

The canyon's edge seemed to snake closer, as if it were moving, crawling over the flat plains, daring Cody to challenge death. One misstep might take him and the horse over the rim and into the black hole. They'd tumble maybe a hundred feet down, barreling over jagged rocks and frozen juniper branches as sharp as spears. No horse or man would survive.

Only tonight Cody wasn't worried. He needed to ride, to run, to feel adrenaline pumping in his veins, to know he was alive. He rode hoping to outrun his dark mood.

The demons that were always in the corners of his mind were chasing him tonight. Daring him to step over the edge and tumble into death's darkness. Whispering that he should give up even trying to live. Betting him to take one more risk . . . the one that would finally kill him.

"Run," he shouted to the midnight mare. Nothing would catch him here. Not on his ranch. Not on land his ancestors had hunted on for thousands of years. Fought over. Died for and bled into. Apache blood, settler blood, Comanchero blood was mixed in him as it was in many people in this part of Texas. His family tree was a tumbleweed of every kind of tribe that ever crossed the plains.

If the horse fell and they went to their deaths, no one would find them for weeks on this far corner of his ranch. Even the canyon that twisted like crippled fingers off the great Palo Duro had no name here. It wasn't beautiful like Ransom Canyon, with layers of earth revealed in a rainbow of colors. Here the rocks were jagged, shooting out of the deep earthen walls from twenty feet in some places, almost like a thin shelf.

The petrified wood formations along the floor of the canyon reminded Cody of snipers waiting, unseen but deadly. Cody felt numb, already dead inside, as he raced across a place with no name on a horse he called Midnight.

The horse's hooves tapped suddenly over a low place where water ran off the flatland and into the canyon. Frozen now. Silent. Deadly black ice. For a moment the tapping matched Cody's heartbeat, then both horse and rider seemed to realize the danger at once.

Cody leaned back, pulling the reins, hoping to stop the animal in time, but the horse reared in panic. Dancing on her hind legs for a moment before twisting violently and bucking Cody off as if he was no more than a green rider on his first bronc.

As Cody flew through the night air, he almost smiled. The battle he'd been fighting since he was shot and left for dead on the border three years ago was about to end here on his own land. The voices of all the ancestors who came before him whispered in the wind, as if calling him.

When he hit the frozen ground so hard it knocked the air from his lungs, he knew death wouldn't come easy tonight. Though he'd welcome the silence, Cody knew he'd fight to the end. He came from generations of fighters. He was the last of his line, and here in the dark he'd make his stand. Too far away to call for help. And too stubborn to ask anyway.

As he fought to breathe, his body slid over a tiny river of frozen rain and into the black canyon.

He twisted, struggling to stop, but all he managed to do was tumble down. Branches whipped against him, and rocks punched his ribs with the force of a prizefighter's blow. And still he rolled. Over and over. Ice on his skin, warm blood dripping into his eyes. He tried bracing for the hits that came when he landed for a moment before his body rolled again. He grabbed for a rock or a branch to hold on to, but his leather gloves couldn't get a grip on the ice.

He wasn't sure if he managed to relax or pass out, but when he landed on a flat rock near the bottom of the canyon, total blackness surrounded him and the few stars above offered no light. For a while he lay still, aware that he was breathing. A good sign. He hurt all over. More proof he was alive.

He'd been near death before. He knew that sometimes the body turned off the pain. Slowly, he mentally took inventory. There were parts that hurt like hell. Others he couldn't feel at all.

Cody swore as loud as he could, and smiled. At least he had his voice. Not that anyone would hear him in the canyon. Maybe his brain was mush; he obviously had a head wound. The blood kept dripping into his eyes. His left leg throbbed with each heartbeat, and he couldn't draw a deep breath. He swore again.

He tried to move and pain skyrocketed, forcing him to concentrate to stop shaking. Fire shot up his leg and flowed straight to his heart. Cody took shallow breaths and tried to reason. He had to control his breathing. He had to stay awake or he'd freeze. He had to keep fighting. Survival was bone and blood to his nature.

The memory of his night in the mud near the

Rio Grande came back as if it had only been a day earlier, not three years. He'd been bleeding then, hurt, alone. Four rangers had stood on the bank at dusk. He'd seen the other three crumple when bullets fell like rain.

Only it had been hot that night, not cold like now, and then the air had been silent after all the gunfire. He finally heard movement in the shadows and wasn't sure which he feared more, armed drug runners or demons. If the outlaws found him alive, they'd kill him. If the demons found him dead, they'd drag him into hell. Reality and nightmares dueled in his mind as sanity seemed to drip away with his blood.

Cody had known that every ranger in the area would be looking for him at first light; he had to make it to dawn first. Stay alive. They'd find him, he kept thinking, until he finally passed out.

But not this time. No one knew where he was tonight. Once he lost consciousness, he'd freeze.

No one would look for him tonight or tomorrow. No one would even notice he was gone. He'd made sure of that. He'd left all his friends back in Austin after the shooting. He'd broken up with his girlfriend, who said she couldn't deal with hospitals. When he came back to his family's land, he didn't bother to call any of his old friends. He'd grown accustomed to the solitude. He'd needed it to heal not just the wounds outside, but the ones deep inside.

Cody swore again.

The pain won out for a moment, and his mind drifted. At the corners of his reason, he knew he needed to move, stop the bleeding, try not to freeze, but he'd become an expert at drifting that night on the border. Even when a rifle had poked into his chest as one of the drug runners tested to see if he was alive, Cody hadn't reacted.

If he had, another bullet would have gone into his body, which was already riddled with lead.

Cody muttered the words he'd once had to scrub off the walls in grade school. Mrs. Presley had kept repeating as he worked, "Cody Winslow, you'll die cussing if you don't learn better."

Turned out she might be right. Even with his eyes almost closed, the stars grew brighter and circled around him like drunken fireflies. If this was death's door, he planned to go through yelling.

The stars drew closer. Their light bounced off the black canyon walls as if they were sparks of echoes.

He stopped swearing as the lights began to talk.

"He's dead," one high, bossy voice said. "Look how shiny the blood is."

Tiny beams of light found his face, blinding him to all else.

A squeaky sound added, "I'm going to throw up. I can't look at blood."

"No, he's not dead," another argued. "His

hand is twitching, and if you throw up, Marjorie Martin, I'll tell Miss Adams."

All at once the lights were bouncing around him, high voices talking at once.

"Yes, he is dead."

"Stop saying that."

"You stop saying anything."

"I'm going to throw up."

Cody opened his eyes. The lights were circling around him like a war party.

"See, I told you so."

One beam of light came closer, blinding him for a moment, and he blinked.

"He's hurt. I can see blood bubbling out of him in several spots." The bossy voice added, "Don't touch it, Marjorie. People bleeding have germs."

The gang of lights streamed along his body as if trying to torture him or drive him mad as the world kept changing from black to bright. It occurred to him that maybe he was being abducted by aliens, but he doubted the beings coming to conquer the world would land here in West Texas or that they'd sound like little girls.

"Hell," he said, and to his surprise the shadows all jumped back.

After a few seconds, he made out the outline of what might be a little girl, or maybe a short ET.

"You shouldn't cuss, mister. We heard you way back in the canyon yelling out words I've seen written but never knew how to pronounce."

"Glad I could help with your education, kid. Any chance you have a cell phone or a leader?"

"We're not allowed to carry cell phones. It interferes with our communicating with nature." She shined her flashlight in his eyes one more time. "Don't call me kid. Miss Adams says you should address people by their names. It's more polite. My name is Melanie Miller, and I could read before I started kindergarten."

Cody mumbled a few words, deciding he was in hell already and, who knew, all the helpers' names started with *M*.

All at once the lights went jittery again, and every one of the six little girls seemed to be talking at once.

One thought he was too bloody to live. One suggested they should cover him with their coats; another voted for undressing him. Two said they would never touch blood. One wanted to put a tourniquet around his neck.

Cody was starting to hope death might come faster when another shadow carrying a lantern moved into the mix. "Move back, girls. This man is hurt."

He couldn't see more than an outline, but the new arrival was definitely not a little girl. Tall, nicely shaped, hiking boots, wearing a backpack.

Closing his eyes and ignoring the little girls' constant questions, he listened as a calm voice used her cell to call for help. She had the location down to latitude and longitude, and described a van parked in an open field about a hundred yards from her location where they could land a helicopter. When she hung up, she knelt at his side and shifted the backpack off her shoulder.

As she began to check his injuries, her voice calmly gave instructions. "Go back to the van, girls. Two at a time, take turns flashing your lights at the sky toward the North Star. The rest of you get under the blankets and stay warm. When you hear the chopper arrive, you can watch from the windows, but stay in the van."

"McKenna, you're in charge. I'll be back as soon as they come."

Another *M*, Cody thought, but didn't bother to ask. Maybe your name had to start with *M* or you couldn't be in this club?

To his surprise the gang of ponytails marched off like tiny little soldiers.

"How'd you find me?" Cody asked the first of a dozen questions bouncing around in his aching head as the woman laid out supplies from her pack. The lantern offered a steady circle of pale light.

"Your cussing echoed off the canyon wall for twenty miles." Her hands moved along his body, not in a caress, but to a man who hadn't felt a woman's touch in years, it wasn't far from it.

"Want to give me your name? Know what day it is? What year? Where you are?"

"I don't have brain damage," he snapped, then

84

regretted moving his head. "My name's Winslow. I don't care what day it is or what year for that matter." He couldn't make out her face. "I'm on my own land. Or at least I was when my horse threw me."

She might have been pretty if she wasn't glaring at him. The lantern light offered that flashlight-to-the-chin kind of glow. With her arms on her hips, she had a kind of Paul Bunyan's little sister look about her.

"Where does it hurt?" She kept her voice low, but she didn't sound friendly. "As soon as I pass you to the medics, I'll start looking for your horse. The animal might be out here, too, hurting or dead. Did she fall with you?"

Great! His Good Samaritan was more worried about the horse than him. "I don't know. I don't think so. When I fell off the edge of the canyon, Midnight was still standing, probably laughing at me." He took a breath as the woman moved to his legs. The pain came sharp suddenly. "I tumbled for what seemed like miles. It hurts all over."

"How did this happen?"

"The horse got spooked when we hit a patch of ice," he snapped again, tired of talking, needing all his strength to handle the pain. Cuss words flowed out with each breath. Not at her, but at his bad luck.

She ignored them as she brushed over the left leg of his jeans, already stained dark with blood.

85

He tried to keep from screaming. He fought her hand now as she searched, examining where something had to be broken it hurt so much. He knew he couldn't take much more without passing out.

"Easy," she whispered as her blood-warmed fingers cupped his face. "Easy, cowboy. You've got a bad break. I have to do what I can to stabilize you and slow the blood flow. They'll be here soon. You've got to let me wrap a few of these wounds so you don't bleed out."

He nodded once, knowing she was right.

In the glow of a lantern she worked, making a tourniquet out of his belt, carefully wrapping his leg, then his head wound.

Her voice finally came low, sexy maybe if it were a different time, a different place. "It looks bad, but I don't see any chunks of brain poking out anywhere."

He didn't know if she was trying to be funny or just stating a fact. He didn't bother to laugh. She put a bandage on the gash along his throat. It wasn't deep, but it dripped a steady stream of blood.

As she wrapped the bandage, the starched cotton over her breasts brushed against his cheek, distracting him. If this was her idea of doctoring a patient with no painkillers, it was working. For a few seconds there, he almost forgot to hurt.

"I don't have water to clean the wounds, but

86

the dressing should keep anything else from getting in."

Cody began to calm. The pain was still there, but the demons in the corners of his mind were silent. Watching her move in the shadows relaxed him. She wasn't petite, but tall and built with curves that her trousers and man's shirt couldn't hide.

"Cody," he finally said. "My first name is Cody."

She smiled then for just a second.

"You a nurse?" he asked.

"No. I'm a park ranger. If you've no objection, I'd like to examine your chest next."

Cody didn't move as she unzipped his jacket. "I used to be a ranger, but I never stepped foot in a park." He could feel her unbuttoning his shirt. Her hand moved in, gently gliding across his ribs. "I put in a few years as a Texas Ranger."

When he gasped for air, she hesitated, then whispered, "One broken rib." A moment later she added, "Two."

He forced slow long breaths as he felt the cold night air pressing against his bare chest. Her hand crossed over his bruised skin, stopping at the scars he'd collected that night at the Rio Grande. The night he bled into the mud. The night he first heard the devils hiding in the shadows.

She lifted the light. "Bullet wounds?" she questioned more to herself than him. "You've been hurt bad before, Ranger Winslow."

"Yeah," he said as he took back control of his mind and made light of a gunfight that almost ended his life. "I was fighting outlaws along the Rio Grande. I swear it seemed like that battle was almost two hundred years ago. Back when Captain Hays ordered his men to cross the river with guns blazing. We went across just like that, only chasing drug runners and not cattle rustlers like they did back then. But we were breaking the law not to cross just the same."

He closed his eyes and saw his three friends. They'd gone through training together and were as close as brothers. They wanted to fight for right. They thought they were invincible that night on the border, just like Captain Hays's men must have believed.

Only those rangers had won the battle. They all returned to Texas. Cody had carried his best friend back across the water that night three years ago, but Hobbs hadn't made it. He'd died in the shallow water a few feet from Cody. Fletcher took two bullets, but helped Gomez back across. Both men died.

"I've heard of that story about the famous Captain Hays." She brought him back from a battle that had haunted him every night for three years. "Legend is that not one ranger was shot. They rode across the Rio screaming and firing. The bandits thought there were a hundred of them coming. But, cowboy, if you rode with Hays, that'd make you a ghost tonight, and you feel like flesh and blood to me. Today's rangers are not allowed to cross."

Her hand was moving over his chest lightly, caressing now, calming him, letting him know that she was near. He relaxed and wished they were somewhere warm.

"You're going to make it, Winslow. I have a feeling you're too tough to die easy." The lights of a helicopter circled above them.

He didn't want to think about dying or being hurt. He pushed the ghosts who always followed him aside and focused on her. "If I live, how about we get together and talk sometime? Any woman who has six kids, can handle injuries in the dark and recognizes bullet wounds is bound to be interesting."

She laughed. "You got yourself a date, Cody."

CHAPTER EIGHT

1 a.m.
Wednesday

A LITTLE AFTER closing time at the Nowhere Club, Dan walked out to his Jeep. The midnight wind blew sideways, pounding tiny balls of snow as hard as gravel against his face, but he barely noticed. His evening with Brandi Malone wasn't over, and that was all that really mattered.

The only person still parked out front was the big guy who'd sat next to Dan during Brandi's last performance. He looked like he was sleeping off a heavy drunk in his old one-ton rig that took up two parking spots. He didn't move when Dan walked within three feet of his window, and the sheriff was glad. The last thing he wanted to do tonight was arrest a man for stalking Brandi. Hauling the drunk in would ruin both Dan's and the drunk's night.

The trucker's engine was idling, so Dan doubted he'd freeze even if he ran out of gas. Hank usually made sure the parking lot was cleared before he did the final lockup. The manager said once that drunks were like fish— they smelled if left out overnight.

Dan started the Jeep. It might not look like

much, but the engine never failed to turn over. He pulled around the back of the bar, and Brandi darted out. She jumped in, squealing about the cold, and Dan laughed as he made a wide circle around the truck out front. He didn't know what it was about this woman, but she made him feel free, like no troubles would find him as long as she was riding shotgun.

"You worried about leaving your van?" he asked, hating that he sounded like a cop. He pulled a blanket from the back and covered her.

She cuddled the wool all the way to her chin. "No, I'm not worried. I left it unlocked. If someone steals it, I've got insurance. If one of the drunks wants to see what's inside, they'll have to go through dirty laundry and a dozen fast-food bags to learn all my secrets."

"You have secrets?" Dan didn't turn on his lights until he pulled onto the highway. The snow fell thick and heavy, making it hard to see, but he knew the road back to Crossroads.

He hadn't asked her which motel she was staying in. There was only one within twenty miles of the bar.

She tugged a multicolored knit hat down over her ears. "Everyone past puberty has secrets. I figured you'd already know that, Sheriff. You tell me one of yours, and I'll tell you one of mine." She grinned as if they were playing a game.

"Right now, you're my secret. Not that I care if

everyone knows we're going out, if that's what you call this thing we're doing, but just for a while I'd like to keep you to myself."

"Any others?"

"Ladies or secrets?"

"Secrets. A man who hasn't been kissed since New Year's Eve a few years ago has no ladies tucked away."

He figured he must seem pretty pitiful. Brandi probably had a lover in every town. "Nope. I'm pretty much an open book. No secrets or lovers, except you."

"It's been a long time since I've been thought of as someone's lover. I'm wild, but I'm picky."

He wished he could see her face, but she was far more shadow than flesh.

Her voice came soft like a whispered song. "I wouldn't mind being someone's secret lover. Keeping whatever happens between us will make it like a low melody that will echo through my mind long after I've moved on. If our story were a song you could dance to, I think I'd like it to be a waltz."

"You'll be a hard woman not to talk about, Brandi, but I'll give it my best try."

"I doubt that, Sheriff. I'd guess you're good at keeping other people's secrets as well as your own. If I wasn't looking at you as a future lover, I might want you for a friend."

"Who knows, I might become both." He wanted

to pull the Jeep over and kiss her. No one ever talked to him so directly. "As long as your secret doesn't involve a crime, I'm not one to talk, so you can tell me anything." He waited then asked, "What's your secret, pretty lady?"

She moved her head back and forth as if trying to pick from a hundred dancing around in her mind. "I guess I can trust you with one. My name's not really Brandi."

"I could have guessed that." Even Dan knew singers usually had stage names. "But Brandi fits you somehow."

"My father named me Elizabeth after the queen of England, and my mother wouldn't let anyone shorten it to Liz or Beth. I always had to have the whole name even when it didn't fit on stuff Mom marked for school. Until I was in the third grade, my lunch box had the last three letters of my name printed on the side because my mother never thought ahead to make sure Elizabeth fit. Kids would call me Eth like it was an elf name."

Dan fought down a laugh. He could just see her three feet tall with wild midnight hair curling down her back and her pale skin glowing white. She probably did look like an elf.

"So when did you toss Elizabeth aside?" It was a nice name, he thought, but it didn't fit her.

"I left home the day after I turned eighteen. Joined a band. The guys I traveled with gave me the name because they said my hair was dark and rich like hundred-year-old brandy." She giggled. "We were all so young and poor, I doubt any of us had ever seen hundred-year-old brandy, but the name made sense at the time."

Dan glanced over and brushed a thick strand of hair off her shoulder, loving that he felt he could touch her so freely, knowing that she wanted it that way between them.

With the silent snow surrounding them, it seemed like right now, right here, they were the only two people in the world, and he didn't mind that feeling at all.

"Did you ever go back home, back to being Elizabeth again?"

"That's another secret for another night." She wasn't looking at him, and he felt like she was moving away, even though she was still beside him.

They didn't talk for a while, and then she told him where to park as he turned into the Canyon Rim Motel a few miles from Crossroads. It wasn't much to brag about. Maybe twenty rooms in a horseshoe shape. The Franklin Bed and Breakfast would have fit her better, but she probably didn't know about the quaint little historical home in Crossroads. He was glad she wasn't staying at the B and B; knowing the Franklin sisters, he wouldn't dare walk her past the front door or he'd be the lead in every gossip story the next morning.

This motel had a blinking sign that reminded Dan of what an irregular heartbeat must look like. The three rows of rooms that formed the U shape had nothing to distinguish them except the numbers on the weathered green doors.

"I'm the last one on the left," she said. "You can park your Jeep on the side, out of most of the weather."

He nodded and did as she suggested, feeling suddenly out of place. He'd cast himself in a role he hadn't played in years. *Lover,* she'd said. Like they already were. Like they'd both known they would be from the first.

Frozen winter branches scraped at the Jeep as he pulled into an abandoned alleyway behind the last room. The bad news was that if it snowed much, he'd be buried within an hour. The good news was that he could walk to his own house from here if he had to. The last thing he planned to do was call for a tow from the town's only motel.

Reality and reason finally rolled around in his tired mind. He needed to tell her he couldn't stay. He had to explain how he'd been up for two days and couldn't spend the rest of the night with her no matter how much he wanted to.

He wasn't sure prospective lovers got rain checks.

Only when he saw her green eyes watching him, he almost forgot why he couldn't stay.

95

Maybe five minutes. Maybe ten. Lauren was sitting up with Thatcher, so no one was at his house to notice he wasn't home. After sitting up all night with his one prisoner, people might leave him alone tonight to sleep.

Tonight? He smiled. It was already morning.

Dan shielded her from the snow with his open coat as they ran for her door. He'd apologize for not staying once they were inside. Then they'd make future plans and say good-night. He planned to kiss her so completely that she'd haunt every moment of his dreams.

Halfway to her room, when she pressed against his side so close they moved as one, he gave up all thinking.

She was laughing as she unlocked her room and stepped inside. He followed, marveling at just how good she'd felt next to him. If she felt this good with her clothes on, he couldn't wait to see how she felt with nothing between them.

When she turned on the lights, snowflakes sparkled in her hair and on her eyelashes. If he believed in elves or fairies, he'd swear he was looking at one right now. Those green eyes told him all he needed to know. She was happy to be with him. It didn't matter that they hadn't gone out to eat or didn't know every detail about each other. She was right for him.

"You've become a walking snowman." She rushed toward him as if he needed help.

He tried not to notice her brushing snow out of his hair and off his shoulders as he started what he knew he had to say before he became lost in watching her. "I just wanted to make sure you got home safe. I . . ."

"I know." She kissed his cheek. "I swear there is something so adorable about you, Sheriff. You want to be my knight in shining armor, but I don't need one. I'm fine, Dan. Stop worrying about me."

He saw her breath as he heard her words.

"It's freezing in here."

"Very observant." She shrugged as if he were simply stating a norm in her life. "The house-keeper comes in to change the towels after I leave and always turns off the heater. I'm guessing the other rooms stay above freezing, but I'm on the end with windows facing north, and it never gets really warm in here if the temperature drops. I complained once, and they delivered two more blankets."

Dan looked around the room. It was bigger than he'd expected, with patio furniture as a living area on one side of the bed and a desk on the other. Along five feet of one wall near the bathroom door was an almost kitchen. Microwave, half refrigerator and a cooktop with two burners. The whole room was depressing. She didn't belong in this place. Everything—the walls, the carpet, the furniture—was beige.

Then he noticed the small touches. A royal-blue scarf draped over the little table. Paper plates and cups with a daisy pattern and a tea set were arranged on the table as if she was expecting someone for dinner.

Unlike her dressing room, all her clothes were organized on hangers and hanging in a closet that was missing its door. Her three pairs of shoes were lined up below the clothes, and he guessed if he opened a drawer in the dresser all would be in order.

"I'll make tea and you turn on the heater. Then we'll cuddle on the bed until we thaw out. Believe me, you do not want to sit on that plastic furniture until spring." She lifted a teapot so small it almost looked like a toy. "I always have tea at bedtime."

He wanted to say that he'd stay for only one cup. He was so tired he feared he might sleep standing up like a horse if he closed his eyes. But he didn't want to leave without at least kissing her one more time. Besides, it wouldn't be polite. She'd offered tea, and though everyone in Crossroads knew how much he hated hot tea, Dan planned to have a cup tonight.

If it made Brandi smile, he'd order a mud cookie to go with his tea.

He pulled off his heavy coat and spread it over one of the flimsy chairs, then put his wet boots near the wall heater that he'd turned up to eighty.

While she moved around on the other side of the room, he crawled, fully dressed, beneath one of the blankets and sat on the bed, leaning his back against the headboard. The heater clanked in rhythm to Brandi's humming.

Slowly, the room warmed, and Dan took in a deep breath, loving the smell of cinnamon tea even though he doubted he'd get more than a few swallows down. She was swaying as she stacked crackers on a paper plate.

Dan smiled and closed his eyes.

BRANDI TUGGED OFF her boots and coat as the tea steeped. She'd never brought anyone back with her before. She wasn't sure what to do, or where to start, but the way Dan kissed she had no doubt they'd figure it out soon enough.

She loved how solid and honest he seemed. She loved the hunger that she saw in his eyes. She loved seeing the delight in his gaze when she shocked him by kissing him. They'd both made it plain that they weren't looking for forever, so maybe this time she could let her guard down and relax in a stranger's arms.

Setting out the cups and napkins on a tray she'd bought at a garage sale in Oklahoma six months ago, and arranging little cookies she kept in a tin, Brandi allowed herself to remember. Her mother had always made tea at night, a ritual Brandi had continued with Evie even when her daughter was in the hospital. Sometimes the cups were filled with milk or juice, but mother and daughter always had their tea before bedtime.

One night almost a year ago she hadn't been able to find a hotel and had to sleep in her van. Using a flashlight, she crawled in the back and dug out her tea set. Even thought the cookies were stale and the tea was imaginary, she pretended, knowing that she needed this one tiny normal thing in life to be able to sleep.

The Dollar Store cups on a cardboard tray were finally ready. She turned around and walked toward Dan, who was sitting in the shadows, his legs covered with a blanket, his chin resting on his chest.

He was sound asleep.

Brandi fought to keep from waking him. This tough guy had no idea just how adorable he looked. But, in the end, reason won out. She stripped down to her silk shirt and climbed under the covers. As the mattress moved, he tumbled over, a silent tree falling. Like magnets, they settled against each other, drawing from one another's warmth. She cuddled her back into his chest and his arm circled her shoulder.

He was doing what he'd said he'd do. He was keeping her safe even in her dreams. No sorrow would sit on her heart tonight. She could let go of the world. She could sleep.

CHAPTER NINE

DEEP INTO THE NIGHT, Thatcher woke to what he thought was a helicopter flying over the town.

At first he guessed it might be the deputy's wife. If Fifth Weathers were back from Austin, she'd be flying home for supper. They'd been married a year and still lived in different towns. But, since she was a pilot, it didn't seem to be a problem.

Only, she wouldn't be out on a night like this, and Fifth Weathers wasn't even in town or he'd be the one babysitting the jail tonight.

Maybe he dreamed he heard a chopper. After his mother left him when he was fourteen, he used to dream that she was calling his name. Then he'd wake up and think it must have been a word that floated, leftover, never heard in the empty house until long after the person had gone. The witch of an old lady who used to live down the road from his mother always said sounds hang around long after folks disappear. She swore she heard her dead husband snoring one night. She swore spirits stayed around even after death found a person. They might not talk, but they sat in the shadows, almost visible, or rattled a door, or ruffled the curtains over a closed window.

Sometimes he liked to think that his mother

was watching over him, but that didn't make sense. She wasn't dead. She'd just run off with her latest boyfriend. Besides, she didn't watch over him when they lived out at the Breaks, so why would she be doing it now?

"Mom," he whispered, "if you're out there sending me good vibes, you might think of sending me a Kevlar vest and a bulletproof helmet. I have a feeling that either way I go on this new problem, I'm going to need protection."

He was safe here. No one could get to him now. He might as well stay awhile. The two babysitters in the opposite cell wouldn't be much help if trouble came. Tim would talk any intruder to death and Lauren would probably run. Thatcher probably liked both of them more than they liked each other. He'd started counting the times Tim touched her and she pulled away.

The thought crossed his mind to tell the sheriff to slow down on trying to get him out of jail. He figured it was just a matter of time before Lauren got tired of Tim and slapped him into tomorrow. Thatcher wouldn't mind seeing that.

The chances were good he'd be stuck here for a while. He wasn't going to apologize to Luther at the truck stop or give any statement.

Not till the guys who threatened to kill him at the trailer left town and Kristi got over hating him. Hell, the snow would be gone by then. With his luck, his youth would be gone, as well. He'd grow old up here on the third floor looking out a barred window as the town grew up around him.

Getting out seemed a long shot. Maybe he should just get used to prison food.

CHAPTER TEN

IN THE STILLNESS of night's shadows, Cody sensed more than saw the woman who'd said she was a park ranger. She moved around him, touching his arm, his shoulder, the tourniquet she'd put on his leg, doing her best to make him comfortable. She'd set the lantern on a high point about ten feet away, but they were still in the circle of its pale yellow light.

He would have thought she was an expert, except she kept muttering her ABC's as if remembering what to do in emergencies. The third time she leaned her ear down close to his face, he whispered, "Still breathing."

"I always check everything at least twice," she said as her hand reevaluated the damage to his ribs.

He thought of saying, *still broken,* but he kind of liked her touch.

"Lie very still, Mr. Winslow. If you do have broken ribs, there is a chance you also have damage to your spine, or have a floating bone that could stab right into your heart."

"I don't have a heart. My first love broke up with me when I joined the rangers, and the last one broke up when I left the rangers."

"Of course you have a heart," she said,

sounding very much like she was talking to one of her tribe of little girls.

"Don't bet on it."

Then she did the strangest thing—she covered him with her coat and knelt above his head. It took him a minute to grasp what she was doing above him, then he realized she was holding his head steady with her knees. He had no intention of complaining about that. The inside of a woman's thighs made a perfect neck brace. Too bad she had on jeans thick enough to stop a rattler's bite.

"You'll be cold without a coat," he muttered, wishing he could see her more clearly.

"I'm all right. I was raised by wolverines." She brushed his hair away from his forehead with her icy fingers. "Try not to move. You're already past my level of skill with first aid. I've been a park ranger for five years and never had anything that couldn't be doctored with a Band-Aid."

He couldn't see her face beneath the shadows of her floppy-brimmed hat. From her outline he'd guess she was tall, athletic build probably, and maybe a little top heavy, but it might just be the layering she wore. He hadn't bothered to ask her name or what she was doing out here with a covey of little girls following her around. Maybe it was part of a park ranger's job.

The loss of blood must have made him light-headed because the woman's voice seemed more in his mind than real.

"Hang in there, cowboy," she kept whispering. "They're on the way."

He raised his hand, as memories of pain in the past blended with reality. He needed to touch her, know that she was beside him, to keep the demons in the corners.

She wrapped her fingers around his and held on tight. "Can you hear me?" she asked when he'd been silent for a while.

It took him a few tries, but he finally found his voice. "What's your name?"

"Tess Adams," she said. "I'm glad you're still with me. I was worried that you might have fallen asleep on our date tonight. We were going to count the stars, remember? They're so bright here, this far from any man-made light."

Cody smiled at her attempt to lighten the situation. "I haven't had a date in years, honey." Dating was something he'd never been good at even before the night he was hurt. After he finally got out of rehab, he figured no woman would want to go out with a man as messed up as he was. Who'd want to live with a man living with his past?

"Me neither." Tess pulled him back from his thoughts. "The last guy I went out with got mad when he realized I was armed. He didn't speak to me during the meal, then he went to the restroom before dessert arrived and left me to pick up the check."

Cody would have laughed if he'd had the energy. "What'd you do?"

"I ate both desserts while I wished I'd broken the date and gone camping. I thought about it while I walked home. Probably should have. Wild animals are easier to understand than most men. That mistake cost me sixty-two dollars plus tip. I would have had more fun camping alone."

He gripped her hand as hard as he could and hoped she felt it. "I got the feeling you're my kind of woman, honey."

"If you weren't already looking like death warmed over, I'd slap you for calling me honey. I'm not the kind of girl who likes men who use pet names."

"You'll get over it, Tess, after we're married."

He liked the way she laughed.

"Oh, we're getting married are we, Cody Winslow?" She patted his shoulder as if she thought he was crazy.

Cody knew what she was doing. Keeping him talking, thinking, awake, until help arrived. If she'd been the one bleeding, he probably would have been yelling, cussing, making her mad so she'd stay with him. Cody liked her method better.

"It's meant to be, you and me." Cody played along. "Otherwise why would you be on my land after midnight?"

"I'm on state land." She didn't sound sure of

herself. "This is my office. I work the canyons all over this area. I've no time to be married to you."

"We'll argue about it in the morning, honey. I make a great cup of coffee, so you can have your first cup in bed."

"I'll hold you to that, Cody. I like mine strong and black. Since we're getting married, do you think you could tell me how old you are and if you have any allergies? It's dark, and you're too bloody for me to even guess."

"Thirty-four. I'm allergic to stupid people. You?"

"Twenty-seven. Almost past my prime child-bearing years." She brushed her fingers slowly through his hair as if she'd done so a hundred times.

"We'll have to get started on the kids right away, then." He liked her touch, and he loved the way the inside of her thighs held him snugly in place. Seemed as good a reason as any to settle down with a woman. "By next winter we could have one born and another on the way."

"You plan ahead, Mr. Winslow."

"I do," he lied, "Mrs. Winslow. It'll be the one thing that'll drive you crazy over the next sixty years or so."

The sound of an engine cut through the night. Moments later a star separated from heavens and headed toward them, growing brighter and louder.

"Promise you'll be with me when I come out of this night." He didn't know if she heard him. There was too much noise to ask again.

The helicopter cut into the canyon and sat down near a van parked along an old Civilian Conservation Corps road that had been plowed out of the canyon floor almost a hundred years ago. Men were climbing out before the chopper settled, all running toward the lantern Tess had set up high.

She didn't let go of his hand until the medics had him strapped on the backboard. She stayed beside him shouting details. Name, age, possible injuries, no allergies. Four men carried him along the uneven ground of the canyon floor.

Cody didn't say a word; he just held tightly to her fingers. They passed a van with tiny faces staring out the windows at him. Cody waved slightly with his free hand and one girl with apple cheeks waved back, but she looked like she was crying.

When they reached the chopper, Tess tugged her hand away and leaned close enough to kiss him on the cheek. "Hang in there," she whispered. "I'll see you in the morning. I promise."

All at once he was circling in a tornado of care. He was strapped down, poked and surrounded by a team working on him. Now there was no questioning, no hesitation. Down to the last man on the team, each knew his job.

A few breaths later, he felt his body relax and whispered, "See you in the morning, honey," even though he knew she was on the ground and the bird was already climbing.

CHAPTER ELEVEN

Wednesday

WHEN DAN ROLLED OVER, watery-blue sunlight blinked through sheet-thin drapes on the motel window. The glass was covered with a layer of ice that looked like it had formed on the inside of the pane. As he shifted farther into the covers, his cheek brushed against soft hair and he closed his eyes.

He took a deep breath, thinking this was the best dream he'd had in years. It seemed so real he could feel the warmth of her body, smell the sweet way a woman smelled in the morning that no perfume could ever compare to.

He moved his hand over silk and cupped a rounded breast. The dream stepped into his reality.

"Morning, Sheriff." Brandi giggled softly when his eyes shot open. "You always wake up like a bolt of lightning just hit you?"

He let go of her breast and fought the urge to slug himself. "Mornin'," he managed to say before he cleared his throat and tried to get his brain working. "Tell me I didn't fall asleep and miss last night."

"Okay, you didn't fall asleep and miss a great

time. It was unbelievable, wasn't it? Best night of my life."

He buried his face against her hair. "I did fall asleep."

She kissed his cheek as she moved her body closer, pressing that nicely rounded part against his side. "You didn't miss the morning, though. I don't have anyplace I have to be until tonight. We can stay right here for a while."

He didn't move, hating the words he knew he had to say. "But I do." He glanced at his cell phone. "In about half an hour, I have to be at my office. In fact, I've probably got the two people I drafted into sitting up with my prisoner wondering where I am right now. I'm sorry, Brandi, I have to run."

She leaned close to his ear. "Give me a few minutes to taste what I'll be waiting for tonight. That is if there is going to be a tonight?"

"There will be if I have to lock up every breathing person in Crossroads."

He knew it was a bad idea to touch her, but he was in bed beside a woman who turned him on simply by making tea. He'd probably self-combust if they ever did make love. A closer encounter with her might kill him if she got any sexier, and he'd die with a smile. One wild, passionate time would last him through eternity.

He couldn't turn away from her now when she

asked for only one thin slice of paradise. Five minutes, maybe ten.

Slowly, he pushed her onto her back and moved his hand down the front of her blouse. There was nothing but skin underneath the thin layer. She closed her eyes and arched toward him as he explored her body. He could feel her breath catch as he touched her. The sight of her smiling, as if having a perfect dream while she enjoyed his caresses, made him think he might go mad if he didn't make it back to her bed tonight.

When he reached her legs, he slowly slid his fingers down so he could brush the soft place behind her knee. She moaned as he learned her curves. They were both lost in pleasure. He longed to know every part of this woman who craved his nearness almost as dearly as he wanted her.

He didn't take off one stitch of clothing or unbutton one button, but he discovered how she liked to be touched. He made love to her with a light caress. With the promise of what would be.

When he finally kissed her cheek, he whispered, "Tonight?"

"Yes." She laughed softly. "I think I'd like that."

He moved away, but he couldn't stop staring at her. He guessed she was like a wild creature no one should ever try to tame, but knowing she was in his world, even for a few nights, made his heart beat faster. "Go back to sleep, pretty lady."

When he pulled on his boots, he watched her tongue move over her bottom lip. Sexiest woman he'd ever seen, he decided, and she was still lost in the way he'd begun making love to her. No woman had ever craved him. The idea that she wanted him as deeply as he wanted her was staggering, heady and a bit frightening.

"Don't open your eyes, Brandi. Just lay still until you hear the door close. I have to go, but I want you to know something." He brushed his open hand over her hip. "I'll be thinking of you like this all day. I'll want more, and tonight I want you just as hungry for me."

She straightened and showed him the outline of her body beneath the thin layer of her crumpled blouse.

He slid his hand down her hip and brushed her bare leg. When she sighed, opening her mouth, he kissed her quick and hard before he ran from the room.

"Just call when you want me to take you back to the Nowhere," he added just before he closed the door.

If he'd stayed one moment more, he wouldn't have been able to leave.

The cold wind hit him as he ran for his Jeep, but the feel of her warm skin on his fingers lingered. For a moment, a beautiful, wild woman had been his. She might be again tonight. This kind of paradise didn't happen to men like him.

Only it had. For once his logical mind didn't want to think. Dan wanted only to feel.

He was already late, so he skipped the stop at his house for a shower and drove straight to the office. Each minute away from her moved him another step into the real world. By the time he parked, he'd managed to get a grip on his thoughts, his schedule for the day, his predictable life. He had duties, a job he loved and a kid named Thatcher up on the third floor he owed his life to.

Right now, he'd do what was needed, but tonight, he'd do nothing but what made the beautiful lady smile.

Pearly didn't look up as he rushed in wearing his coat over his off-duty clothes. She appeared to be letting the phone ring while she got a knot out of her knitting.

"Morning," he said as he passed.

She grabbed the phone and said, "Hello," to both him and whoever was on the line.

Five minutes later he'd changed into a fresh uniform he kept in the back and looked almost presentable. In a few hours, when he went out for breakfast, he'd switch his cruiser for the Jeep now parked in his county spot. Maybe he'd take a few minutes to shower and shave while he was home. No one would know he'd been out all night.

It crossed his mind that he'd slept with her. They might have done little more than sleep, but he swore he could still feel her in his arms, still smell her perfume in the air around him. He'd slept with a woman for the first time in years. He took a deep breath. He'd forgotten just how good it felt to simply sleep next to someone.

Or maybe it wasn't just someone; it was Brandi who made it perfect.

Dan opened the window an inch, letting cold air blow in. He needed to clear his head. He had a full day. There would be time to think about tonight while he listened to her sing at the bar. He planned to be there, making sure she was safe, and when she was finished, he'd be the one to take her home.

By the time he sat down at his desk, all was back to normal. The sheriff was on alert and preparing for a busy day.

Only the feel of Brandi still lingered on his fingers and the promise of tonight whispered deep in his lonely heart.

CHAPTER TWELVE

Wednesday morning

LAUREN BRIGMAN STOOD in the space between the two jail cells on the third floor of the county offices and watched the sun come up over her hometown, now covered in snow. She missed waking up in Crossroads. People seemed to think that everyone who grew up in a small town should fly away. She'd even bought into the idea for a while, but now, all she thought about was finding her way back home. Dallas wasn't where she belonged. Here was.

She watched Tim's thin frame walk across the street to Dorothy's Diner. His head always appeared to be a step ahead of his body. Maybe that was because he lived in fantasy so much. Invisible stories were probably circling around Tim O'Grady even when he wasn't talking about them.

That's the way of writers. Add one more reason she'd never be one. No stories circled around her. A famous writer who lived on the canyon's edge once told her that she'd write, but Lauren had decided even sages sometimes made mistakes.

She tried. She'd taken classes. She'd read

a dozen books. She could do the exercises, but she couldn't put a story together. It wasn't likely she'd complete a book when she couldn't even think of a beginning.

After her pop had disappeared last night, she and Tim had stayed up most of the night watching movies and talking while Thatcher slept a cell away.

Tim had told her all about his new book, and she'd avoided his questions about how her writing was going. Finally, he'd slept a few hours on the cot in the open cell, and she'd played games on his computer until the battery ran down.

Thatcher was still asleep in his locked cage. He'd told them not to wake him until breakfast arrived at eight, as if he thought the place was a hotel.

Of course, Tim woke starving and insisted that he be the one to go after their breakfast. Lauren knew she was worrying about nothing, but she'd seen him wake sober and down a few drinks before breakfast, so it didn't surprise her when he stopped at his car for a few minutes on his walk to the diner. Long enough for a drink, she thought.

He'd said once that he needed the alcohol to relax his mind so he could let his imagination roam, but Lauren knew him better than anyone. He was given to mood swings even when they

118

were kids. The life of the party one minute, the one who thought his world was ending the next. Tim drank when he was down. Deep inside, she feared she might be part of his depression now. He'd wanted to be more than friends. He wanted commitment and she couldn't give him that.

How was it possible to love someone, she thought, and know that you couldn't be with him?

The front door opened, and Lauren guessed her father was finally getting to work. He sometimes came in for a few hours before he went over to breakfast. Maybe she'd walk with him this morning. Tim could probably eat both trays he brought while he watched Thatcher sleep.

The door opened again and again. The county offices were waking up. Doors were banging, phones ringing, people moving about.

She glanced toward Thatcher, curled in his blankets. He'd tried to call his girlfriend back a little after midnight. She hadn't answered.

After that, Thatcher turned his face to the wall and acted like he was asleep, but she'd noticed it was a long time before he settled. The kid had been abandoned by his family years ago. He had no clue how much the people of the town cared about him. Charley Collins had taken him in but never tried to be his parent. Thatcher, at fourteen, wouldn't have allowed that. Charley being a friend was far more important to the kid.

He might have nothing to his name, but Thatcher figured since he was tall enough he'd stand equal to the rancher and Charley had been smart enough to treat him that way.

Everyone in town knew Charley loved Thatcher like a son, but Thatcher called him by his name. Pop had said that when Charley Collins visited with the boy, he'd ask Thatcher how he could help. The kid might have taken every suggestion Charley made, but it was Thatcher's call.

Lauren walked the length of the two-cell jail. All night the place had felt like a tomb.

The sheriff's and county business offices on the main floor were the oldest part of the building, so every sound carried up like smoke from a greenwood fire.

The two courtrooms on the second floor sat silent most of the time.

The jail had been added on later and was usually used for weekend drunks. The smaller third floor had always reminded Lauren of a hat on top of the building. When she was little, the entire place fascinated her. This was her playground while her pop worked. Then, sometimes, long after dark, he'd step to his office door and whistle. The sound carried up the stairs, and she knew it was time to go home.

At twenty-five it was probably too late to ask Pop to whistle, but a part of her wanted to come home, really home. She was shy, quiet, not meant for the big city. She needed grounding, not anonymity. Lauren wanted to belong somewhere.

She heard voices below.

Curiosity got the better of her. After a few minutes, she decided Thatcher wasn't going anywhere. She might as well check downstairs. In her stocking feet, Lauren moved down the steps. Pearly was opening blinds and didn't see her pass.

Lauren could hear a voice that sounded familiar. She stood at her father's open office door, afraid to go in, afraid to move. A man in a black suit sat on the corner of Pop's desk. His legs were long. His shoes polished. She couldn't see his face, but he didn't dress like he was from around here.

Black hair, perfectly styled, curled over his white starched collar.

"Lauren," her father called; he'd spotted her. "Come on in. You remember Lucas Reyes."

She'd expected him to change in the years since college, but the man who turned toward her was far more a stranger than a friend. His eyes were the same dark brown, but now they seemed cold, almost formal, as he offered his hand like they were meeting, were touching, for the first time.

Lauren played along. "Hello, Lucas. What brings you back to Crossroads?" She wasn't about to tell her father that she'd called him at midnight last night.

"A friend told me a kid was in trouble. I'm between cases right now and thought I'd take a few days off and see if I could help." His smile was formal, practiced. "I'm betting my folks will be happy to see me, too. It's been a while since I've made it back. My dad told me the next time I came, arrive ready to help out. He'll probably have me working all week. I can almost hear him now saying, 'Saddle up, boy, the cows don't know it's Thanksgiving.' "

Pop frowned. "If Tim O'Grady called you, he's wasted your time. It's just a matter of hours before this whole thing will be cleared up. I've almost got Luther talked into dropping the charges if Thatcher will apologize. Once Luther thought about it, he saw the truth."

Her father didn't seem to notice no one in the room was listening to him. Lucas was staring at her so hard she doubted he was blinking, and she was doing the same. Somewhere in this polished man was the seventeen-year-old who'd saved her when she'd almost taken a fall one night in an old abandoned house. The boy she remembered was thinner, shy, not as certain of himself. He'd been the first boy who'd kissed her, so innocently, the night she'd turned sixteen.

Finally, Dan stepped between them and added, "Don't pay any attention to Lauren not joining the conversation. She's got to be dead tired after driving in from Dallas yesterday and then

122

up all night watching the prisoner and probably listening to Tim. If he could write as fast as he talks, he'd be a walking library."

Lauren realized she was standing there like a mute. She moved over to her father's coffeepot and pretended to consider a cup.

"I'd like to look over the report anyway, Sheriff." Lucas had turned away from her and back to the sheriff. "I know we'd all hate to see this kid's life messed up just because he threw one punch."

"You're welcome to everything, Lucas. It's public record. Lauren will even take you up to talk to the kid, but I don't see that it would do any good."

"Thanks, Sheriff." Lucas stood and shook Pop's hand then turned to her. "Will you show me the prisoner?"

"Sure. Follow me."

Pop waved them on as he glanced at his phone. "Stay with Thatcher another hour, Lauren. I've got an errand to run."

She smiled back at him. "Yeah, I noticed, Pop. You forgot to shave."

"Right," he said, as he put his phone to his ear and turned his back.

Lauren slowly climbed the stairs, trying to think of something to say to Lucas. The last time she'd seen him was outside the hospital after her father had been shot a few years ago. He'd driven half the night to make sure she was all right.

They'd talked and then fought. He'd made it plain he'd wanted to be on the fringes of her life even then. After that night, when she yelled at him for breaking up with her before they'd even started dating, he dropped off the fringes completely.

His footsteps sounded several feet behind her now. He didn't say a word or make an effort to catch up. It occurred to her that he was probably as lost for words as she was.

"Tim and I spent the night with Thatcher, and he didn't tell us anything new," she called back to him. "He's eighteen, but Pop didn't want him to feel alone, and the only deputy he has right now is in Austin for training."

She unlocked both the outer doors quickly and rushed into the open space between the two cells. Thatcher was still in his cot sound asleep.

Turning, she watched Lucas as he stepped from the hallway shadows. She could see him more clearly now. His black hair wasn't as in place as she'd first thought, and dark whiskers dusted his jaw. For a moment he almost looked younger. Maybe not the guy she first got to know in high school or the cowboy he'd become on weekends to earn money during college, but more the man who'd evolved from them and not the slick lawyer she'd seen the last time they'd talked.

"Lauren," he said in his low voice, slightly

124

flavored with his Spanish heritage, "I drove all night because you asked me to help. You must have known I'd come when you called. Are you all right?"

Maybe it was because she hadn't slept or because she'd wanted to see him for an eternity, but Lauren shattered. With one gulping cry, she ran full out to him.

Lucas caught her in his arms and swung her around. He held her so tightly she couldn't breathe, but Lauren didn't care. Then, as if they'd been lovers, he kissed her.

She melted, remembering how he'd been the first boy to kiss her, the first to touch her with passion and the first and only one to break her heart.

She'd kissed him one night in a bar hallway while she was still in college and he'd already graduated and was out working. They were both back in Crossroads for a weekend. Neither had planned the meeting. They'd shared something hot and wild for a few moments, then she'd run, disappearing before they could finish what she'd started.

Only now she was older, wiser. She wasn't holding back from what she wanted and neither was he. Maybe it was only one kiss. Maybe they were ending something more then starting. Right now, she didn't care.

The kiss was explosive with need, and they

held on to each other as if both feared the world would pull them apart again. She let her mind shut down and her body simply feel.

"I may be wrong—" Thatcher's voice came from ten feet away "—but I'm guessing you two know each other."

Lucas groaned and pulled away. For a moment, he looked down at her, smiling, with a promise in his eyes. "We'll continue this discussion later, Lauren."

She nodded. Then turned and introduced Lucas Reyes to Thatcher Jones as formally as she could muster.

Thatcher tilted his head sideways and stared at her as if he weren't at all sure she hadn't had her brain replaced in the ten minutes she'd been gone, but he didn't say a word.

Lucas, on the other hand, did turn into someone she had never met. All at once he was friendly, outgoing, a take-control kind of guy. All the shy, hesitant boy was gone. The man before her was confident and polished.

The lawyer in him seemed to have forgotten she was in the room.

"Glad to meet you, Thatcher Jones. I've been called in to visit with you. After we've talked, if you decide we'd make a good team, I'll work my hardest to get you out of here."

Thatcher frowned. "Do you even know what I did, mister?"

"No, but you've got someone who believes in you, and that's enough for me."

Lucas must have realized that his polished style might not work here, so he transformed like a chameleon, relaxing his body, leaning against the bars. "Look, I haven't had any sleep, and I'm pumped up on caffeine. Give me a few hours, and I'll know all about what got you to this place. You think I could come back about noon and we could talk? It may look like we have nothing in common except both knowing Lauren."

"I'd say you probably know her better than I do." Thatcher scratched his head.

Lauren wouldn't have been surprised if fleas didn't start jumping out in mass evacuation. When Pop got back, she'd suggest allowing Thatcher to shower.

Lucas grinned at the kid. "I grew up here, too. Lauren and I go way back."

"Yeah, I'm guessing all the way to the tonsils." Thatcher froze. "Wait a minute, you're Lucas Reyes. I've heard of you. You rode with Yancy Grey and Staten Kirkland that night they rounded up rustlers on the Double K. I was just a kid then, but I remember everyone talking about it. You've been in a shoot-out, almost got killed fighting rustlers on Kirkland land that night. Man, you're a legend. What you cowboys did was straight out of a western."

Lucas laughed. "I was there. We rode the canyon at night and came up behind the men stealing cattle. When Mr. Kirkland gave the signal, we all raised our rifles. The rustlers gave up when they saw forty armed men on the ridge. It wasn't the battle it's become. Just a good plan."

"Heroes always do that." Thatcher nodded. "They talk down what they do."

Lucas agreed. "Like you did when you took fire saving the sheriff out on County Road 111? That story made the news all over Texas. You faced bullets to get the sheriff out."

"Anyone would have helped. I just happened to be there. I didn't even know I was hit in the leg until we were halfway back to town."

Lucas shook his head. "No, some men act while others just watch, Thatcher. You're one of the good guys, and I'm here to help you get out of this place as fast as I can."

"I can't pay you much."

"I'm not asking much."

They shook hands and began to talk. Lucas had a way of getting information from Thatcher without seeming to ask questions. Lauren listened, admiring his skill.

Tim showed up with two boxed breakfasts from the café about the time Daisy Franklin delivered Thatcher's "prison meal," which included a dozen cranberry muffins with a jar of homemade plum jelly.

Tim greeted Lucas like an old friend, and the three sat down to eat, even though Thatcher's table was on the other side of a line of bars.

By the time Lauren went downstairs and brought them back two cups of coffee and a Dr Pepper for Thatcher, the three of them had decided to share the Franklin sisters' breakfast with sides of the diner's pancakes and French toast.

Lauren declined any breakfast, and said she wanted to go home and check on Pop. He'd been working far too hard. After being up for two days, he'd probably gone home for more sleep.

She slipped away without any of the guys commenting. In truth, she needed time to think.

Halfway down the stairs she remembered that she'd left her shoes in the open cell. When she turned, heading back up, Lucas was five feet behind her.

He smiled as he handed over her shoes. "When this is over we need to talk."

"No," she whispered. "Whatever was between us was over years ago." She couldn't let herself believe there could be something between them. She'd believed it too many times before.

"You're wrong, and saying it is doesn't change a thing."

She looked into his brown eyes and realized she'd probably hurt him as many times as he had her. Maybe there was something between them, maybe there always would be, but they weren't meant to be together. They were oil and water.

He was still standing in the same place on the stairs when she made it to the main floor. She glanced up at him and knew Lucas was right. There was and had always been something between them that needed to be settled. Be it love or lust, it needed to be dealt with before either of them could move on.

When she reached the lake house, Pop wasn't there. The shower was still steamy, but he'd vanished. Something important must have pulled him away.

Again. As it had a thousand times when she was growing up. She'd always been proud of her father. He was vital here, needed.

If she left Dallas, no one would even notice she was gone, but reason told her she wouldn't find herself in Tim or Lucas.

At twenty-five, it was about time she grew up.

CHAPTER THIRTEEN

CODY WOKE TO the sound of giggling. He knew he was in the hospital. His leg felt like it had been stretched, tortured and wrapped in concrete. His head must have been stapled back together with power tools. His chest hurt every time he breathed, and the soundtrack in his torture chamber resembled the whispering of little girls.

He opened one eye. Bright lights sparked through his brain. Why couldn't the nurses turn down the lights when they left? He wasn't likely to want to read or land an airplane in his condition, but the nurses had the room ready.

The girls' chatter finally stopped.

Before he could relax back into unconsciousness, a high voice from the side of his bed whispered, "Does it hurt, mister?"

"No," he lied, and moved his head slightly to the left.

A head of sunshine hair was peeking over his bandages. "Who are you?"

"I told you last night, I'm Melanie Miller. You probably have memory problems. Ranger Tess said that sometimes happens with head wounds. She called it am-nose-sia. Said you might not even remember your own name."

It was coming back to him. The fall, the little

girls, the woman who'd touched him. "Where are the others?"

"We're all here." A cute little redhead popped up beside the one with blond braids. "Except for Chloe. Her mother said she got a cold last night from being out in the night air, but I think it's probably pneumonia."

Melanie nodded at the redhead he remembered as Marjorie, but Melanie obviously wasn't finished talking to him. "Do you know your name, mister?"

"Sam?" Cody said.

She frowned.

"Pete, maybe?" he added as they both shook their heads.

"Jack? I'm almost sure it's Jack."

Melanie looked at the redhead. "Obviously permanent brain damage."

Marjorie agreed, then whispered, "Don't ask him any more questions. Let's just talk about Chloe. Maybe it'll get what mind he has left off his troubles." They both looked in his direction and gave that smile women must learn at birth that says nothing was going on.

Cody never dreamed he'd find any female under twenty-five interesting enough to talk to, but who knew, these girls were adorable. He hurt in so many places he'd thought laughing would be out for months, but these little girls achieved a miracle.

"People die from pneumonia, you know, mister, if they aren't careful, and it was cold out in the van last night," Marjorie said. "We watched them take you away. You looked dead lying there on that board they put you on."

A few more heads popped up, all nodding. One who hadn't mentioned her name told him that the rescue was far more fun than staring at stars.

Another asked how long it would be till he was dead because they had to all leave pretty soon.

He tried to look like he was serious. "I don't think I am going to die. Unless you all are angels, but to tell the truth I don't think I'm heading in that direction."

"You're not if you keep cussing. My momma said so," a chubby girl in the back added. She'd been the one in the van, he remembered, who'd cried as she'd watched him. "She says cussing is the devil's language."

This tenderhearted one was missing most of her front teeth and didn't seem to care as she smiled at him. Before he could ask her name, the door opened.

"I said you could look at him, girls, not talk to him," a familiar voice whispered as if he wasn't wide-awake. "Now say goodbye. Your rides are waiting just beyond the double doors."

Cody wanted to look at the woman he'd talked to last night. Tess, she'd said when he'd asked for her name.

But moving his head seemed far too much effort. He knew her voice, her touch, but he couldn't remember seeing her face clearly.

One by one the girls patted his unbandaged arm. Melanie warned him to stay still and Marjorie told him to keep breathing. The rest just said goodbye. The one without front teeth was crying again.

Cody closed his eyes when silence settled around him. He tried to piece together all that had happened last night. He'd been in a dark mood over nothing really, more than halfway drunk and needing to feel adrenaline pounding through his body. He'd climbed on a horse, half wild on a calm day, and they'd raced along the canyon's edge as if they both thought they were immortal.

A warm hand brushed his forehead, moving back what was surely muddy and dirty hair. Cody knew the park ranger named Tess was still in the room. He'd felt her touch before.

"Did you find my horse?"

Her voice was low. "Two other rangers and I went over to your place at dawn thinking we'd find her dead at the bottom of that canyon you flew over, but apparently she'd been smart enough not to take the flight. When we drove up to your house, I spotted a black horse you would call Midnight standing outside the corral in the shelter of trees. She looked tired and hungry, but unharmed and still saddled."

Cody lay his hand over hers resting on his chest, now covered in white gauze, but he couldn't bring himself to look at her. "Thanks. I was worried about her. She's about the only friend I have left."

When she huffed, he added, "You know the kind. A friend who doesn't hesitate to come along on any crazy thing you want to do. The kind who'll never tell you to slow down. The kind who'll watch you get drunk and never say a word."

"No, Winslow, I don't have that friend and you don't either. Midnight is a horse."

"She's smarter than most buddies I've had."

Tess pulled her hand away. "I've no doubt. If either of you had had any brains, you wouldn't have been racing along the canyon edge after dark."

Cody decided he'd be wise to stop talking. He was dropping IQ points with every word. He leaned back against his pillow and listened while she gave what he was sure was her planned lecture.

"We went into your barn and fed all your horses. You keep a very organized barn, Mr. Winslow."

Cody wondered when he'd become Mr. Winslow to her. He'd thought they'd be on a first-name basis by now. After all, she'd pretty much felt every part of his body, and she had

135

kissed him goodbye when they'd lifted him on the chopper.

"I wasn't sure what kind of shape you'd be in this morning, so I called the sheriff's office over at Crossroads and left a message." She continued her report. "The secretary said she'd find someone to feed the horses tomorrow if you didn't call in saying you'd made arrangements for them. I couldn't see much difference between the pigpen and your house, so I asked if the sheriff knew someone who could clean both. For a man who takes such good care of his horses, you'd think you'd at least make an effort at housekeeping."

She was at the top of his bed, and he was hurting too bad to even try to look up at her. Besides, what could he say? She was right. The only things he kept in working order were the barn and corrals. He hadn't even bothered to fix the gate. Who'd want to turn into his place anyway?

Only he didn't like being reminded of his problems. She'd probably think he was completely mad if he told her that some nights he slept in the barn. The horses' low noises kept the demons away.

She added in a soft tone, as if just remembering he was hurt and shouldn't be lectured, "Your house will be clean when you get out of here. The pigs are out of luck."

"You taking over my life, Tess?" he asked.

"Somebody needs to, Winslow. You don't seem to be doing a very good job of it right now." A slight laugh took any harshness out of her words. "The mailman even stopped me when I was trying to close the broken gate into your place. He told me you haven't bothered to pick up your mail in over a month." As she moved to his side, her hand slid along his arm. Her touch was featherlight and comforting even if her words were not.

He frowned and braced himself as he opened one eye. Any woman this bossy had to be as ugly as hell. Maybe the lantern's light last night had favored what little he saw of her face. The jack-o'-lantern glow might be her best look.

The shock brought him fully awake. She was taller than he thought she'd be. No makeup. Chestnut-brown hair tied back at the base of her neck and honey-brown eyes. She wasn't the kind of woman he'd ever try to pick up in a bar, and she wasn't the sweet, meek kind his mother used to introduce him to every time he came home. She had an intelligent stare, and light freckles crossed the bridge of her nose. There were tiny lines at the corners of her eyes when she smiled. His grandmother would have said she was a "handsome" woman, but nothing about Tess Adams was soft or simply pretty.

She leaned closer. "You all right? You got that

137

eyes-fixin'-to-roll-back-in-your-head look about you."

He stared at her and took her measure. She was younger than he thought when he'd first seen her in shadow, but he knew without any doubt that she'd grow old gracefully. Tess Adams was a strong woman who didn't look like she needed someone to take care of her, and that one trait drew him to her. In fact, he found it as sexy as hell.

He had a feeling if he ever stepped out of line with her, she'd knock him to the floor before he saw it coming. "I'm great, honey. Thanks for saving my life."

She sat on the edge of his bed. "I believe you would have crawled out of the canyon and lived if I hadn't been there to help. You could have called a neighbor or friend, and they'd have eventually found you and carried you home."

"I don't have a cell phone, and I don't know my neighbors."

"Let me guess, you don't have a friend either," Tess added.

"I do have a few left, but they're all in Austin and probably barely remember me. I haven't called them in months." He almost added that some were dead, but he didn't want to explain.

She frowned at him. "You obviously don't have any brains either. Riding on a night when rain is turning to snow. Telling no one where you're

138

going. Not being able to contact anyone if you hit trouble. Which you did."

His head was throbbing, but he decided offense was the only way to go. "At least I wasn't down in the bottom of the canyon with a bunch of little girls. What kind of parents send their kid off with a ranger who forgot to check the weather?"

She took the criticism. "You're right. I should have gotten them out an hour earlier, but I hoped the rain would wait until the stars were bright. They're unbelievable in that spot."

"If you hadn't waited, no one would have found me. And you're right, I would have crawled out, but I might not have made it back to my house before freezing. So thanks, Tess. I mean it."

She patted his hand. "I'm glad I was there. I have a confession. I looked you up on the internet. Saw lots of articles about you from three years ago. Those bullet holes on your chest came from a battle with drug runners down at the tip of Texas. You were left for dead then."

He saw caring in her honey eyes and looked away. He didn't need sympathy or worse, pity. He'd seen enough of that to last a lifetime. He'd rather face the demons alone than put up with someone smothering him.

"I guess I was too mean to die." He might not be looking at her, but his fingers folded around her hand. "One of your little girls told me I needed to stop cussing if I want to get into heaven. I learned three years ago that neither heaven nor hell seems to want me."

"Maybe you just need direction, Winslow. Maybe you should get married. That seems to give most men direction. You shouldn't have any trouble, not with those steel-blue eyes, and there are women who wouldn't care that you don't have any social skills."

"I don't take to a lead rope, Tess. It's not my way. But if I was the kind of man to settle down, it'd be with a woman like you." He almost grinned. She might be bossing him around and pointing out his faults, but at least she wasn't crying or patting on him like he was a lame horse they were about to put down.

"Like me?" She pulled her hand away. "I don't think so. I'm the kind of woman who never really got into dating and lives alone with her cats. I'm taller than most men, smarter by half and don't play the games women play."

He frowned. He didn't see her that way at all. Sure, she had no makeup or fancy hairstyle, but she didn't need it. "How many you got?"

"How many what? Dates?"

"No, cats."

"Three."

"Any other pets? Fish, birds, rattlesnakes?"

"No. Why?"

"I want to ask you out on a date. A real date, Tess, even if you advise against it."

When she didn't say no right away, Cody continued. "Not one of those 'having a drink or cup of coffee' as friends date. I want to pick you up and take you to the best place I can find for dinner. I want to stand on your front porch and kiss you good-night and then walk away knowing that next time you'll invite me in."

"You do have a death wish, don't you? I've already told you I'm not the kind of girl who does well on dates." She studied him. "All right. You get out of this hospital and we'll have a date. But I should warn you, you do anything inappropriate and I'll break your other leg."

"How about I promise not to do anything you don't love?" He covered her hand again, deciding he liked hanging on to her.

"All right, but it's been my experience that I am terrible when it comes to men. My prom date brought me home at nine, then went back to the dance."

"Tell me all the bad experiences you got, Tess. It's not going to change my mind. We're still going out." Cody made up his mind. He was taking her out.

She shook her head. "I can't stay here and argue with a man too weak to stand and too dumb to stop talking. I have to go. Visits in this wing are limited to fifteen minutes. I'll save all the other horror stories about dating for our evening together you seem to think we're going to have, but I'm telling you right now, I'm only ordering appetizers until I see how long you can last."

"Fair enough. Maybe I'll still be on drugs, and it won't sound so bad."

She laughed, and he decided he loved her laughter even if he did hate cats.

He closed his hand around her fingers. "Kiss me goodbye, Tess."

"What?" She looked more like she was thinking of hitting an injured man. Him.

"You heard me. Kiss me before you go. On the mouth, not the cheek this time."

"Why?"

"I want to feel your lips. Come on. My mouth is about the only part of this body that isn't swollen, bruised or broken." He let go of her hand. If she was going to run, so be it.

"All right. Why not." She leaned over and kissed him on the mouth. A soft kiss that lingered too long to just be friendly.

When she straightened, he whispered, "See you tomorrow, honey."

"When you heal, I'm going to slug you for calling me that." She moved to the door, but she was smiling.

"As long as you're around, I won't care." He smiled. "It wasn't so bad, was it?"

Tess brushed her fingertips over her lips. "No, it wasn't."

"We'll practice some more later." He swore he saw a blush just below her freckles.

She disappeared, and a moment later a nurse came in with a cupful of pills. "Nice-looking visitor you've got there, Mr. Winslow."

"She's my wife," he said. "But don't tell anyone. We're keeping it a secret for a while."

The nurse crossed her heart with the thermometer, and Cody knew without a doubt she'd spread the news as soon as she left the room. By noon tomorrow it will have reached Crossroads that the loner, former Texas Ranger out on Wild Horse Springs had married the park ranger. The next time he went to town, he'd see it in their eyes and they'd smile at him, silently telling him they were keeping his secret.

Except when the whole town kept your secret, it wasn't much of a secret.

Tess was probably going to drag him to the canyon herself and toss him over when she found out. If they did see much of each other, he predicted death threats in his future coming in regular intervals until they got this marriage lie straightened out.

But until then, folks would be looking at her in a different light.

CHAPTER FOURTEEN

BRANDI TRIED TO go back to sleep after the sheriff left, but it was useless. She'd lost his warmth next to her, and she was shocked at just how much she missed it.

She didn't want to ask herself why he'd felt so right, but Dan Brigman had. From the first kiss a few days ago to holding her all night long, this stranger had simply stepped into her life as if he'd been there all along. When he'd knelt to help her on with her boot a few minutes after they'd met, she'd known he was different from any man she'd ever encountered.

She'd noticed the sheriff was exhausted last night and hadn't minded when he fell asleep. It told her one simple fact: he felt safe with her, just as she did with him. Maybe she simply needed him near last night. Any more might have been too much for her to handle, but this morning she knew one night would never be enough.

In a way, sleeping with him seemed far more personal than just having sex. In her traveling days years ago, she'd had sex now and then, but she'd never stayed the night with anyone. Unless she counted the drummer who once passed out in her bed by accident. She'd watched him snore until he sobered up enough to lean over the side of the bed and throw up. Then at dawn he'd muttered "sorry" as he patted her on the bottom and left. She hadn't bothered to remember his face or name, but the smell of whiskey vomit sometimes lingered in her nose.

She laughed, remembering how he'd bragged to the band about sleeping with her, leaving out the part that he'd been passed out the entire time. Most of the guys she'd known back then were either jerks or potheads, or both. It was refreshing to meet an adult male who was simply too tired to stay awake, and she had no doubt that the sheriff would never say a word to anyone about their night together.

Brandi wrapped up in her blankets and drifted, half asleep, half dreaming. So much for memories of the wild life she thought she'd lived after she'd run away from home at eighteen. Mostly it was long nights of working for little money, or worse, tips. Then hoping the band had enough gas to make it to the next town.

There had been a few memories of hurried sex in bar bathrooms or the back of cars. She could never remember taking off all her clothes, and not one of the parade of boys during her traveling years had ever touched her as Dan had this morning.

He treated her like a treasure almost too precious to touch. They'd both known they were stealing a few minutes, but he took his time. He made her feel cherished. No one had ever done that before.

Not her family, or any guy she'd met on tour, or Evie's father. She did remember his dark good looks, his rush to live fully, his fist against her cheek.

The last time she saw Marty, the man who got her pregnant, he had accused her of trying to force him to grow old. He'd yelled that the last thing he wanted was a baby to drag around on tour. Her heart shattered as she realized he wasn't half the man he pretended to be. He was simply a frightened boy. She'd mistaken recklessness for adventure and lust for love.

He was right about one thing though: the pregnancy made her grow up that morning, while he'd shrunken to spider height. She'd decided to become an adult that day, even if it meant going back home and giving up on her dream to sing.

Marty simply moved on, giving her up without looking back.

Reaching into the nightstand drawer, she pulled out Evie's baby picture. She'd had her father's eyes, big and coffee brown. The picture had been taken before Brandi knew something was terribly wrong with her beautiful little girl. Brandi thought of the photo as her sunny-day picture. All the rest were shadow days. Hospital shots with birthday cakes on a tray table in front of her frail body or Christmas collages of the staff smiling around a child slowly dying.

The last picture she hadn't kept. It had been framed by a hospital hallway with all the doctors and nurses wearing green scrubs as they pushed her nine-year-old into surgery. Brandi hadn't known it then, but her only child's eyes already reflected death in their depths that day.

"Morning, angel," Brandi whispered, even though Evie had been gone fourteen months. She'd never grow up. She'd never have children or another birthday. Evie would never laugh, or smile, or hold her mother's hand again.

She'd give it all up again, the freedom, the career, just to have one more day to hold her daughter. One more hour to hold her so maybe her arms would stop aching.

Sometimes Brandi thought her little girl hadn't died, she'd simply let go of her hand. Once, she'd reached out in the night as if a little hand might be waiting just beyond. When she felt nothing, grief flowed into her heart as if new.

She didn't cry now as she stared at the picture. She'd already cried her lifetime quota of tears. She'd had a daughter no one but her wanted, and when Evie died, the family had all said it was for the best.

Brandi had always been the one Malone child who never fit in. If her father hadn't left her a fourth of the ranch, the other three children would have kicked her out of the family tree years ago. They never let her in on the decisions, and the only contact she had with them was when the accountant deposited her share of the profits into her account.

At first she'd thought she wouldn't touch the money, but it was needed to cover hospital bills. It was enough to live on so she could spend her time taking care of her child.

When Evie died, Brandi left the day after the funeral. No one seemed to notice. She was as far away from Wyoming as she could get both in miles and in her mind. The huge Malone ranch would run just fine without her.

For over a year she'd been living one day at a time. Trying to find where she belonged. Trying to outrun heartache.

Brandi shivered as she climbed out of bed. She kissed Evie's picture and put it back in the drawer. Someday, if she ever settled down, she'd take it out and set it in the sunshine, but this wasn't a place for her angel. Her baby would need a quiet place where peace whispered over calm waters. A place where pain never visited and laughter smelled lavender sweet.

Smiling, Brandi switched her thoughts to how grand it had been to sleep in someone's arms. Once she'd moved home, alone and pregnant, she'd never gone out with anyone. When Evie was born, there had been no time to date. Evie needed her.

Since she'd been on the road again, no one had seemed right. She'd thought about having sex with a few men, but she realized there were none she wanted to cuddle with. Or maybe it simply wasn't worth the effort of getting to know someone and then having to explain how she had to walk away. How could she clarify that she couldn't love anyone because she'd sworn she'd never watch another loved one die?

Until Dan. He'd made her feel safe. She'd let down her guard and slept soundly for once. He didn't want a relationship. They both only wanted a fling. She could handle that.

As she dressed, Brandi laughed at how Dan thought she was wild. Of course she must be. She worked in a bar, she traveled around, she wore rhinestone boots.

"I'll never tell him otherwise," she whispered. "I'll be the wild dream he's always wanted and when it's over, I'll walk away just as he expects me to do."

She applied her makeup a little bolder and wore a blouse that showed more skin than usual. She'd learned her lesson fourteen months ago. There was no forever. No happily-ever-after. No love that lasted a lifetime.

The motel phone sounded just as she pulled on her fancy boots. No one called her but Hank from the bar. No one else knew where she stayed.

"Morning, Hank, it's a little early for you to be up and around."

"Brandi, are you all right?" His deep voice, as big as the man, sounded strangely high, near panic.

"I'm fine. The storm was so bad last night that I asked the sheriff to drop me off at my motel on his way home."

"Thank God." Hank took a moment to breathe. "The back wall of the Nowhere caught fire just before dawn. Fire department says it looks like someone emptied a few five-gallon cans of gasoline on the back door right where your dressing room is or more accurately, was."

He took another breath. "I almost had a heart attack when I got here and saw the blaze and your van still parked close up to the back door. I thought you were still in there." He took a moment to gulp down a few cuss words then continued, "Sorrel finally calmed down enough to say he thought you went home with the sheriff, but he wasn't sure."

"I didn't . . ." she started.

"I know. I figured Sorrel meant that the sheriff took you back to your motel. It's only a few miles from his office. I should have offered, Brandi."

"I'm fine, Hank. How much burned?" Thoughts popped like a string of firecrackers in her head. Her clothes, her guitars, her equipment might all be gone. Most could be replaced.

"Anyone hurt?"

"No." Hank slowed down. "But I'm afraid you're out of a job. I'll never get it open in two weeks, and your agent says you're booked for the rest of the year."

She couldn't seem to focus on one thought.

"It's not as bad as it could have been," Hank admitted. "My drunk bartender was sleeping in the hallway. I swear he empties the beer bottles down his throat as he cleans up. But when the fire hit, he called 911 right away and got out."

Brandi fought down worry over her things enough to ask about Sorrel. "Is he all right?"

"He's fine. Burned his arm a little." Hank swore again. "Said his wife kicked him out again yesterday and now that the cot in the back is burned, he's double homeless. He doesn't know it yet, but he was damn lucky. Rain and wind put out most of the fire before the trucks got here." The big guy was talking himself down. "If the weather improves and I can get enough help out here, we'll take a look at the structural damage."

"Is there anything I can do?" She guessed she was about to be as homeless as Sorrel. Money wasn't a problem. She had plenty in the bank. But what would she do with her time? She suddenly didn't have a direction.

"The fire's out. If you want to come rummage through what's left of your stuff, there might be something that survived the fire, the icy rain

151

and the water the fire department dumped on the place."

"What about my van?" She'd been afraid to drive it on bald tires in the snow. It was already time to buy another. Nothing fancy. The last thing she wanted to do was look too successful.

"It was parked next to the wall that caught fire. I don't know, but I'm guessing it's totaled. Windows look like they've been knocked out. Probably by the heat, or maybe whoever brought the gasoline also brought a bat and your van was simply in his way."

Brandi didn't care about the van. The only thing she'd left at the Nowhere that mattered to her were her guitars.

Forcing her words to be calm, she asked, "My guitars? Did they burn?" She couldn't lose them. They were the one link back to her past. Memories of being happy and free in her younger days. Memories of playing to Evie every night.

"Sorrel grabbed one of them when he woke and saw the flames. It's in the front hallway. I don't know about the other. If it was on stage, it may have survived."

"I'll be there as soon as I can catch a ride," she said.

"I'd come get you, but I'm needed here. Maybe the sheriff could bring you over. I heard a deputy here saying he was calling Brigman in on the investigation this afternoon. Firemen are still rummaging through the place making sure there are no hot spots, so there is no need to hurry over. I'm not leaving until I can board up enough to secure the place, so I'll be here all day."

She hung up the phone. She only had two weeks left on this gig, but if she had to buy new clothes, more equipment and a van, she'd need time. Money wasn't a problem, but what to do with her time was.

She'd need help getting around, and the only friend she'd made in this part of Texas was the sheriff.

CHAPTER FIFTEEN

LAUREN, ARMS OUT WIDE, fell onto her bed face-first. Stuffed animals bounced and tumbled off the quilts as if escaping a tsunami.

She laughed, kicked off her shoes and cuddled in. The slightly dusty smell of home surrounded her. No matter how hard the world got, this room, her house, would always be her safe haven. The sound of water lapping against the dock out back. The smell of dried lavender in a vase she'd forgotten to toss. The feel of a cotton quilt washed a hundred times and left in the sun to dry.

The sky grew cloudy outside her window, bathing the morning's glow in the colors of twilight as she drifted to sleep.

In her dream she was fifteen again and back in the old run-down place people called the Gypsy House. It was almost midnight and frosty cold in the nightmare. Tim O'Grady and Lucas Reyes were with her.

Reid Collins, the third boy who'd been with them that night, had almost faded from her dreams, but the other memories were still there. The smell of rot soaked into the walls. Trash on the dug-out floor that rattled in the wind. The feel of ghosts pressing against her skin as light as humidity.

154

They'd gone in on a bet, thinking they'd have a story to tell at school. Lucas, the oldest of them, had dropped through the window first, then caught her. They were laughing, trying not to act afraid as they began to explore. They talked of spirits and legends about the old place as they moved around the moonlight-striped rooms.

Tim was the last one heading up the stairs when the second floor gave way, and decaying lumber that had held for generations tumbled through to the basement.

His cries were the soundtrack now to this old scene she played over and over in her mind. He was hurt, trapped below, screaming in pain. Then the floor disappeared out from under Lauren, too, and she started to fall.

In no more than the pause between seconds, Lucas grabbed her and pulled her against him. They stood on the tiny bit of flooring left as Tim yelled for help and Reid jumped out of the second floor window, still thinking they all were playing a game.

Lauren moved deeper into the dream. She could feel Lucas's heart pounding against her. His arm held her tight, and she almost believed she was safe.

His hand moved beneath her sweater and over her lace bra.

Lauren's eyes flew opened and the dream vanished. "Tim!" She screamed his name before she glanced behind her. "What are you doing here? Get out of my bed."

Tim sat up and scratched his head, making his mass of red hair even more out of control, if that were possible. "The sheriff told me to go home and get some sleep. I just stopped at the first bed I came across. I thought you might enjoy the company, since we spent last night jail-sitting and not touching."

She elbowed him and climbed off the bed, since he didn't seem to be moving. They'd had sex for the first time in this room when her pop had been in the hospital after being shot. She'd needed comfort then, but what they did had never been *making love*. Not for her, anyway.

He reached for her with one hand while he rubbed his rib with the other. "It was nice holding you, L, when you were asleep. Not near as many sharp edges." He put his finger in his ear. "I think I have hearing damage. For a quiet girl, you sure do wake up loud."

"You're fine, Tim, and the damage you're complaining about is nothing compared to what would happen if Pop came home and found you in my bed."

"We're adults. So we sleep together. We should just tell him and let him deal with it. We're both out of college and single." He frowned. "There is no crime to report here."

"Okay, you tell him."

Tim stood. "Not while he's armed, or within ten feet of a weapon. Oh, hell, L, your dad could probably kill me with his bare hands. You should tell him. He wouldn't murder his only offspring."

"I'm not telling him because as of right now we are not sleeping together." She should have told Tim before, like the morning after the first time they'd slept together or the last time he'd been in Dallas for a visit and she'd pretended when they'd had sex. She'd known it wasn't right between them; it seemed mechanical, almost like something they just did. Dinner, movie, sex. But neither ever mentioned going further. No hint of marriage. *Forever* or even *someday* weren't words they used. Sleeping with Tim was like trying to dance to a rhythm you've never heard before. All the actions were there, but she didn't feel anything.

There were a hundred reasons why she should have stopped it, but only one kept her silent. She didn't want to hurt Tim; he was her best friend. She couldn't remember the time before he lived just down the shoreline. He'd always been a part of her life. He'd always cared about her and been on her side.

"You know I love you." She patted him on the chest, wishing she felt differently. Life would be so much easier if she wanted him in her bed.

"I know. I love you, too." He wrapped one arm around her and pulled her against him. He wasn't hugging her, just holding on for one more moment.

"But not that way." She stepped backward, and he didn't try to stop her. "I don't want to be lovers anymore."

"Not what way?" He repeated her words as he turned his back, unable to look her in the eyes. "You know, L, I'm not sure we were ever lovers. We could have been, but you wouldn't let that happen."

She knew he was hurt, but she didn't want to fight. "Can we stay friends?"

He grabbed his coat from where he'd dropped it on his way in. "I don't know, L. I don't think so."

As he walked away, she heard him say again, "I don't know."

Maybe it was because she hadn't slept all night or maybe she feared she'd just lost her best friend, but Lauren curled back into bed and cried herself to sleep like the lonely little girl she'd been all her life.

CHAPTER SIXTEEN

BRANDI COULDN'T BREATHE deep enough to get all the air she needed after she finished talking to Hank. The fire had not been an accident. He'd repeated it twice.

She sat on the corner of her bed and watched ice melt off the inside of the window glass like a tiny glacier skating toward oblivion. The day was warming, but she felt cold inside, hollow, afraid. Someone meant the club or her harm. Why else would he set the place ablaze?

But who? She'd turned down dates, but no one seemed that upset. Not enough to want to hurt her. Hank kicked drunks out on a regular basis. It was almost part of sweeping up every night. Surely one didn't come back and try to burn the place down? Sorrel's wife seemed to hate the bartender, but killing him in a fire seemed a bit extreme.

Slowly, numbness blanketed her, more than worry. Someone could have been hurt. Or killed. In her months of drifting, singing to crowds who seemed no more than blank faces watching, she rarely had to step so fully into reality.

Brandi wasn't sure she liked it outside her dreamy cocoon. She'd learned the hard way that the world could be a cruel place to live.

Now, with the fire and its damage, she had to deal with the world. She couldn't run without a car. She didn't want to step away from Dan yet. She had nowhere she'd rather be than here.

It crossed her mind that she needed the memories they'd made to put in her dreamworld, but she also needed the real man to help her to step back into the real world. Dan Brigman's head wasn't full of daydreams. He dealt with life head-on. Maybe, if she stayed around awhile, he'd help her learn to do that also.

She could have died in the fire. But she hadn't.

If Dan hadn't offered to take her back to the motel last night, she would have slept in her dressing room. She would have been there.

Closing her eyes, she tried to imagine the fire starting at the back wall. One spark would have set the stored paper goods in her room on fire, and if the hallway were already blazing, she would have been trapped.

Drunk Sorrel, who usually passed out on the cot after Hank left, could have been killed trying to save her or been too drunk to wake up in time to run. He would have left four children and a desperate wife behind.

Brandi's stage outfits, which were probably destroyed in the fire, didn't matter. One of her guitars had been saved. That was all she really needed to perform. She could get another van, new clothes. She could move on down the road, running, as always, away from her troubles. Or she could stay for a while and deal with the world for a change.

She'd been thinking that at some point she might settle down for a while. Once, when she'd been driving through Arkansas, she'd seen a little place on a back road. The sign on the gate read Sunflower Farm, Make an Offer.

Someday, maybe she'd drive back through Arkansas and stop. But right now all she was able to manage was a few days here before she moved on and continued drifting with her music.

"Don't worry about tomorrow," she whispered. "Tomorrow might never come."

Since her job at the Nowhere was over, nothing was keeping her in Crossroads. The next job was six hours west in New Mexico. If she wanted to, she could rent a car, drive to Taos and buy something there.

The memory of Dan's warm body next to hers drifted through her mind, calming her. "A reason to stay." She said the words as if they were the beginning of a song. She wasn't looking for love. But it wouldn't be so bad to have a memory.

It was about time for a vacation, if people took breaks from running away from life.

She didn't want to miss the chance to feel alive again, if only for a while. Men like Dan Brigman didn't come along often, and if he knew all the baggage she carried, he'd probably run like hell.

He didn't seem all that interested in sharing conversation, and she'd just as soon skip talking to him altogether.

After all, that's what wild people did.

She made a cup of Earl Grey tea and drank it while she packed. Her mind drifted to another kind of fire, the one building inside her. It was time she had a bit of fun with someone who looked like he could handle anything she suggested. Maybe they'd make love like two wild kids or maybe she'd torture him with a long, slow surrender.

As she closed the last suitcase, she heard a car pull into the empty motel parking lot. Glancing out, there was no mistaking the cruiser or the sheriff climbing out of it.

Dan looked different in his uniform. Cold, hard, official. She liked him better in his rumpled cotton shirt and jeans.

He tapped on the door, then removed his hat as she answered.

"Morning, Sheriff," she said, as if she barely knew him. "How can I help you this morning?"

The maid's cart was one door away, and Brandi had no doubt the chubby little maid, the one who always turned off her heater, was within hearing distance.

"I wanted to inform you, Miss Malone, that there has been a fire at the place where you work."

"I know, Sheriff. My boss called me an hour ago. He said you might be heading over to help out with police work, and he'd send word for you to give me a ride if you had time." She said the words with the emotions of one reading prescription instructions.

Dan nodded. "I'm headed over now, if you're ready? Don't know how much help I'll be, but I might be able to add a few names to the list of folks who were there last night. Listening to you sing was worth the snowy drive. I considered it an honor to have heard you before you hit the big time."

His eyes said he was telling the truth, but she suspected the compliment was more for the maid's benefit than hers.

She fought down a grin. "Thank you, Sheriff, that's very kind of you." Brandi felt like she was in a school play. "I've already packed and called the office to check out. It's been a lovely stay, but it's time I moved on."

Without a word, he reached in and took her huge suitcase. Brandi followed him out with the rest of her things.

They were pulling onto the highway before he glanced at her. "Where you going from here, pretty lady? You have no dressing room, and you just checked out of the only motel around."

She almost told him the truth. She knew small towns. They might have gotten away with him bringing her home in the middle of a snowstorm, but someone would see them if he parked, even in the back, again. "I was hoping you'd know another motel I could switch to. Maybe something out on the highway to Lubbock? I only picked this motel because it was the closest to Nowhere."

"That means you'll be within driving distance if I get a night free?" He wasn't looking at her, but she saw the corner of his smile.

"It does. I thought I'd take a few days off. My next gig isn't for two weeks. Hank says as soon as he can find a few minutes he'll take me in to buy a new van. In the meantime, if I can find a place, I thought I'd hole up and write a few of the songs dancing around in my head."

"You're not worried where you're headed, are you, Brandi?"

"Nope. It was just stuff that burned in the fire. No one was hurt and always-drunk Sorrel even managed to save my guitar. I've nothing to worry about, and I can think of at least one reason to hang around this part of the country for a while."

He winked at her. "We could share a little time."

"We could. I'll make sure the next hotel isn't too close to Crossroads."

"I'd appreciate that. I doubt anyone would ever think we're together. If they saw my cruiser outside your door, they'd probably assume

I'd stopped by to check your insurance papers."

"Or you might want to question me about the fire. Maybe I'm a disgruntled employee and set the fire?"

She touched his arm. "You are the only one who knew exactly where I was all night."

Dan slowed the car and looked at her, laughter in his warm, honest eyes. "Sorrel knew where you were, might even have seen you go out the back door. No one else would have known you left the building, so maybe you were the target. You got anyone gunning for you, pretty lady?"

Brandi's hand shook as fear plowed through her veins. "You really think someone might have been trying to kill me?" Impossible.

"Maybe. I talked to the bartender on the phone. He said he'd been moving around in the place turning on lights during the night. If someone was outside watching, they could have thought it was you. Sorrel's car wasn't in the lot because his wife dropped him off. Her last words to him when he asked if she was coming back to get him were 'when hell freezes over.' So he could have been the target, except she had four kids under five in the car with her when she drove away. Women with that many toddlers don't usually have time to plot a murder. Plus, even drunk, he was bringing in income."

"That's probably why he sleeps at the bar. It's quieter. Or maybe he doesn't want number five."

Dan shrugged. "Or maybe he's too afraid of her to ask for a divorce."

"Or maybe he loves her," Brandi whispered, knowing she was allowing her thoughts to drift in the dreamworld again.

She stared out the window for a while, watching the landscape. Spikes of tall, brown grass poked from the snow-covered ground, and tumbleweeds almost as big as Volkswagens bumped their way across the flatland. Desolate, lonely, barren.

Like her, she thought.

Dan stopped the car on the side of the deserted road. "You want to talk about something, Brandi?"

"No," she whispered as she turned toward him. "I want you to kiss me. I'm hungry for the taste of you on my lips."

"Right here? Right now?"

"Right here. Right now," she answered, pushing her worries back as if they were no more than bangs in her eyes.

To her surprise, he leaned toward her. She leaned toward him, too.

His lips were cold when they touched hers, but they warmed as he kissed her lightly. She'd expected him to pull away quickly, before anyone came along, but he didn't.

Smiling, she finally straightened. "Aren't you afraid someone will see us?"

"It's a chance I'm willing to take. Another mile and we'll be in sight of the bar." He rested his

166

hand on her knee. "Part of me couldn't care less if the whole town sees us. I'm not in the habit of doing things I'm ashamed of, and I'm not ashamed of being with you."

She laughed. "Oh, but think of what knowing you could do to my reputation."

"In that case, I'll back off."

She shook her head. "I don't want you to back off, Dan. I want you running full out toward me. Only in private. Not public. I'll be gone in a few days, and I don't want to leave the town a story to tell about their sheriff." She'd lived in a place where stories from the past hung on you like funeral clothes never letting you step into a new day, a new life.

A delivery truck passed them. The driver waved at the sheriff.

Dan cut the wipers. She watched snow slowly curtain them off from the world.

His hand moved up her leg, warming her through the wool slacks she wore. "Then private is how we'll have it. A wild affair no one will ever know about. Something between just you and me."

"A memory we'll share forever." She leaned back, loving how he touched her, knowing that she needed a few great memories to stack up against all the bad.

When she turned toward him, his eyes had darkened.

He whispered, "I'll call you up every fall and

say one word, *remember,* and then I'll hang up and know that wherever you are, you're remembering me." His bold hand moved up her body and inside her coat.

"Sheriff, I think you missed your calling. You should have been a poet."

Big flakes had covered the windshield. He leaned across the car and pulled her to him. His kiss was now hungry, and she loved pushing him further onto passion's edge.

With a sigh, he pulled away. "I want far more of you than this."

"So do I," she answered. "I've been thinking that I'd like to see you exhausted from making love to me. Maybe you'd better get some rest, Sheriff. You're going to need all your strength."

Laughing, he winked at her. "You stay around, pretty lady, and I'll take up running."

He straightened and put the cruiser into gear. Neither said a word. She knew what he was thinking. To do any more sitting in the middle of a road in morning light would have been too much. To do less would never be enough.

It was good that people would be around at the club. Another kind of fire was building inside her. What they were both planning would be best tonight if it was left to simmer all day in their thoughts.

As they pulled up to the Nowhere, fire trucks, pickups and cars were everywhere. The place had never been this full, even on a Saturday night.

Hank stepped away from a crowd of firemen as they climbed out. "You two missed all the fire," he said.

Brandi didn't dare look at Dan.

Hank was high on adrenaline. "When I got here, I feared I'd lose the whole place, but it appears most of the burn was along the back wall. We may be able to even save the stage. Too bad you won't be able to perform tonight, Brandi."

She swore she could feel Dan's gaze on her, but she didn't move.

Hank rattled on, explaining details.

Brandi moved around the edges of the still-smoking ashes. She noticed a leather notebook in which she often wrote lines for songs. It must have been on the stage. The cover was cracking and the pages were wet, but she picked it up anyway.

What would she have saved? Of this life? Of her past? Nothing. Only memories.

When the sheriff's cell sounded, he stepped back as Brandi continued to walk with Hank. A few firemen joined them, all talking about what might have happened. All signs indicated that the fire had been set. Hank complained that his list of people he'd made mad by not serving or had to kick out would be four or five pages long. Any one of them could have driven by and dumped gas on the back wall just to get even.

About the time Hank was listing every moment and every feeling since he'd got the call from Sorrel, Dan pulled Brandi out of the crowd and they walked toward his car.

"I have to go back to Crossroads. Will you be all right?" He wasn't looking at her as he asked. He was watching the crowd.

"I will." Something had to be wrong because the sheriff's voice was curt, all business. "I'll get Hank to take me somewhere to stay. Call my cell later, and I'll let you know where I am."

"Will do." He climbed into his cruiser.

"What's happened?" she asked. The man who glanced at her was so different from the one who'd touched her leg when they'd been driving over.

He shoved the car into gear. The moment before he turned away she heard him say, "My one prisoner just escaped. I have to get back to town."

She watched him go, knowing no matter how long it took, he'd come back to her. What was building between them wasn't over.

CHAPTER SEVENTEEN

CODY WINSLOW HAD slept most of the day after Ranger Tess Adams left him at the hospital, but he'd dreamed about her. Her thick, chestnut-brown hair was undone from the braid she'd worn. The tiny freckles across the bridge of her nose fascinated him. Something about the woman drew him. She didn't seem to have a helpless bone in her body.

As the day aged, the hospital seemed determined to kill him. When he wasn't being moved or tested or tortured in general, he slept. The good news was his leg was a clean break that would heal quickly. The ribs were cracked but would also heal without surgery. His head wound didn't appear to have caused any brain damage. The cuts on his shoulder and arm were stitched up and dressed.

Basically, Cody felt like the Thanksgiving turkey. He might be bruised and swollen, but he knew what he had to do to get out of the place.

He never asked where the park ranger was or when they thought she might come back. He'd wait. She would come.

One day passed, then another.

Mostly, the staff talked about the weather. A few mentioned having to work double shifts because roads were closed and their relief couldn't make it. Once two men cleaning the room talked about a fire at some nightspot, but Cody barely listened.

He didn't talk to any of them more than to answer in one-word sentences. He recognized the drill; he'd been hurt much worse than this before. He knew when his leg took his weight and the pain didn't make him scream that he'd be out of the hospital.

Once he was home, he'd trash the drugs the doctors were feeding him and let whiskey wash away his pain. In life's crappy pickings gallery, Cody figured he'd rather be a drunk than hooked on drugs.

He told himself that he didn't want Tess to see him like this, hurting and weak. If she stayed away a week, he'd be through the worst part. She was a strong woman, and he'd face her on that level.

He wanted to be walking up to her door on their first date, maybe pull her chair out for her at the restaurant and lean down a few inches to kiss her good-night on the porch. Cody figured he didn't have a romantic bone in his body, but he wouldn't mind kissing his way across her face the way the sun already had with freckles.

He'd never spent much time dating, and between the army and being a ranger, he didn't even know many women. Cody didn't know the right things to say to a woman he'd like to get to know. He felt like he was still in grade school where relationships were concerned and most of them were in middle school. But Tess might be worth the effort to learn. Maybe he'd just try being honest, tell her what he wanted, and see how she reacted.

What was the worst thing that would happen? He'd be alone. He'd already worn that spot out.

Long after dark, he'd been given a sleeping pill to help him rest when he sensed, more than heard, her in the room.

"That you, honey?" He felt her hand slide into his. "I've been waiting for you to come back." He closed his fingers around hers, which were ice cold. "You shouldn't have come. I've heard the roads are still bad."

"You're right, the weather's terrible, but I wanted to check on you. I had to work an extra shift and . . . of course, run your place while you were napping up here in this warm hospital and having folks bring you meals."

"Of course." Dear God, how he'd missed her humor. Her touch. Her voice. "Did you feed the animals, check the backup generator and pay the bills?" he joked back.

"I think I did." She didn't sound so sure. "Now where's that generator?"

"In a shed a few feet from the north side of the barn. It'll kick on if the electricity goes off."

"Oh, then it's fine. The lights are still on. It's

like a beautiful winter wonderland out on your place. The evergreens along the windbreak look fat and heavy like giant snowballs." She stood at the head of his bed, just beyond his vision.

Cody hated winter. To him there was nothing pretty about cold weather. Mud, naked trees, work that couldn't get done and disaster waiting around every corner. "Anything else to report?" He didn't want to think about the snow; he just wanted to hear her voice.

"The gray mare had her foal last night. I was the midwife."

"You know how to deliver a foal?" He was starting to believe she could do anything.

"No, but I Googled it." She laughed. "In truth the mare did most of the work."

He felt Tess's weight on the bed beside him. She must have leaned down because her whispered words brushed near his ear. "It was unbelievable. The colt's the most beautiful creature in the world. He stood up on his thin, wobbly legs and looked right at me like he was a duckling and I was his mother duck. I started cleaning him up, but the mare pushed me out of the way as if to say she'd take care of the details herself."

Cody smiled. He'd seen horses born all his life. His father was a veterinarian, and by the time Cody could help, he was the assistant. He knew that rush of excitement. He was glad the first birthing she watched went easy.

"What are you going to name him?" she asked, wiggling closer as if she wanted this conversation to be private.

Cody wondered if she was simply his first dream for the night and not real. If so, it was a great way to start. "You name him, honey. He's yours." He opened his eyes to see her face but, for once, the nurse had turned down the lights and she was mostly shadow.

"Sure, you say that now, but wait until you see him. He has the cutest milk coat and funny little tail. I kept trying to hug him, but the mom pushed me away. I think she wanted him to nurse."

Cody loved this dream. It was almost as if they were lovers and simply discussing the workings of the day, not strangers who met at the scene of an accident. His accident. "How's everything else? Did the shipment of grain come in that I ordered last week?"

"There was a message on your machine in the house from someone named Whitaker. He said he'd be dropping off the load as soon as the road cleared. He said to leave him a check by the coffeepot."

"Did you?" he asked.

"Sure. I'm running your life now, remember."

She laughed as if she was telling the truth, but he knew she must just be joking again.

"You might as well take over, honey. I haven't been doing much of a job at it lately." For a man who'd lived and breathed his job with the Texas Rangers, there wasn't much left after he was shot. He was too old to go to his folks. They wouldn't know what to do with him anyway. He was too young to buy a rocking chair and sit on the porch.

How did a man go from being a Texas Ranger, the best of the best, to being nothing? Now, the outlaws he fought were demons in his head who haunted his world at night. Some nights he'd stay awake, walking the floor, reading, riding, anything to keep them at bay. Other nights he'd drink until he passed out.

He wasn't just relieving the night he'd been shot on the border; his nightmare had expanded and warped into something far darker. Some nights he crossed into hell and fought there.

Tess cuddled next to him, pulling him from his dark thoughts. Her head rested on the other half of his pillow, her cheek almost touching his. She seemed to be testing to make sure it was all right to be so close.

He wished he had the words to tell her that it was. They might be almost strangers, but she'd saved his life. She was the one person who could come as close as she liked.

When he didn't turn away, she moved an inch closer and slowly relaxed.

"Yesterday afternoon, when the snow started again, a section of the back storage room caved in." Tess kept her voice low, as if they were lovers whispering, and it dawned on him that she probably didn't know how to talk to men any more than he knew how to talk to women. But with her so close, it didn't seem to matter.

"Too much weight on the roof, I think." She lightly touched his arm.

"I'll fix it when I get home." He relaxed, deciding to forget his problems and just enjoy this dream. He covered her fingers with his hand. He thought of asking her to come closer, but right now just not having her leave seemed enough.

"Well . . ." She hesitated, and he wondered if she knew something about his condition that he didn't.

"Well, what?" How bad could any news be? He already hurt all over. "Did the doctor tell you something they're not telling me?"

"No."

"Then what, Tess?"

"The roof, it's taken care of, Cody. It's fixed with double the braces."

He moved his hand and brushed his fingers along her side from just under her well-rounded breast to the flare of her hips. Their conversation had nothing to do with what they were communicating to each other.

She might be a strong woman, but there was no way she'd fixed a roof in bad weather. Maybe this whole conversation was just part of his dream. "How'd you do that? Fairy dust?" His hand moved along her side once more, bumping into the bottom of her breast before he switched directions and moved back down.

There was a catch in her voice and her breathing quickened, but she tried to calmly answer his question. All she had to do was move away; he was in no shape to follow. "I . . . I . . ."

Cody grinned. She wasn't moving away, and this wasn't a dream. Tess was real, and he was touching her. He rested his hand at her waist and waited.

Slowly, she calmed, but she didn't retreat. "I called the bank to ask if there was a cosigner on your account who could tell me what to do. They weren't open yet, but one of the tellers had come in early. She was so sweet when I told her who I was and how badly you were hurt. She said the whole town is worried about you. She's Melanie Miller's father's second cousin, so she'd heard all about your accident."

"Is this going anywhere, Tess? I don't know how long I have to live. I'd hate to die on you and miss the end of this story about what happened to the storage room."

"Oh, sorry." She didn't sound the least bit sorry. "Anyway, Melanie's father's second cousin called her boss, and the bank president called me back and told me he was sure it would be all right if I signed on your account if checks needed writing. And he had a brother-in-law who was out of work and would probably handle the job right away."

"What!" Cody found it impossible to believe some banker gave her permission to write checks on the ranch account.

"That's what I said, but he assured me the brother-in-law was a good carpenter."

Cody leveled his voice. "Not the carpenter, Tess. How could the banker allow you to write checks?" Not that she could write many. He doubted there was more than a few thousand in the account. He hadn't balanced it in months.

"Oh, that. When I asked how that could possibly be, he laughed and whispered that it was a secret."

Cody would have rolled his head to the side and confronted her, but his brain would have probably exploded. This had to be illegal. The bank couldn't just pick someone to take over when a man has an accident. He'd never signed any papers or given over power of attorney. She wasn't even kin to him.

He gulped in what he feared might be his last breath. Surely a heart attack or brain aneurism was on its way, and he wouldn't even fight. He deserved whatever hit him. When he took another breath, a light came on in in his mind. He was too dumb to die.

The secret! He'd told the nurse that first night at the hospital that Tess was his wife. Somehow

179

the news had already reached Crossroads. He'd asked the lady in scrubs to not tell anyone that he and Tess Adams were married. He'd said they were keeping it a secret.

A secret the bank president obviously knew.

Tess was talking. He realized he hadn't been listening, so his drugged up, tired pea-brain tried to catch up.

". . . so after I got the brother-in-law out to fix the roof, I decided you'd want me to pay all those bills stacked up on your desk and deposit several checks made out to the ranch."

"Thanks," he managed to say, still not believing what he was hearing. "Do I have any money left?"

"Several thousand. I started a list of repairs around the place you might want to start on when the weather calms."

"Good," he said and almost added, *like that was going to happen.* He moved his hand along her side, making sure she was still real because what she was saying seemed impossible.

"I tossed all the junk mail and some of the magazines, too." Tess talked now, obviously comfortable with his touch. "Are you aware there are probably libraries that don't keep copies as long as you do? One stack I thought was *on* the coffee table I was surprised to discover they *were* the coffee table."

He'd lost the ability to form words. No one had

ever tried to run his life or tell him what to do. From the time he was in double digits, his parents simply asked him what he wanted. He'd been an only child of parents who seemed to be counting the days until he'd grow up and move away. When he didn't leave by seventeen, they signed the ranch, which he didn't want, over to him and moved to Galveston. His father had decided to shift his career to small animals, and his mother said she'd always wanted to live by the sea.

The ranch pretty much ran itself. Money from leased grassland paid the taxes. Cody kept his personal accounts separate just in case his parents ever decided to come back or he took off. Neither option seemed likely. They were happy on the coast, and he had nowhere else he wanted to go.

From the time his parents left, they were on the fringes waving, wishing him well as he left for college, the army, the war. They'd been there in the background when he'd won a Silver Star, graduated from the police academy, got accepted into the Texas Rangers. But they didn't want to participate in his life. They apparently had their own to live.

When he'd been in the hospital with three bullet wounds, they'd visited him once a month and stayed all day. His mother fussed over him, and his father read every paper the gift shop had. After three months, they switched to weekly calls.

The sandman was pulling a wool blanket over his mind. He'd deal with the problems at Wild Horse Springs in the morning. After all, how much damage could she do to a run-down ranch?

In the few minutes he had left awake, he wanted to feel her next to him. His hand slid up her side and gently bumped into the bottom of her breast. Through the layers of clothing he could barely feel her softness, but his hand settled here.

She started that rapid breathing again, but she didn't pull away.

He moved his head toward her. "Kiss me goodnight."

She put her now warm hand on his cheek. "I thought you'd never ask." Her words brushed his lips as she kissed him softly.

Somewhere between dream and reality, he added, "Sleep beside me, Tess."

"I will for as long as they'll let me. I don't know why, but the nurse said she'd give me a little extra time to visit."

She touched his lips with hers, and he wished he had the energy to kiss her deeply.

He drifted then, thinking how grand it was to have someone by his side.

"Good night, honey," he whispered as if he'd said the words to her for years.

CHAPTER EIGHTEEN

LAUREN'S CELL MUST have rung a dozen times before she finally woke up enough to answer. Watery sunlight streamed through her west-facing window.

Afternoon. She'd slept the morning away.

"What's up, Pop?" she said, glancing at his office number on her cell. "I'm trying to get some sleep."

"It's not your father, Lauren, this is Deputy Fifth Weathers."

"Hi, Fifth." She tried to clear her head. He sounded so formal; surely he hadn't forgotten her since last summer. "I guess you're back from Austin. Great, Pop needs the help. How was training?"

Fifth, always polite, answered, "Fine. Training went just fine. Can you come up to the sheriff's office as soon as possible? We have a situation here."

"What's wrong?" She was wide-awake now. As the daughter of an officer of the law, the call she never wanted to get was always lurking in the corners of her thoughts. "Has something happened?" When he'd been shot, she'd gotten the call while she was walking across the Tech campus.

One call and her world shifted. Lauren squeezed her eyes closed as if bracing for another blow. "Is Pop all right?" The words scratched across her heart before they came out.

"He's fine, Lauren. I swear, nothing has happened to your dad. I just talked to him. He's over in the next county working another case." Weathers's words came fast now, almost panicked. "But we have a problem here at the office, and the sheriff wants everyone who might know anything to be present as soon as possible for questioning."

Lauren did exactly what she'd heard her father do a hundred times. She lowered her voice and said calmly, "Start from the beginning."

To her surprise the deputy didn't argue. "Thatcher Jones is missing from his cell."

"Don't tell me the kid broke out?" She jumped out of the bed, swearing if she could get a good grip on Thatcher, she'd slug him. After staying up watching him all night, worrying about him, even calling Lucas to come home to help with his case, the kid escaped. His cell door was probably left unlocked. Tim let him out twice yesterday to go to the bathroom because Thatcher said he wasn't peeing in public even if the facility was in the cell with him. The last time, Tim was too tired to even go downstairs with him. He just threatened the kid and told him he'd better be back upstairs in five minutes.

When Thatcher came back, maybe Tim forgot to lock the cell door. They'd already stopped locking the two outside doors that led to the jail. It was too much trouble to keep locking or unlocking them every time someone needed to go for coffee or snacks.

Lauren tried to get her sleep-deprived mind to work as she dug through clothes. "Maybe Thatcher was released earlier. Lucas said he'd get him out on bond, if not freed sometime today. Maybe Lucas dropped by and Pearly let him out. She knows where the key to the doors and cells are, and she might have forgotten to call Pop or you to inform you."

Closing her eyes, Lauren imagined Thatcher going downstairs to the restroom, slipping past Pearly, taking the keys off the wall in her father's office and then waiting for his chance. Easy, but why? Thatcher didn't seem worried about being a prisoner.

"You're right about one thing, Lauren," Weathers agreed. "He would have been free to go today, but before Lucas could get here with the paperwork, he disappeared." Fifth sounded like he was gulping down a bucket load of swearwords.

Lauren rolled her eyes. Weathers was a great deputy, and someday he'd make a great sheriff, but right now everything had to be done exactly by the book. She was used to this kind of talk. If

185

Fifth Weathers wasn't younger and a foot taller than her pop, she'd think the two lawmen were clones.

She pulled on an old sweater, grabbed a coat and headed for the door. "I'll come down to the office, but I don't know how much help I'll be. He was locked up when I left this morning. That's all I know. Lucas and Tim were eating breakfast with him, or more accurately eating his breakfast." She grabbed her purse and keys off the bar. "Have you called Charley Collins? If Thatcher left, he's heading somewhere safe. The Lone Heart Ranch is as near a home as he's had for years."

"Charley is standing right in front of me," Weathers said. "He hasn't seen Thatcher. He was the first person I called. Thatcher's old pickup is still parked out in front of the office with two days' worth of snow piled on top."

Lauren slipped into her muddy shoes and headed toward her car. "What are you *not* telling me, Fifth?"

"Pearly checked on him an hour ago. He was fine. Reading one of those paperback westerns he always keeps in his pocket.

"Pearly reported that he said he was hungry. She came downstairs and called the Franklins to see if they could deliver lunch a little early. Thirty minutes later when she took it up, he was gone."

As she opened the front door, cold snow and

one chilling fact hit her at once. Weathers had sounded panicked when he called. Now he was rattling off way too many facts. Like people do when they're nervous or scared.

"I walked in about the time she was running down the stairs screaming that there had been a bloody jailbreak." Weathers's voice shook a little. "Rose and Daisy Franklin were in the lobby waiting for their dishes, and they started screaming, too. As soon as I got them settled down and checked out the crime scene, I called your dad. He told me to round up everyone who'd seen Thatcher today as fast as possible. The sheriff's on his way now."

Lauren started her car and headed toward the office.

"What else?" Something was wrong. Too much screaming and police procedure talk for it to be a simple story.

Fifth hesitated, then lowered his voice so much she pressed the cell hard against her ear. "When I went upstairs, there was blood all over the cell. Something happened in there, something bad."

"Thatcher hurt himself?" She pushed the accelerator, ignoring the stop sign as she left the little lake community outside town.

"I don't think so. Charley and I agree he didn't seem in any hurry to get out. He wasn't suicidal or anything. The sheriff said to call in CSI, but they won't be here for an hour. Pearly's out in the

187

snow marking off the whole building with crime-scene tape."

Lauren was halfway there. The windshield wipers shoved snow around as the road blinked in and out of sight. "Two scenarios." She tried to think like her father. "If he didn't hurt himself, then someone hurt him. Someone broke into the jail cell and hurt Thatcher!"

"The offices were empty. All but Pearly went home because of the snow. The sheriff was thirty miles away at another crime scene." Fifth was silent for a moment, then added, "There is a third scenario, Lauren. The third one is Thatcher hurt someone. The blood in the cell might not be his."

Lauren forced herself to slow. She could see Crossroads. If she went any faster, she'd slide off the highway. "How could he do that? He's the one locked up. You think someone snuck past Pearly, made it up two flights of stairs, opened two locked doors and broke into Thatcher's cell so the kid could beat him bloody?"

"Yeah, something like that." Weathers sounded just as confused as she felt.

A few minutes later, Lauren pulled into an empty parking spot, jumped out of her car and ran into the county offices.

Pearly was sitting at her desk as usual, but she didn't look so good. One of the volunteer firemen was giving her oxygen from the tank they kept at the firehouse. Someone must have brushed her hair away from her face, and without her glasses, Pearly had a wild screaming monkey kind of look about her.

Lauren decided not to ask the lady how she was doing. The answer was obvious.

So, she marched into her father's office, looked up at Fifth and finished her argument. "What makes you think the blood in the cell was not Thatcher's?"

Fifth straightened to his giant height and said simply, "It wasn't his ear."

She followed the deputy's gaze down to her father's desk and a white paper towel spotted with blood. In the middle, looking almost dainty, was one ear.

The room started circling. If Lauren had had the energy, she would have run out to the reception room and fought Pearly for the oxygen tank. Suddenly she felt there was way too little air in the building.

Charley Collins stepped forward and circled his arm around her waist just in case she toppled. His concerned look wasn't much help, but his arm gave her the support she needed.

Fifth covered the ear with paper and pulled up a chair for her.

She continued to stare at the corner of the desk where the evidence rested. She'd seen it, a human ear not attached to anyone. One layer of paper couldn't erase what she'd seen.

"How do you know it's not Thatcher's ear?"

"Charley said he's cut Thatcher's hair enough times to remember what his ears looked like. He swears it's not Thatcher's." Fifth moved away from the desk. "Plus, I think I would have remembered if the kid had hairy ears. We're guessing the head this ear was attached to has seen many more than eighteen summers. But seeing an ear alone like that is creepy.

"I should have left it at the crime scene, but I didn't want anyone to step into the cell unaware that it was there." Weathers was looking a little pale. "There is blood everywhere and three sets of footprints tracking down the stairs to the second floor."

Just hearing the words made her want to throw up. Right now someone, somewhere close probably, was missing what had been on the side of his face for all his life.

"Right ear," Fifth added as if he'd left out an important fact.

Tim rushed in, and Lauren had to relive every detail. Every clue. When they showed Tim the ear, he threw up in the trash can. Now her father's office not only had a detached ear on the desk, the whole room also smelled of vomit.

Lauren just sat in the corner. The CSI team arrived about the same time Pop did and clomped up the stairs like a herd behind him. Then, an hour later, they clomped back down. They took the ear with them. Pearly fainted when they asked her questions, and two firemen carried her off to the clinic next to the fire department's shed.

Pearly did admit she'd called about Thatcher's lunch from the sheriff's desk, so someone might have come in or had already been in the building, and used her absence to climb the stairs. "And," she'd whispered to Lauren, "I did run to the ladies' room."

Deputy Weathers nodded at Lauren as if to say, *the window of escape.*

It didn't add up to Lauren. What was the chance that One-ear and Thatcher were upstairs waiting to run, and they caught that few minutes' window when Pearly went to the bathroom? If Thatcher was kidnapped, he wouldn't go quietly. Pearly would have heard him even from the bathroom. Plus, the Franklin sisters were waiting in the lobby, so when Thatcher and two other people left, they didn't pass the sisters or the two ladies would still be screaming.

The office filled with people asking questions and demanding to know if Thatcher was all right.

Lucas Reyes showed up in a suit and took over answering questions from the concerned public, as he called them, and the press—one woman from the weekly paper.

The art teacher at the high school called in to offer to do a sketch of what the other ear might look like.

A few old guys from the retirement homes across the street took over traffic control out front, but the snow had gotten so bad people were talking more about the weather than Thatcher by then.

When her father and Deputy Weathers finally shoved everyone out of the office so they could concentrate on police work, Lauren was starting to feel like she was in one of Tim's terrible novels. Alien zombies in need of human ears were kidnapping young men. They'd accidentally left part of their bounty behind. Of course, the reason Pearly hadn't seen them come or go was because they controlled her mind.

Which wouldn't be too hard. Pearly couldn't even control her mouth most times. Lauren figured in the plot of things she was probably the next character to be abducted.

Tim brought her a cup of coffee, but he didn't lean close or talk to her. He was still angry about their breakup. When he finally had some time to think and climbed over his pride, he'd realize it was for the best. Now maybe at least one of them could move on.

She had a feeling it would be him. In her experiences in life, she'd decided that she wasn't that good at moving, period. Up, on, or out. Most twenty-five-year-olds didn't dream of moving back home. Something must be wrong with her. She wanted to stay in the nest and never fly.

Only right now wasn't the time to worry about it. She had Thatcher to find.

Pop organized the facts like a man working a thousand-piece puzzle. He might not keep his filing cabinet in order, but he squirreled away details forever in his mind. She'd seen him talk to a stranger for a few minutes and remember everything about him six months later.

When no one was looking, she climbed half of the flight of stairs to the landing and sat in the corner. No one below would notice her. The air was warm on the landing, and the evening shadows played across the old wood in long lines like tiny railroad tracks crisscrossing.

One flight higher was a crime scene still bloody. One flight below was chaos, but here in the middle was silence.

Lauren leaned her head back, wishing she could come up with one idea as to where Thatcher might be. He couldn't have simply vanished. No one saw him go out the front door or into the street. The back door was kept locked, and an alarm sounded if anyone opened it.

Why would he run, anyway? It wasn't like he was doing time in a prison. The sheriff even had her and Tim sit up with him last night so Thatcher wouldn't be lonely. He was eating like a king. There was a good chance the charges would be dropped. Everyone in town was on his side.

When that direction of problem solving didn't

work, she tried piecing it together from the other end. Someone had come in, without anyone noticing, and made it all the way to Thatcher's cell. The footprints in blood showed it was more than one person. They'd kidnapped the kid. Thatcher fought and managed to cut off one of the attacker's ears.

The hammering of the men building the gazebo in the lot across the street echoed up to her like an old clock that didn't tick in rhythm. The workers all wore furry caps that covered their ears. Her pop had mentioned that they worked from dawn to dusk every day until the job was done. They were way behind schedule.

She ran down the stairs and into her father's office. "I know how . . ."

Weathers, Pop and Tim all looked up from where they'd been sitting around her dad's desk. In the middle rested a furry cap with blood soaked into one side. The right side.

"I guess you figured it out too." She let her shoulders drop.

Her father stood. "We did, about half an hour ago. Weathers found the hat in the trash out back. One of the construction workers said it was stolen out of his truck. We also found drops of blood in different spots outside, but the snow's falling too fast to follow a trail."

"Do you think whoever took Thatcher was one of the workers?"

Weathers shook his head. "Foreman said all his men are accounted for. They've been working in tight quarters under the framed roof today, trying to stay out of the worst of the weather."

Pop nodded, then added, "They're a rough crew, and I'm not sure I trust the foreman's word. After we find Thatcher, I think I'll go back and have another talk with the man. Not one of the crew looked me in the eye the whole time I was talking to the boss."

She looked around. "Where's Charley?" Collins was as worried as any father would be. He wouldn't have just left.

"We also saw a trail of blood moving down the alley and back behind the retirement houses. There's a place back there where Ransom Canyon's shallow end dips close, then continues on down to where the lake fans out. From the looks of it, someone who was injured or maybe an animal who was hurt either slipped down into the canyon, or was tossed. It's not very deep there, but the wind blows through and builds up the snow."

"Where's Charley?" she asked again, dread already settling in the pit of her stomach.

Pop frowned as if he didn't approve. "Charley's gone to get horses. Lucas is changing into riding gear. They plan to head down to search the canyon before it gets dark." Her father suddenly looked very tired. "I want this search kept quiet.

We don't know if it's the guys who came after Thatcher, or if it's the kid, or even if it was a dog hit by a car. The last thing I want is a bunch of people who have no business being out in the cold looking for someone bleeding in the middle of a snowstorm."

"It'll be dangerous on horseback," Fifth said. "Impossible on foot or in an ATV." He glanced at the sheriff. "But a man can search fast on a horse, and at the very least we'll learn which way they didn't go."

The sheriff nodded.

Just then Lauren heard the slight jingle of spurs. She turned. She almost didn't recognize the cowboy standing in the doorway. Tall, dark, lean. Outfitted in leather boots, chaps, vest and coat. His dark eyes stared right at her as if he was hungry for one last look.

She couldn't move. The man she'd always thought Lucas would grow up to be was standing before her. Folks called it *being born to the land,* and today he looked to be just that.

Lucas finally turned his gaze to the sheriff. "I know what I'm getting into, Sheriff. I've grown up riding the canyon in every season. In an hour we'll have covered as much ground as anyone on foot could have made. In two hours, three at the most, we'll be back."

The sheriff nodded. "No matter what, Lucas, I want your word that you and Charley will climb out of the canyon by twilight. The last thing I want is someone else missing."

"If he's in the canyon, we'll find him by then."

The office phone rang.

Lauren couldn't stop staring. Lucas had been handsome in a suit, but he was perfect in western clothes.

"Charley's unloading the horses over behind the bungalows." The sheriff held out the phone.

"Tell him I'm on my way." Lucas moved so fast he seemed to vanish. All she heard was the slight ring of spurs remaining.

Pop turned back to the phone, but Lauren ran for her coat.

Once outside, the wind seemed to blow the snow sideways. It blew and swirled like sand, too light and dry to stick.

If she hadn't known the way to the retirement center, she might have walked into the street. The late-afternoon sun provided little more light than a low-watt bulb burning in a dusty cave. She could see the spot of light, but it didn't do much to illuminate her way.

The hammering across the street had finally stopped. The workers must have given up for the day on Crossroads' great building project. No one believed it would ever be finished anyway. In January, the contractor had said he'd have it up by July. No one thought to ask what year.

Lauren walked as fast as she dared, using the

cute little retirement houses as her guide. Today they reminded her of covered wagons that had circled to weather winter. Just behind them was a long row of carports and just beyond the shallow canyon.

She heard the horses before she saw them. Two more steps and the whole scene came into view. One man was unloading a third mount while Lucas and Charley readied their horses and saddles. Both had grown up cowboying. Charley had even rodeoed some. They knew horses and they knew the canyon. If any two men could find Thatcher, it would be them.

"Go back inside, Lauren," Charley yelled as he looped the lead rope from the third horse onto his saddle.

"I have to give Lucas something," she said above the wind.

Lucas turned. His wide-brimmed hat was too low for her to see his eyes. He didn't say a word, but she knew he was watching her.

Lauren pulled the ear muffs from her pocket. "I thought this might help."

He lifted his hat and she clamped the covering around his ears, leaving the band running behind his neck.

When he put his hat back on, it fit tight above the wool ear muffs.

Suddenly, she was in the shelter of the wide brim of his hat. All around them a winter storm raged, but under the hat all seemed calm.

She felt like she'd been sleeping for years, and the hunger in his dark eyes shocked her full awake.

He didn't move and she couldn't.

Then Charley's order broke the silence. "Kiss the girl, Reyes, and mount up. We don't have all day."

Lucas smiled, kissed her hard and fast on her frozen lips, and was atop his horse before she thought to react.

"I didn't feel a thing," she said, more to herself than to him.

He touched his fingers to his hat in salute and said, "You will when I get back."

Charley was already ahead, walking his horse down the narrow path behind the parking sheds and into the canyon.

"We were over a long time ago," she said as Lucas moved away, disappearing into the blizzard. The wind caught her words and carried them.

His voice also drifted to her on the wind. "We haven't even started, *mi cielo*."

Lauren walked slowly back to the county offices. She was a total idiot. Why'd she let him kiss her? How many times did she have to be hit in the head with a sledgehammer to learn that Lucas wasn't hers? He sometimes pretended to be. He seemed like he was. But every time she got close, he disappeared.

She'd loved him at fifteen, and he'd wanted to wait until they were both in college to see each other. Then, when she got to college, he never had time for her. She thought they'd be together after graduation, but he moved to Houston and she went to Dallas. If he'd just suggested he wanted more from her, she would have been packed and moved in a week. But Lucas never seemed to have the time. He never wanted a commitment.

Tim had, though. He'd suggested it many times. Not anything like marriage, but more like moving in together. She'd been the one to always want to keep things between them as they were. Friends with benefits, nothing more. Maybe she wanted it that way because she knew Tim just wanted to be in a relationship.

Lucas wanted the opposite.

By the time she hit the office doors, she was fighting mad. Maybe she should forget them both and go for door number three.

The only trouble was finding door number three.

CHAPTER NINETEEN

THATCHER HAD TALKED Pearly into calling about his noon meal and was deep into his newest western when he heard the light tap of footsteps on the stairs heading up. It didn't sound like children, more like a couple people trying not to make a sound.

He glanced over and noticed Pearly had left both doors that led to the room with the cells open. She probably knew she'd be returning soon with lunch and was just thinking of saving herself the hassle of unlocking, but it didn't make Thatcher feel safe.

Prisoners, even him, should be kept locked up safe and sound.

He liked knowing there were three locks and two flights of stairs between him and outsiders. The footsteps came close like reindeer tapping up in stocking feet. Too late for Halloween, too early for Christmas.

Every cell in Thatcher's body came alive. He'd lived life in the Breaks long enough to smell trouble like snakes sensed the heat of predators. Danger was tiptoeing up the stairs, and he was locked in, unable to run.

A tall, thin guy in overalls and stocking feet slithered around the first open door as silently as

201

a cat. He wore a funny fur hat that looked more like it belonged in Alaska than Texas. The flaps over his ears were sticking straight out, almost making his head look like a fat tiny airplane atop his stick of a body.

Another man followed, shorter, out of breath from the climb and holding a knife in his fat, porky fingers. The blade was long and looked razor sharp.

Standing on full alert, Thatcher played his options over in his mind. He knew the sheriff had left the office an hour ago, heading to the scene of a fire a county over. He'd also heard people tromping up and down the stairs a while back. Pearly mentioned they'd decided to close all county offices except the sheriff's office because of the snow.

Thatcher moved to the back of his cell as the two men slithered closer, both smiling a hungry carnivore's grin.

Thatcher decided to handle this problem. If he yelled, Pearly might be his only backup, and he didn't want to get her hurt. After all, the men were on the outside of his cell. They couldn't touch him.

"Look, guys, if you're here about what you thought I saw at the trailer, I can tell you right now, I didn't see anything and I swear I'm not going to mention to anyone what I didn't see." He wasn't sure they were two of the men he'd seen at the little girl's trailer, but they could have been.

The short one laughed, a hiccupy kind of squeal. "We told you we'd find you and shut you up." He drooled as he giggled. "How about we go for a little walk? If you're real quiet, we won't take the old lady downstairs with us."

"You're going to need more than that knife." Thatcher felt brave with the bars and five feet between him and them. "My guess is you didn't bring a gun. One shot would have half the town here before you two could get down the stairs."

The thin one smiled with what few teeth he had left. "We don't need a gun. We found this in the sheriff's office."

He pulled a key from his pocket. The key to Thatcher's cell.

Thatcher stopped talking and started acting. As they opened the door, he threw everything he could find at them. Books, blankets, Dr Pepper cans.

Nothing stopped the short guy from coming at him, knife pointed in his direction, while the skinny bum made a funny cheering sound like he had a front row seat to a fight. Now and then, Slim would jump and swing at Thatcher, then dart back into place, but the short one slowly marched straight toward his prey.

Thatcher suddenly felt more irritated than afraid. It was downright insulting to be attacked by these two losers.

"We went ahead and beat the girl for letting you

follow her home. Her stepdad let us all give her a few swings with the belt, but you're not getting off that easy."

Thatcher's blood began to boil. "Is she all right?" She'd been so tiny in her faded red coat that was two or three sizes too big. One swing from a belt would knock her down.

Shorty shook his head. "What do I care? She ain't my kid. She ain't anybody's kid. She's just a whiny bother. By the time it was my turn to hit her, she wasn't even screaming. She was just lying there taking it without a sound."

Thatcher turned his back, hoping to find something to hold off Shorty, or better yet, kill the bastard.

He grabbed the blankets from his bed, and, with a wild charge, threw them over the short guy's head. He got in three or four good punches before he felt the short man's knife slide along his side, just deep enough to draw blood.

Then Thatcher realized he'd forgotten about Slim. The tall guy's blow hit him across the back of the head, not hard enough to hurt, more of an irritation.

Thatcher jumped to avoid the second blow, but another slice cut across his shoulder from Shorty's blade as the tall guy moved in to sucker punch him when Thatcher wasn't looking.

For a few minutes, they both came at him, the slim one punching and the short one slicing. Each cut went a little deeper.

When Thatcher curled on the floor in pain, Shorty stuck a knife in Thatcher's back just enough to draw blood again and said, "You make a sound, I'll skin you right here in the cell."

Thatcher froze. He didn't know what to do, but he knew he wasn't going with these two so they could murder him somewhere else. If they killed him, they'd make sure no one found the body. He couldn't do that to Charley or the sheriff. They'd both never stop looking for him.

Only Kristi would probably give up in a day or two. Even hurt and bleeding, he had enough brains to realize she wasn't going to stay with him through the bad times. She hadn't even thought of driving down to visit him. She'd said she had plans on campus this weekend. Being mad at her took his mind off the pain.

When Thatcher didn't move, Shorty got angry, like their suggestion was the only fair option and Thatcher should jump at the chance to leave. Shorty kicked him hard, demanding Thatcher stand up; they were all leaving.

The short guy started sweating as he whispered deadly threats if Thatcher didn't start walking. His bony partner just stared, like a man watching his dog play with a wild rabbit.

Finally, Thatcher had had enough. Fast as a rifle shot, Thatcher stood and swung around, grabbing for the knife handle.

The short man hadn't expected the attack. He

hesitated a fraction of a second, and Thatcher grabbed the knife. They fought for control. Thatcher tightened his grip and pulled upward. He might have only one chance, so he threw every ounce of strength into the move.

Shorty's body felt more like mush then muscle. He wiggled and tried to get his footing as his hand lost control of the weapon. Thatcher jerked harder, knowing his life depended on it.

The blade sliced Shorty's ear off as easily as slicing through warm butter.

Thatcher didn't slow. He shoved the short guy into the slim one with the force of his whole body. As they both tumbled, Thatcher bolted out the open door and ran for his life.

When he reached the stairs, he looked back, trying to believe what had just happened. The high cry of a wounded animal seemed to echo through the third-floor hallways.

The stout little man knelt in the center of the cell, staring at the ear on the floor. He didn't seem to realize all the red around him was his blood. His taller partner finally pulled a knife of his own, but he made no move to follow Thatcher until Shorty started cussing. He might be just as mean as Shorty, but drugs had clearly dulled his reactions.

Shorty grabbed the thin man's hat, strapped it on tight over the spouting hole that had once been his ear and shot out words between crying,

"He's going to die slow." He tried to stand, slipping on his own blood. Rage had won out over pain. "I'm going to cut off pieces of him until he's nothing but a stump when I'm finished."

Thatcher knew he should be running, but the scene before him was surreal. He had a feeling when he talked about what had just happened, no one would believe a word.

The moment he caught the look in Shorty's eyes, he ran. At the second-floor landing, he knew he couldn't go down and put Pearly or anyone else in danger. He veered off into the second-floor courtroom and heard the men ten feet behind him.

He ran for a back window behind the judge's bench and tumbled out. The snow was so cold it masked the pain from his cuts. He ran into the wind, thinking of only one thing: escape.

The only out. The only way to lose them. Cross the street. Steal a car. Get as far away as possible.

The line of metal carports that held all the Evening Shadows retirees' cars came into view. A few loose panels were flapping in the wind, waving to him. Thatcher didn't have time to think. He had to act or he'd be dead, or buried in the snow.

He ran for the first old car without looking back to see if the men were following. Cap Fuller's old boat of a car was unlocked. The keys fell when he flipped the sun visor. A moment later he hit the accelerator and shot out of the shelter like a racer.

Snow blew around him, brushing away any tracks within seconds.

As the fuzzy lights of Crossroads faded behind him, Thatcher finally took a long breath and started to believe he'd made it. No sign of Shorty and Slim. No car lights following him.

He clunked along the snowy road in his old friend's car. The only good thing about the piece of junk was that it was so heavy it would take a tornado to blow it off the road. He should have stolen a fast car, but they were a little hard to find at the retirement home, and it wasn't like he'd had time to be picky.

He didn't even know, or care, which way he was going. All Thatcher knew was he had to get away and he was bleeding on the leather seats. Cap would make him clean that up when he found out.

Technically, he reasoned, he didn't steal the car. Cap had told him where the keys were years ago, and the retired captain of the Crossroads' fire department would have taken him home, even in the snow, if Thatcher had asked.

Only he hadn't had time to ask, and Cap didn't need to be out in this weather. Old guys like that probably froze quicker than Popsicles.

"Think!" Thatcher shouted to himself. He had to hide until he could contact the sheriff. The car or the blood or the cold didn't matter. He had to get somewhere safe, contact Brigman and together they had to find the little girl. Knowing that they'd hurt her made Thatcher want to go back and "accidentally" run down Shorty and Slim a few times. If this huge car didn't kill them the first few times, he'd keep trying.

But he'd have to save that for now. First, he had to stay alive long enough to help the little girl.

He thought of trying to make it to the Breaks where his mother's shack might still be standing. Maybe she'd come back with common-law husband number twenty-seven or so by now. Maybe she'd have a fire going in the stove, and she'd patch him up while they talked about where she'd been the past four years.

For a while, after she left, he'd missed her, then he got comfortable not missing her. He used to worry about her or about what would happen to him, but all that seemed minor right now, when he knew two men were hunting him like it was open season on eighteen-year-olds.

He pushed the car as fast as he dared and tried to think about something, anything, so he'd calm down and maybe not bleed so fast.

If Kristi didn't stay with him in this tough time, maybe he should think about looking for another girlfriend. He had no idea where to look. Kristi had found him in the eighth grade. Maybe he'd just hang around, waiting to be found again by someone else.

Not that any girl would look at him twice. Right now he was bleeding, an escaped prisoner, had two men wanting to kill him and had probably blown any chance of getting into college.

Thatcher pulled his hand away from the wound on his upper arm. Warm blood dribbled out. It might be wise to worry about staying alive before making any further education plans.

He needed to get somewhere safe fast before the two men chasing him had time to finish him off.

Thatcher didn't have time to double back and see if they were following now. He had to keep moving. Think it all out.

"So here I am, in the middle of some back road, bleeding all over Cap's upholstery, an escaped prisoner with a record on file and two dumb-ass hit men trying to kill me." Saying it out loud didn't make his situation sound any more hopeful.

Thatcher swore. "Man, it's getting harder and harder to look at the bright side." He never thought he'd be praying to get back in jail.

Nothing but the wind whistling through the gap in the window answered him.

"Mom!" he yelled. "If you're seeing me now with your same-colored eyes as mine, you might want to look away.

"Oh, one other problem," he yelled and slammed his hand against the wheel. "If Shorty dies, I also killed one of the bums who came to take me out of a jail I was perfectly happy being in."

Thatcher should have started yelling his head off when the two men walked in, but he didn't think the whole thing was real. Who sent hit men in stocking feet? It had to be some kind of joke, right?

Thatcher just wanted this mess to disappear so he could worry about passing algebra. The whole thing, including the ear flying through the air, had happened so fast, like fanning through pages of a graphic novel.

Gripping the wheel, he tried to stop shaking.

A rusty gate, leaning on a fence pole, blinked in and out of view as the wipers fought the snow. Last summer's weeds had grown up knee-high in the dirt road that turned off the pavement. A good sign. A place to hide.

"Thanks, Mom," he yelled like she'd seen him. Like she cared.

Thatcher twisted the wheel and slid off the road. If the gate was open and needed repair, this probably wasn't a working ranch. It would be as good as any place to hole up. If he was lucky, there would be a working phone and he could call the sheriff. Of course, if Shorty was dead, the sheriff probably wouldn't want to talk to Thatcher at all. Sheriff Brigman thought Thatcher's goal in life was to make his job more difficult. Thatcher practiced the call while he bumped down what had once been a dirt road. "Hey, Sheriff, it's me again. What can I say, shit happens."

A farmhouse blinked into sight. The yard and barn lights were on. Good chance there would be folks to help, he thought. If they weren't friendly, they'd call the sheriff. He won either way.

He parked the car in the barn shadows where it wouldn't have been seen from the main road on a clear day. Then, feeling light-headed, Thatcher ran to the barn. "Hello. Anyone in here?"

Only a few horses answered with neighs and stomps.

He turned back to the house, but the wind blew against him, almost stopping his progress. Thatcher closed his eyes and put one foot in front of the other. He had to get inside, to a phone. He was starting to lose feeling in his hands and feet.

The front door wasn't locked. One light had been left on in the house. He could see a kitchen, a living area, a desk in the corner with a phone on top of what looked like several years of phone books.

Moving to the couch, Thatcher dropped, deciding he'd rest for a minute before he made the call.

Dreams whirled in his mind, dark visions of an ocean he'd never seen, with huge black waves, water as thick as oil and as cold as ice. He had to fight to keep his head up.

Slowly, the water warmed. He couldn't open his eyes, but he felt something tight wrapping around his arm and leg as if pulling him down into the black ocean.

Thatcher fought to move and felt firm hands press against his shoulders. He didn't have the strength to fight, so he drifted back into the dark water.

CHAPTER TWENTY

"STOP STRUGGLING OR you'll start bleeding again." Tess Adams hoped this time the kid she'd found in Cody's house would hear her. She wasn't sure if he was alert enough to listen or if he'd simply passed out, but he'd finally settled back down, mumbling to himself.

She'd seen blood on the steps when she walked into Winslow's farmhouse just before dark. The minute she turned on the lights, she saw a boy of about eighteen collapsed on the worn-out couch. His clothes were wet, bloody and mud covered, reminding her of a wild animal who'd been hurt and sought shelter.

Her hands moved slowly down his body. She felt no broken bones. Saw no head injury. His breathing was strong. The socks had frozen on his feet, so they must have been wet at some time. He was more man than boy, but right now, hurt and cold, he'd curled up like a baby.

She tried both her cell and the house phone. No reception. The storm was raging, and she'd barely made it to the farm. There would be no chance getting back to town after dark.

So Tess did what she'd been trained to do. She found the places where he was hurt and went to work. The cuts weren't deep. Butterfly stitches from the first-aid kit she found in Cody's bathroom worked fine. She wrapped the wounds in gauze and tried to wash off most of the blood.

Unlike when she'd doctored Cody less than a week ago, now she was prepared. She had light and water and supplies.

"What is it about this ranch?" she said aloud as she worked. "It's like camp suicide. The roof collapses in the barn, I find a snake curled up around the generator and now I got some kid dropping by like this is a flophouse for bleeders."

Thatcher opened his eyes a bit. "Where am I?"

Tess relaxed. If he was asking questions, he was all right. "You're on Cody Winslow's ranch. It's called Wild Horse Springs."

She studied her newest patient. "You're Thatcher Jones, right?"

"I was," the kid answered. "There's not much of me left." He took a minute to breathe, then asked, "You a sheriff or something? If so, I'd like to surrender to you."

She looked down at her second blood-splattered uniform this week. The greenish-tan material did nothing for her mousy brown hair and eyes. "I'm a park interpreter, but most people just call us rangers. I'm stationed north of here at the state park. We're not allowed to collect criminals. Law enforcement gets a kick out of doing that. What'd you do?"

"Just pick a crime, I'm guilty. How'd you know

my name?" The kid was looking pale, but at least his brains weren't scrambled.

She stood and dug through one of the grocery bags, then passed him a half-gallon jug of milk with a straw. "Drink this. I want to see if you leak."

Thatcher didn't laugh at her joke. No one ever did.

"Looks like someone sliced into you pretty bad." She didn't want to mention what else was wrong with him. His left eye would swell closed by morning. His jaw was badly bruised, and if she hadn't got his frozen socks off, he would have had frostbite.

When she'd cut off the bloody leg of his jeans, she'd noticed that, just like Cody, he had a bullet hole scarring his skin from an old wound.

As he drank, she talked. "I know who you are because every emergency service is out looking for you. They think you've been kidnapped."

"I was, or maybe they were just trying to kill me. It all happened so fast. I was waiting for the Franklin sisters to bring my lunch one minute and running for my life the next."

Tess moved across the room and started a fire in the beautiful old rock fireplace.

Thatcher kept talking to himself more than to her, like he was trying to put it all together in his own mind. "I'm not sure the two losers who broke into my cell had a clear plan. They might have been hired killers, but they looked like they were paid in quarters. There's a whole other story about why I was locked up in the first place."

He scratched his matted hair, and she wouldn't have been surprised if something living didn't jump out.

"Back to the two idiots who tried to grab me. I think they wanted me, their victim, to walk to the kill site. Now that's the height of laziness, if you ask me."

"What did you do?" She handed him a paper towel so he could wipe at his bottom lip, which slowly dripped blood.

"I decided to fight." He looked at her. "I cut one of their ears off, then I ran."

"I don't think it's illegal to break out of jail if someone is trying to kill you." Tess tried to sound positive. "Well, maybe it is. Where was the sheriff?"

"He had a call and left Tim O'Grady and Miss Pearly in charge. Tim said I didn't need babysitting, and he was tired of watching me read. So he went home to get some sleep. Everyone else in the county offices left a half hour later because of the storm. I have no idea where Miss Pearly was but once a few years ago when I was looking around the place, I found her on one of the benches in the courtroom snoring away. She claimed she was just resting her eyes."

He leaned back, mumbling something about checking on a little girl in an old red coat. She was hurt, he kept saying. "We got to get to her! We got to."

"I'll tell the sheriff," Tess whispered, hoping he'd also rest his eyes for a while.

She took the half-empty milk jug. "We're stuck here for a while. A snowstorm with winds up to fifty miles an hour isn't something to go out in. They're probably closing the roads, and phone service is out." She covered him with an old quilt, realizing she was talking to herself. Thatcher Jones, the great criminal, at least in his own mind, was sound asleep.

Tess went to the kitchen and pulled out supplies. If she was going to be stuck here, she might as well make herself useful. She could paint the kitchen. Cody wouldn't be able to do it for months, and she'd noticed the cans of paint by the back door.

Pulling off her blood-spotted uniform, she decided her T-shirt would be fine to paint in.

As she worked, she thought of how much she liked helping out. It was almost as if she was playing house. She had someone to care for, someone to think about, someone to talk to.

During her childhood, her parents had always insisted she be able to survive on her own, be it in the woods of North Carolina or the snow of Alaska. She knew what plants were edible and how to set a trap with sticks and string or build a fire that would last the night.

When she left for college, her parents didn't think about taking her shopping for clothes like normal parents would. They arranged several lectures on how to manage her money and how to protect herself on the wild streets of Austin. While other girls were probably thinking of decorating their dorm space, Tess took a self-defense class.

She'd gone to the university knowing how to kill, skin and cook her own meat, but having no idea how to order takeout. They'd taught her how to live alone and survive, but they never taught her how to live with people. In her two years in the dorm, she'd never had a roommate she was close to. She moved out and lived by herself after that, finding it no more lonely than living with people.

Only now, Cody had told her to "take care of things," so that was exactly what she planned to do. He'd be so surprised when he came home. She'd already spent a few hours cleaning the house and organizing canned goods, his bills and his shaving supplies.

After all, they were friends. He'd asked her for a date. A real date, he'd said. Not a blind date, or a group date, or a "just friends" date. And last night she'd slept on half of his pillow for a few minutes. That must mean something, but she wasn't sure what.

By the time Cody got out of the hospital in a

few days, he'd have a clean house, be stocked with good food and have a kitchen painted bright yellow to cheer him up.

She hummed as she worked. Growing up, the closest she'd ever got to a home were cabins that sometimes came with the park host jobs. Her parents were born for adventure, and they saw no reason to slow down when they had kids. So the Adams offspring grew up in a trailer, traveling all fifty states. When they stopped, they usually set up camp in a national park or a geological dig or a place on the map her father would claim no one had ever been.

Maybe that's why she became an interpreter. She was working in the backyards of where she grew up.

Her dad taught wilderness classes all over the country. Her mother published "back-pocket cookbooks" that were sold in every camping supply store. The small cookbook had the basics with a flare. Fresh Fish Cooked on a Stone, Road Kill Barbecue, Apple Pie Baked in a Leftover ean Can, and so on. By the time Tess and her brother left home, their mom had published twenty-seven cookbooks and had squirreled enough money away to pay for their college tuition.

Tess was homeschooled before then, and never knew her address growing up. That first semester it came as a shock when she discovered that the rest of the world didn't live like she had. She met girls who screamed at spiders and didn't even know the names of stars, much less how to navigate by them.

She looked around and smiled. Even though this little house was neglected and run-down, she would have loved living in a place like this growing up. It felt solid around her.

A few hours later when Thatcher woke, the storm was still blowing against the windows so hard it sounded like knocking, and the phones were still out, but a little color was back in his face.

Tess checked his wounds, gave him two aspirins and a peanut butter sandwich, and studied him while he ate. No dying man could down a meal so fast, so she figured he was on the mend.

When Thatcher drifted back to sleep, she finished painting the kitchen, then washed the blood out of her uniform shirt in the sink. The fireplace had warmed the room so that it was almost toasty. In her T-shirt and the yoga pants she always wore under her trousers in winter, she snuggled into a makeshift bedroll and slept on the floor a few feet away from her patient.

At dawn she woke to the sound of her phone buzzing.

Tess checked on a sleeping Thatcher, then

slipped into the kitchen area of Cody's house and answered, "Hello, Mom."

"I heard about the storm and thought I'd call."

"I'm fine, Mom. The phones were out last night, but they must have got it fixed."

"Where are you? Surely you didn't go into work. No tourist is going to step foot in the park today."

Tess frowned at the cell phone. Her mother would let her run wild in the Appalachian Mountains or try to climb Denali, but she worried about her living in an apartment in town. "I'm staying over at a friend's ranch, Mom."

"A man friend?"

"Yes."

"Oh."

Tess couldn't tell if her mother was surprised or hopeful. She didn't want to tell her too much, or she'd never stop asking questions. "Dad would like him. He was a Texas Ranger." Basically, if he knew how to fire a rifle, her father would probably love him.

"Oh," Mom said again.

Definitely hopeful. Her mom had kept a score-card on Tess's record with men, and it wasn't pretty. Even the guy who her brother paid to take her out a few years ago brought her home early, claiming he had a cramp in his neck from looking up.

She hadn't been bothered that she was three

inches taller than him, but some men couldn't handle a woman almost six feet. Or maybe they just didn't want to?

"I have to go, Mom." Tess almost said that she had to call the sheriff. After all, an escaped criminal was sleeping on the couch. Mom would explode if she heard that.

"All right, dear. Now don't do anything wild. Don't hit your new friend or . . ."

Tess had already heard the list, so she cut her off. "I only slugged that one guy, Mom. He deserved it, and I paid for the dental work." She'd told her parents he'd been rude. She hadn't told them he'd grabbed her breast fifteen minutes into the date. If he'd been nice, she might have been interested, but Tess didn't enjoy feeling like she was a squeeze toy. "I've got to go, Mom."

She hung up before more questions came along.

When she turned, Thatcher was propped up on one elbow, obviously listening. "Your mom call you every morning?"

The bruises on his face were darker, one eyelid was bright purple, but she thought he looked much better. "I'm afraid so."

"It might not be so bad." He shrugged. "She complaining about you shacking up with the ranger?"

"I'm not shacking up."

Thatcher looked around. "This is a shack and you're sleeping here."

"I'm just helping Cody out. He took a fall from a horse and is in bad shape." It was a little more than that, but she didn't want to get into details. They'd kissed a few times. He'd called her honey and asked her to marry him, but that was after the drugs kicked in. None of which was this kid's business.

Tess turned back to the kitchen and started making breakfast. She didn't want to talk about it. She shouldn't try to make more of it than it was. Cody would get out of the hospital, thank her and maybe they'd decide to be friends. Once Cody was on his feet, he'd realize she wasn't the kind of woman men chased or even gave a second look. She was too tall, too plain and could take care of herself.

As she worked, she said more to herself than to Thatcher, "I hope Cody Winslow doesn't get any ideas just because I painted his kitchen."

"He won't," Thatcher answered. "But he might if you walk around in that T-shirt in front of him. Just saying truth. Don't mean no disrespect."

"What's wrong with what I'm wearing? People wear clothes like this to the gym all the time."

"Not with a body like yours. You got some nice curves, lady. Maybe I'm just used to high-school girls, but you're filled out nicely for an older woman." Thatcher turned red under all his bruises. "Not that I'm looking, but I'm thinking

224

if this Winslow comes home and you're standing in his kitchen in that outfit, he'll be staring at you with a goofy smile, if he's breathing."

She shook her head. "I'm only twenty-seven." Tess knew he was complimenting her in his own way. The uniform didn't do much for her figure, but she'd grown comfortable in it. In fact, her off-duty clothes were starting to resemble the uniform. Baggy trousers and plain cotton shirts. Still, it was not good when a kid gave her fashion advice.

"You up for breakfast?"

"Sure," Thatcher answered. "I'm starving."

"How about I call the sheriff first and tell him I'll watch over you until the roads clear?"

"You not afraid I'll escape or cut your ear off?"

"No, but if you don't cooperate, I'll forget to feed you." She tossed him an energy bar.

He picked it up and studied it. "What's this?"

"The appetizer."

Thatcher frowned. "Man, I miss my home in the cell. I had fresh muffins delivered every morning and some kind of pie brought at both lunch and dinner."

"Right, but you also had two men who dropped by to kill you." Tess laughed. "At least here, you've only got to worry about that bull snake in the box by the door."

She was surprised he didn't look the least frightened.

"Any reason you keep company with a snake?" Thatcher asked.

"I found him near the generator. I didn't want him getting in the barn and scaring the horses and he'd freeze if I turned him loose outside. He's the biggest one I've seen in a long time. Over six feet, I'd guess."

"You know folks confuse them with rattlers all the time. You'd think they'd notice that bull snakes don't have a rattle." Thatcher was fighting to stay awake long enough to finish his sentence. "I used to hunt snakes for a living." He leaned back on the arm of the couch. "Mind if I take a morning nap while you cook breakfast? I'm a little tired."

"After I make the call, I'll finish breakfast, then wake you."

She moved back to the kitchen and dialed the Ransom Canyon County Offices.

A woman answered the phone. "County Offices."

"This is Tess Adams with the Parks Department. I'd like to speak to the sheriff."

"He's very busy, Miss Adams. Could I have him call you back?"

"It's an emergency." Tess wasn't about to talk to anyone but the sheriff. She waited the receptionist out.

After a pause, the woman huffed and said, "I'll put you through."

Tess had never met the sheriff, but she'd talked to him a few times about Cody. Once to ask him to find someone to take care of feeding Cody's horses and another to inform him that she'd be taking over the job herself.

Dan Brigman had seemed to know where Wild Horse Springs was and said he'd met Cody a few times when Winslow was working for the Texas Rangers.

Finally, the sheriff picked up. "Brigman here. How's our night rider doing, Miss Adams? Word is he's healing. Hope there's no problem." He sounded like he was in a hurry to be finished with the call. He was saying the right words, being polite, but they came in rapid-fire.

"Cody's fine, I guess. Haven't seen him since yesterday around two," she said calmly, "only I found another man injured when I got to the ranch last night."

She paused. "My phone was dead, and I was afraid to take him back out in the storm. I patched him up."

"Who do you have?" Dan's voice shot through the phone and the background noise on his end died.

"Thatcher Jones." She could tell his end of the call had been switched to speaker. "He's okay, Sheriff. A few cuts, beat up some. Hungry every few hours."

"That's Thatcher." Brigman laughed.

She lowered her voice. "I think someone's trying to kill him."

"I know. Tell the kid I'm on my way." He sounded relived and tired.

She heard voices in the background as she shouted, "The roads are . . ."

"I'll get there. And tell the kid I'm bringing his cell phone. I don't ever want him without it again." The phone went dead.

Tess stared at it for a moment. The sheriff wasn't much of a talker. She had no idea how he'd get down the half mile of icy dirt road, but she had a feeling he'd be here soon. She'd better get dressed.

CHAPTER TWENTY-ONE

BRANDI MALONE SWORE she could pay for a hotel. All the bar owner had to do was take her to one, but after spending hours talking about the fire with everyone who dropped by, Hank insisted on putting her up in the best place he knew about.

The Franklin Sisters' Bed and Breakfast in Crossroads, Texas.

Brandi frowned when Hank drove past the Ransom Canyon County Offices, then stopped half a block away. Great. How was she going to keep a wild affair with the sheriff secret when she was practically on Main Street?

Cars and pickups surrounded the building, so the sheriff was obviously still working. As near as she could tell, Dan Brigman worked so hard he only slept every other night.

Brandi settled into the B and B and decided she'd wait him out. Eventually he'd have to crash, and when he did, she planned to be there to catch him.

Late the next morning Dan finally called. "Hank said you got a room last night. Sorry I didn't have time to drop over. I was dealing with a suspected kidnapping here in Crossroads."

She laughed. "You're running out of excuses. Was it or wasn't it a kidnapping?"

"Thank God it was not. I found out this morning that the victim escaped and managed to find a safe place last night. I'm relieved, but I'm going to make sure he stays hidden for a few days until I round up the suspects. It'd help if I knew more about them, but the kid couldn't tell me much."

"How will you know them when you see them?" Brandi had already heard most of the details from the Franklin sisters, but she liked listening to Dan's voice.

"Easy, a tall guy will be with a short guy who only has one ear."

"And the other?" She could hear a hint of happiness in his voice even when he was trying to be serious.

"The other will be missing a right ear." When she stopped laughing, he added, "It doesn't look like I'll be able to drive out to your hotel for a few hours. I need to talk to my escaped prisoner, the one who was almost kidnapped. Although he technically hasn't escaped, since the charges were dropped yesterday. As soon as it warms up a little, I'm heading out to question him again and take him a cheeseburger."

"Don't worry about me," she said. "I'm settled in and warm. I slept like a rock last night."

"I slept in my office chair. It felt like a rock. How far down the road did you have to go to find a room?"

"Half a block." She tried to laugh. They hadn't even gotten their clothes off yet and they'd become star-crossed lovers. "I'm at the best bed and breakfast in town."

"Brandi, don't tell me you're at the only bed and breakfast in Crossroads."

"I am. I thought I'd have to go all the way to Lubbock to find a vacancy last night, but with the roads so bad, Hank insisted on helping me find a place."

"Tell me the bright side."

Though he sounded tired and disappointed, there was still laughter in his voice.

As she began, she kept her voice low and sexy even though what she had to say wasn't the least like phone sex. "I've spent yesterday afternoon and this morning visiting with two little old dears, a couple from Utah who love the canyon walls and a lonely groom who just found out that his wife is a shopaholic."

"Tell me more," he whispered, as she heard a door close and guessed he was alone.

She could hear him relaxing. "If the bride ever comes back from the antique mall, he plans to have it out with her. Oh, a point of interest. The groom isn't speaking to the innkeepers because they told the bride the mall would probably be open and she could walk. They even loaned her one of the half-dozen pairs of snow boots left behind by former guests."

"The mall is three junk stores in a row, and I don't think it's open yet." He'd lowered his tone, midnight smooth. "I passed there a little after dawn, and they have two feet of snow in their six-space parking lot. If the bride's been gone more than thirty minutes and she hasn't called, she's left him. Anyone else at the B and B that I should worry about?"

"There were two little ladies from Oklahoma with bowling-ball haircuts, but they never added more than a nod to the conversation."

"I love talking to you," he said.

"Me, too. Almost as good as watching you. I like surprising you, Dan."

"How about coming home with me for supper? My daughter is in from Dallas for a few days. She says she's making chili tonight. I've got this ache to see you even if other people are around." He was silent for a moment, then added, "I just want to look at you, too. Maybe feel your hair." His voice lowered. "Maybe touch that nicely rounded—"

"Okay, I'll come." Brandi wasn't sure it was a good idea to meet any of his family, but she wanted to see him, too. It seemed his was an addiction that came on fast.

A few hours later, Dan picked her up at the bed and breakfast. He told the sisters that he needed her to look at a few mug shots.

Since Rose and Daisy loved mysteries, they

232

acted like they knew just how involved mug shot identification could be. Rose packed Brandi a snack so she could concentrate, and Daisy told her to study the eyes because that's where the criminals showed their true heartlessness.

The sheriff was formal, calling her Miss Malone, opening the door for her. Not standing too close. Not standing close enough.

"How's Thatcher?" she asked, trying to get her mind off what they were both thinking.

Dan shrugged. "I'm guessing you got the whole story from the sisters. I didn't mention any names this morning."

"Rose said you've been watching out for him all his life. This wasn't just some kid who skipped out of jail, was it?"

Dan drove toward his office. "No. I guess that's the blessing and the curse of being a small-town sheriff. You get involved. There was nothing I wanted more than to be with you last night, but I had to find him."

"And you did?"

"I don't think I stopped worrying for a moment until I got the call he was safe. We talked it over and decided he should stay exactly where he is until we find the two men who tried to kill him."

She nodded. If Dan had been another man, a different man, she wouldn't have believed him, but anyone could see that Sheriff Brigman *was* his job. It was part of him, bone and blood.

"How about we stop for coffee before we go to my office or the house? It's as private a conversation as we'll probably get for hours."

She agreed, and they pulled into a little café within sight of the county offices.

When they walked in, everyone stopped and stared. It didn't take much to figure out that the sheriff usually didn't enter the place with a lady. Once he opened his notepad and pulled out his pen from his vest pocket, people turned back to their meals. They all thought he was simply doing his job.

"Let me guess," she whispered even though he'd picked a booth in the corner, out of hearing distance of anyone else. "Everyone in town has a sister or mother or cousin they want you to meet. If you even hinted you were seeing someone, they'd be mad you didn't give their relative a try."

He smiled. "Maybe, but I'm not interested in the sisters, mothers and cousins."

She pulled her foot from the oversize snow boots Rose loaned her and stretched her leg across to his side of the booth. As her sock rubbed against his thigh, she said, "No one knows you want to walk on the wild side except me."

He laughed. "Doesn't seem to be working for me, but I'm still hoping."

Brandi pulled her foot out of sight when the waitress dropped by to take their order.

"Two coffees, two pies," he ordered without looking at the menu.

"Got it, Sheriff." She tapped her pencil against her cheek until he looked up at her. "Word is Thatcher is somewhere safe. You wouldn't happen to know where? Everyone is guessing. Some say he's down at your place on the lake. Some say he's in a real jail a hundred miles away. Some even say you drove him to a safe house during the storm late night."

The sheriff didn't bark at the nosy waitress. His words were calm and even. "Tell all the 'somes' that Thatcher is okay. You're right, he is at a safe house, under guard, and I'm not bringing him back until we catch whoever tried to hurt him."

"I'm thinking . . ."

"Sorry, Sissie, I have to interview Miss Malone right now. You mind if we talk later?"

"Oh, of course." The waitress smiled at Brandi. "So you're Brandi Malone. I heard all about the fire at the Nowhere. A trucker who stopped here for lunch yesterday said he drove slow past it but couldn't see much, except that the whole back side of the building was on fire. Who do you think did it?"

"Sissie, coffee," Dan reminded her.

"Oh, yeah. Sorry."

When she vanished, Brandi studied him. "You brought me here on purpose, didn't you, Sheriff."

"Maybe. I told you I'm not ashamed of being seen with you. You're a beautiful woman, and someone I'm looking forward to knowing completely."

"But you won't come up to my room tonight." She wasn't asking; she already knew the answer.

"Right. I want what happens between you and me to be private, and I know it wouldn't be in the Franklins' house."

She loved the way he looked right at her when he talked. "Let me guess. You've never gone out with a woman in this town since your wife left you. You've never put your arm around one in public, or even flirted with a lady for all the world to see."

"Correct."

"And that kiss on New Year's Eve was the woman's advance, not yours, right?"

"Right."

Brandi leaned back, trying to understand the man before her. It wasn't her he refused to touch in public, it was anyone. He'd brought her here to let her know he didn't mind being seen with her.

"So tell me, Sheriff. What do you plan to do with me in private?"

He smiled. "Everything." His gaze never wavered from hers.

"I think I'll wait around until you keep that promise. Then I'll move on after we make memories neither of us will ever forget." She raised three fingers as if giving a Girl Scout salute. "Nothing in public and everything in private. How can a girl turn down an offer like that?"

Sissie delivered the coffee and pie but didn't interrupt what she thought was an interview.

Brandi took a bite of the chocolate pie. "You didn't tell the waitress what kind of pie, and I saw several in the case when we walked in."

"I like chocolate. I guess after ordering it a couple times a week for twenty years, they probably figured it out."

She took another bite. "What if I didn't like chocolate?"

"Then I'd eat both and order you what you want." He ate a third of his pie in one bite then added, "Anything you want, Brandi?"

She had a feeling they were no longer talking about dessert. "We'd better get back to the interview, Sheriff. I'm starting to get the feeling I might be on the menu."

Dan finished his pie and then asked her several questions about the night of the fire. Who she saw. What she heard. What employees left before her. Who she thought remained in the building.

She moved her foot back beside his leg and felt his hand gently stroking her calf. The man turned her on simply by looking at her. And she could so get used to his touch.

When they got back in the car and the doors were closed, she looked at him and said, "I want you so badly I feel like I'm starving, Sheriff."

He didn't say a word; he just drove through the snow that was quickly turning to slush. He parked in front of the county offices. She followed him into his office to look at mug shots. Miss Pearly never left her side. Dan sat at his desk, thumbing through notes, but Brandi could feel him watching her.

"I'm so starstruck. I've never met a real singer," Pearly gushed.

"It's just a way to make a living," Brandi said, as she turned the pages of mug shots.

"I bet it's real exciting. I've seen how music folks live. One wild party after another. Did you ever trash out a hotel room? I've heard that's almost expected of bands."

"I'm not in a band. It's just me and my guitar on stage."

Brandi was polite. The sheriff professional. Thirty minutes later, when they left, Brandi felt like she was trapped. "Am I ever going to be alone with you?"

Dan laughed. "We'll find a way."

When he pulled into his lake house drive, though, he was silent.

"Are you sure you want to do this?" Brandi asked. "You could take me to the grocery store, then we could go back to the B and B and I'd try to sneak you in the back door. We could eat junk food in bed and forget about dinner."

"No. I'm fine." His gloved hands gripped the steering wheel. "I just don't know if I can keep this up much longer either. Since you kissed me at lunch a few days ago, all I've thought about is being with you. If we'd never met, I think I could have gone on with my life the same way forever, but now . . ."

"I know," she whispered. "*Keep it private,* remember? Your words, not mine."

"All I've thought about is the way I touched you yesterday morning. It was like one perfect moment."

He cut the engine.

"Me, too," she said. With the car turned off, she could see his outline in the pale sunset. "You tell me one of your thoughts about me, and I'll tell you one I had about you. Then, when we're inside, we can think about them even if half the town comes to dinner."

"I don't usually talk about things like this," he said.

"You just do them?"

"No. I don't do much of the *doing* either."

She thought of saying she also didn't. Now and then she'd imagine having a sexy time with a movie star filling in as a lover. But she couldn't tell him the truth. She was wild, remember. And the fantasy of her would always be with him when she left. "I'd like to watch you take off your uniform," she began. "When your shirt is gone, I want you to stop so I can move my fingers over your chest for a while. Until you grow used to my touch and want more."

"Really? I promise you taking my shirt off won't be exciting, but I could get into the touching." Dan turned toward her and lowered his voice. "I wouldn't mind watching you, though. When you were singing the other night, I kept wishing you'd touch me with the tenderness you do your guitar."

She loved the way his voice sounded, low and sexy. "I have a tattoo you'll have to examine."

"Where is it?"

"You'll have to explore to find it. Would it bother you if we leave the light on when we make love? I'd like to see your face when I drive you mad."

"No, I don't mind. I'd have more to remember. Give me a hint where the tattoo is."

Before she could answer, something moved across the windshield, brushing the newly fallen snow aside. A gloved hand.

"Pop. You all right? You didn't come in," a slender blonde in her early twenties yelled. Her hair was up in a braid around her head, almost like a halo.

Dan opened his door. "We're fine, just waiting for the snow to let up a little. I brought someone

240

home for dinner, since you were making chili."

Brandi climbed out of the car. "I hope it's not any trouble," she said as she offered her hand. "Lauren, right? I'm Brandi Malone."

"No trouble." The sheriff's daughter had her father's honest eyes. "I rounded up a few strays, too. I mean, I invited a few people, too, friends from high school."

Lauren led the way up the steps. "Nice to meet you, Miss Malone. I've heard you're a great singer. Sorry someone set fire to the Nowhere. Tim and I were talking about going there one night while I'm home."

"Call me Brandi."

The angel of a woman gave a quick nod and hurried to the door.

There was no doubt Lauren was nervous. Another hint that Dan had never brought a woman home before. The guy lived like a monk. She was going to have a grand time taking him to the edge of sanity, assuming they ever had time alone.

Brandi wasn't surprised at Lauren's comment about the fire. She probably knew more about what was going on with the investigation than Brandi did. Once Hank found out his insurance would cover all the damages, he stopped talking about the fire and gave all his attention to planning the remodeling. Backstage was really the only part of the place he hadn't mentioned redoing for the grand opening.

Dan took Brandi's arm and steadied her across a wide porch and into his home. She was amazed at how welcoming the lake house seemed. It wasn't big, but it felt lived in.

Dan pulled off his service belt while Brandi stepped out of her snow boots and left them at the door. She followed Lauren through the living area, which had a fireplace mantel covered with pictures of Lauren at every age. A worn recliner sat directly in front of a TV. There was a desk, almost as cluttered as the one in Dan's office, a great stereo system along one wall, and floor-to-ceiling bookshelves on the other side of the room that seemed to wrap around and continue into the hallway.

Two young men stood on either end of the kitchen. Neither looked happy. These must be the strays Lauren had brought home.

Dan took over the introductions. "Brandi, meet Lucas Reyes, the finest lawyer in Crossroads. He was a great help looking for Thatcher last night. We were afraid he fell into or was tossed down the canyon. Lucas worked with me all night searching, and we were both very relieved to hear he was safe this morning."

"He's the only lawyer in Crossroads," the man at the far end of the kitchen said. "And he's only passing through. Lucas lives in Houston."

Dan introduced the other man, who also looked to be in his midtwenties. Tall, very thin, with a red beard that gave him a pirate look. "Tim O'Grady, who lives down the shore a few hundred feet.

"Tim's a writer, Brandi, and I think he looks like a young, redheaded Hemingway, don't you?" Dan seemed more interested in the hot sauce and chips than talking, but he'd done his duty as host by introducing everyone.

Tim barely gave her a nod before he turned to the sheriff. "You said Thatcher's safe, but where is he?"

Dan's face hardened. "He'll be safest if no one but me knows that answer."

"So you're leaving me, your daughter and even the great Lucas Reyes out of the circle, Sheriff?"

"I am, at least until we find the men who attacked Thatcher. I've got two investigations keeping me busy right now, and the last thing I need is a crowd of people interfering." Dan's voice softened. "What's the matter, Tim, something bothering you? You usually have a little more patience with investigations."

Brandi didn't miss the way Tim's gaze darted to Lauren. As an outsider guessing, she'd say "lovers' quarrel," but Dan had mentioned that his daughter wasn't dating anyone.

Later, when she saw Lucas brush Lauren's side as he passed her, she reconsidered. A love triangle was more likely, and the sheriff was totally unaware. For a smart man who made a habit of knowing details, Dan Brigman had a blind eye where his daughter was concerned.

All three were obviously friends. They talked of growing up together, but tonight there was something between the two men. A tension. An anger. She'd bet a month's pay that it had to do with Lauren. The sheriff's daughter might be shy, but she was the only one in the room who knew exactly what was going on.

Brandi did her best to fit in. When she asked Tim a question about his occupation, Lucas's dark eyes flashed at the redheaded man. "Tim O'Grady is the only writer in town, so I guess that makes him the finest. But don't look for his books in print. They're only made of air."

"They're ebooks, man. Where have you been?"

Dan looked at Brandi and raised an eyebrow, as if to say he had no idea who the two men having dinner at his table were or why his daughter had invited them.

Brandi grinned and tilted her head toward the sheriff's daughter, who was busy collecting dessert and not looking at either of her guests.

He shook his head slightly as the two men continued their discussion of what counted as a real book. Dan moved his chair closer to Brandi.

"They're not fighting over books, Dan, they're fighting over your daughter," she whispered.

"Impossible."

"I'll bet you." She watched Lauren, shy and adorable. She seemed to ignore both Tim and Lucas as their argument grew.

"You're on." Dan bumped Brandi's shoulder, well aware that no one in the room was paying any attention to them. "Name the bet."

Brandi leaned closer and whispered, "Loser has to strip completely while the winner watches."

"You've got a bet." His honest eyes had sparks of fire dancing in them. "I'm going to love every minute of watching you."

"You're losing this bet, Sheriff."

He turned back to the kitchen and yelled over the argument. "How about Brandi and I do the dishes and you three take your dessert with you? I know you kids want to go over to Tim's place and watch movies."

Lauren laughed. "Pop, we haven't done that since we were in high school."

"Well, then, you've got lots of shows to catch up on." He looked from Lucas to Tim. "I remember when you were hurt, Tim. Lucas used to come visit you every day and help you with your homework."

Both the young men settled. They'd been friends once, good friends, and the sheriff was reminding them of that before the argument turned into a fight.

The redhead nodded at Lucas. "I only agreed to dinner because we all need to put our heads together and figure out how help Thatcher. Not only is he ruining his chances at getting into a good school, the kid's only eighteen and there are two kidnappers looking for him. Somehow I have a feeling the jail attack is related to the incident at the truck stop. It's just too much of a coincidence that both things happened within a few days of each other."

Lucas nodded. "I agree. We get to the bottom of one, and we solve the other." Lucas looked straight at Dan. "We're going to help, Sheriff. You might as well know it."

Dan gave a quick nod as if giving in to the fact he'd have help whether he wanted it or not. "Thatcher's got more survival skills than all of us put together," he admitted as he pulled Brandi's chair out and brushed her shoulder by accident as he stepped away.

The sheriff was smiling at Brandi until he noticed the other two guests at dinner were fighting over who would pull Lauren's chair out.

Lucas asked Lauren if she wanted to go for coffee to discuss helping Thatcher. She didn't look too interested.

Then Tim said he'd tag along. If possible, she looked even less interested.

"Go on." Dan ended the speculation. "You three go and talk it out, or you can stay here and I'll take Brandi home while you three wash up."

Suddenly everyone under thirty was pulling on coats and hats. In less time then Brandi would have imagined, all three were out the door.

Dan watched them drive away. "You're right. Something is going on with those three."

"Both men either are or want to be sleeping with your daughter." Brandi laughed. "And from her body language, she doesn't like either one of them right now."

Dan shook his head. "I'll never understand women and I raised one. When she was little, it was so easy. Even from the first after her mother left, she was always trying to take care of me."

Brandi moved behind him and gently placed her hands on either side of his waist. "Dan, we're finally alone and you lost the bet."

CHAPTER TWENTY-TWO

A SILENCE SEEMED TO settle on the little lake house like velvet lace. Brandi could hear herself breathe. She'd wanted to be alone with Dan Brigman since she'd first seen him, but the time was either too short or people were too close.

Now finally, it was just the two of them.

He slowly turned, reached around her and clicked off the kitchen light. The glow from the living room made the small space, even with dishes everywhere, seem romantic.

"How about we stop talking altogether?" He leaned against the counter and tugged her to him.

"I'm just fine with that," she said, moving into his arms without hesitating.

Their first kiss was tender, almost too gentle to be real. When he pulled away, he stared down at her. "You fit perfect against me. I love the feel of you. The way you move."

"I thought we weren't going to talk."

"Right." He kissed her again. A little deeper this time. They were settling into one another, and she knew he felt the same as she did, just right in his arms. From the first time he'd touched her when he'd helped her put her boot on, she'd craved the stroke of his fingers.

"Shouldn't we do the dishes first?" she whispered in his ear.

"No, we have hours." His hands moved along her back and over her hips. "I have an important investigation to do right now."

"What's that?" she asked, unbuttoning her blouse slowly as he stared.

When the silk opened, revealing her bra, she saw the hunger in his eyes.

"I need to find that tattoo."

She felt suddenly very young again as he took her hand and led her into his bedroom. Neither thought of turning on a light; the glow from the deck lamp was enough to see.

The room was plain, no pictures on the walls, no junk scattered around. Everything had its place, and right now, her place was here with him.

When he locked the door, he whispered that from now on there would be no talking.

She nodded in agreement as she let her blouse drift to the floor.

He sat on the room's only chair and unlaced his boots. When she put her foot on his knee, he stopped long enough to tug her sock off and slide his hand up her leg to the calf he'd been feeling earlier in the café. "I like this part of you, pretty lady, among other parts."

"Take your time. I'm not going anywhere until you're finished." She loved that he didn't hurry the beginning. It somehow made the ending so much sweeter.

"Lift your other foot," he ordered, and when she did, he tugged off the other sock with the same care. But he took his time stroking her leg, pressing hard enough to almost leave a bruise one moment and featherlight the next. "Your skin's warm, Brandi," he said. "Tell me, are you warm all over?"

She stood close in front of him as she unbuckled her belt and started to slip out of her pants, but his hand covered her, stopping her progress.

Raising her arms in surrender, she let him push the pants down slowly, taking his time watching as she appeared before him one inch at a time. When the fabric bundled just below her stomach, she let out a little cry when he leaned forward and kissed her there.

His strong fingers on either side of her hips held her still as he kissed his way up to her waist and back down again. The pleasure of it, the pure raw enjoyment he took, almost buckled her knees.

He pushed the material lower and kissed her bare body now, and she was so hot she felt like she was on fire.

When he finally looked up, her hands were on the clasp at the front of her bra. She wanted more, much more, all over.

As she stared into his eyes, she slowly released

the clasp. Breathe, she silently ordered as she watched him staring, admiring. She turned her back to him and tossed the bra on top of her blouse.

"Do you have any idea how beautiful you are?" he whispered as his hand curved over her hip.

He waited until she was down to skin before he admitted that he'd been the one who lost the bet.

"You complaining, Sheriff?"

"Not a chance. You're so much fun to watch undress I couldn't make myself admit I should be the one undressing first."

"I told you I wasn't shy," she whispered, as she sat in his lap, facing him.

He kissed her then, the way she'd always dreamed of being kissed. His hand caressed her bare body and she laughed with pure joy at how great it felt to be touched so lovingly.

Then, she insisted on helping him strip.

They made love with a caring that surprised and delighted her. They kissed and explored and whispered to each other all the way. This slow, passionate journey was new to her, and she couldn't get enough.

Whenever he turned her body to explore, to truly see her, she gave him a show and loved seeing passion fire in his eyes. She wasn't hesitant with him. He wanted to make her happy, please her, and she wanted to return the pleasure.

After they made love the first time, he barely gave her time to let her heart slow before they started again. This time he was even bolder and just as hungry. The kisses were deeper. Only she kept pushing him away when he got too close. She teased him until she was convinced that no man had ever wanted a woman like he wanted her.

The surrender wasn't sweet, but wild and maddening. It left both too exhausted to move. She could feel his breathing slow against her chest, but his hand still moved over her.

"I've never . . ." he whispered.

"Me neither," she answered. "I didn't even know it could be like this. Once in a lifetime. The Fourth of July and Christmas rolled in chocolate."

He laughed softly. "If I ever recover, we should do this again just to see if that's true."

She pushed him to his side. "I can't. My heart won't take it again."

He was gently caressing her now with his fingers along her side. Every now and then, he'd move a few inches and brush the side of her breast. She lifted her arms and let him explore, knowing that there would be a next time, and a next. She'd never been so open with a man, so free, so loving. She trusted him, and she knew she was the drug he was quickly becoming addicted to. The next few weeks with him would be one long high. Even now, when they'd already made love twice, his nearness was turning her on again.

When she curled in his arms under the covers, Brandi realized that she'd never felt this way before. Safe, cherished, loved. For the first time in her life, she'd met a man who wouldn't be easy to walk away from. But she would. It's what they both wanted—a memory. Nothing more.

Even in his sleep he moved his hand over her body. He was making love to her in his dreams. She drifted, half asleep, half wrapped in the pleasure of him near. Deep in the night, she woke him silently, demanding satisfaction. He surrendered without a fight and gave her what she wanted.

The sheriff had kept his promise. He'd given her something she'd never had: a memory to take with her forever. A perfect night of lovemaking. Sanctuary in his arms. No matter how cold the nights got, she'd have this one time to remember, to hold on to.

She'd have one night in her life when she knew she was cherished by a man with honest eyes.

CHAPTER TWENTY-THREE

CODY HAD SUFFERED through a hell of a day, and Tess still hadn't shown up at the hospital. She'd said she would check in, and if he got released, she'd come get him, but that obviously wasn't happening.

If he had a cell phone, he'd call her.

If he knew her number.

The sun was shining, melting off snow and ice as fast as it melted away any hope of ever having Tess Adams as a friend. He didn't need her. He didn't need anyone. *If you depend on people, they either let you down or die on you.* He needed to get used to that fact.

Cody swore. If she didn't show up soon, he'd tell the nurse that his wife had run off with a biker. If he could make up a wife, he might as well make up her biker lover.

Finally, half asleep and tired of waiting, he heard the door to his room slowly open. "That you, honey?" he snapped.

A man in a sheriff's uniform stepped in. "No, it's not, darlin'."

Cody swore again. "What are you doing here, Sheriff Brigman? Near as I can tell, falling off a horse isn't a crime. Of course, I've been missing a park ranger for two days who said she'd come get me. You think I could file a missing person's report while you're here?"

Dan Brigman walked to the side of the bed. "I haven't got time for any paperwork right now. I'm your taxi back to your land. Miss Adams isn't missing, she has got her hands full at your place with another injured man." He looked over at the stack of supplies. "I see you're packed and ready."

"I have been for hours, but I didn't know home deliveries were part of the sheriff's job." Cody frowned. "What other man is at my place?"

"I'll explain in the car. I'll also have plenty of time to talk you into doing me a favor on the ride home." He grinned. "Lucky for you Tess called to tell me to bring you something to wear. All I had handy was this coat. Sorry about the dust."

Dan handed Cody a long raincoat that looked like it had been riding around in a police car for years.

"I don't care." Cody scooted to the edge of the bed and put his good foot on the floor. "I just want to get out of here. I need air that doesn't smell like medicine. Hell, everything smells around this place."

He opened the coat and shook it out. Dust flew, but Cody breathed in deep. "Ah, I never thought I'd say it, but dirt smells good after this place. At least this coat will keep the back of my butt from showing. Then you'd have to arrest me for indecent exposure."

255

Two nurses came in to help. By the way they were smiling, Cody guessed he hadn't been an easy patient to handle.

While they worked getting the coat over his broad shoulders made even wider by the bandages and tucked him into a wheelchair, Cody told the truth to the sheriff. "I'm not worth much, lately. You might look for a favor somewhere else."

He knew the sheriff was surveying his injuries, but it was the scars inside that made him unfit for duty. "I'm not sure I could be of any help, but I appreciate the ride home."

Dan leaned down while the nurses were busy and whispered, "Can you handle a weapon if I need a guard?"

"I can." Cody had never turned down an assignment. When he was put on leave, he was fighting mad and that hadn't helped. He wanted to be in the field working, not behind a desk.

Officially, he was still a ranger on leave, but mentally, Cody knew he was messed up. Nightmares still haunted him, even though he'd told the psychiatrist that they didn't. Cody wasn't sure how he'd react if he heard gunfire again. After you've lain in the mud for hours listening to it, you started to wonder if you were dead and your hearing was simply the last sense to go.

Brigman picked up a plastic bag of things like bedpans, little pitchers and tissue boxes. The two nurses started rolling Cody into the hallway.

"Let's get you home, Ranger Winslow, and we'll talk about the assignment waiting for you." Brigman led the parade to the elevator.

One nurse pushed Cody in the wheelchair and the other followed with a cart.

"You want this junk?" Brigman lifted the plastic bag of plastic stuff.

"No," Cody answered.

Brigman dumped it in the first trash container they passed.

Cody smiled for the first time in days. "You've had a stay in a hospital before, I'm guessing."

"Yep. And believe me, you'll never miss a pink pitcher."

Right then Cody decided he liked the sheriff. Whatever this favor was, he'd do it. He'd been delivered here by the chopper with nothing but his clothes, and most of them were cut off during the flight in. He was leaving with one hospital gown under a borrowed raincoat, a pair of crutches, a walker, a shower seat and his cowboy boots. At least the medic hadn't cut them off.

Cody raised an eyebrow, wondering if the sheriff was playing a trick on him. Brigman must be pretty hard up for help if he was recruiting out of the hospital. Maybe the nurses had called and said they planned to murder him in his sleep if someone didn't come get him. It was possible. His main physical therapy had been fighting with them.

When they rolled him to the passenger side of a one-ton truck that had HARRY'S WELDING painted on the side, Cody asked, "Undercover vehicle?"

"It was all I could find in a pinch," Dan said.

Cody shrugged. "I'm surprised Harry, whoever he is, loaned it to you."

"He didn't exactly, but when he gets back from Hawaii I'll ask him. He told me to watch over his place while he was gone."

Cody lifted himself slowly up into the truck as both nurses shouted orders and tried to push, as if he were an overweight Santa Claus being stuffed down the chimney.

Once he was seated, the head nurse leaned in to tuck a blanket around him. As she backed out, she kissed him on the cheek. "You're a hard man, Cody Winslow, but you couldn't be all that mean or that sweet wife of yours would never love you or put up with you."

"What makes you think she does?" Cody grumbled.

They both laughed. "We see it in her eyes," the other nurse answered. "She's got the most expressive eyes."

Great, Cody thought. *My imaginary wife loves me.* The nurses must have been dipping into the drug cabinet. He and Tess Adams were barely on the *like* shelf, and once she got to know him better, she'd fall off that, too.

On the way home, Dan told him all about Thatcher Jones and how the kid had ended up at Cody's place. "He's not hurt bad, but he needs some time to heal, and I need to have him safe so I can work."

Cody understood. This actually sounded like something he could do. How hard could it be to watch over a hurt kid? He could hear any car when it turned off the road, so no one was likely to sneak up on the house.

"I'll take the assignment," he said. "If you'll help Tess move the half bed in the spare room into the living room, I'll never let the kid out of my sight."

Dan was silent a few miles, then said, as if it was no big deal, "I've asked Tess to stay at the ranch. I don't even want her going after the mail or groceries." The sheriff laid out his plan. "I want you two to isolate Thatcher until I know it's safe. I've okayed it with her boss, so as of right now you both are on twenty-four-hour duty. A ranger in plain clothes or I will deliver anything you need every other day. I'm hoping this assignment you've been drafted into will all be over in less than a week, but I'm not taking any chances with Thatcher's life. Since I couldn't protect him in my jail, I'm counting on you to do a better job."

Cody knew the routine. Even laid up with a broken leg, he could do this. "Any chance you could get me another partner? I don't like the idea of putting Tess in danger."

Dan shook his head. "She knows the risks and she's already accepted the assignment. I know it's unusual, but Ranger Winslow, this time your wife is also going to be your partner."

Cody let his head fall back against the headrest so hard he added another knot on his skull to the half dozen he already had. The secret marriage he'd made up had spread to the sheriff.

Now didn't seem the time to admit to lying. If she was playing along with the farce, he could, too.

"You all right, Cody?" Dan slowed the truck.

"I'm fine," he answered. "I just have a headache. It'll pass." *Or get worse,* he decided. Once he was alone with Tess, she was going to kill him. Teasing about asking her to marry him was one thing; making everyone believe it was a done deal was another.

The sheriff spent the next half hour telling Cody how lucky he was to be alive. There had been a few others fall into the canyon over the years, and Cody was the first he'd ever heard who survived.

Cody didn't want to hear how lucky he was. People had said that when he'd lived after the battle with drug runners at the border. He hadn't felt very lucky then, and he didn't feel lucky now. "What else is going on?" he asked, needing to change the subject.

Dan filled him in on the fire at the Nowhere Club over by the county line. It was obviously set, but no one could come up with a motive.

Cody got the feeling that Dan Brigman needed to talk things out with someone in the profession. Who knew? Cody might be able to help with the investigation. This was a safe subject. One he could handle.

"Check the other bars around, Sheriff. Sometimes competition can heat things up, if you know what I mean."

"I'll look into it."

The two lawmen moved from the fire to the attack in the jail.

"When I talked to Thatcher, he mentioned a little girl in an old red coat that he was worried about. Said the guy who cut him may have beat her. He guessed she was about the same size as Charley Collins's kid, Lillie, when he first met her."

"How old was Lillie when Thatcher met her?" Cody asked.

Dan thought a minute. "Lillie Collins was about five then. She's about nine now."

"How does this kid at my place know the red coat girl?"

"He admitted he'd seen her stealing canned goods at the truck stop. He gave her a ride home, gave her money and was taking the cans back when Luther, the truck stop owner, caught him."

Dan was silent for a minute then added, "I think she reminded him of Charley's Lillie. Thatcher was just trying to help out. He's like a big brother to Lillie."

"Where is the little girl he's worried about now?" Cody asked.

"We can't find her. I walked through the trailers behind the gas station in Crossroads where Thatcher said he dropped her off. With all the construction going on, the mud hole they call a model-home park has doubled since spring. There must be forty or more trailers parked out there. There's no order to most of it, no roads, not enough hookups. Most of the folks out there are workers on a construction project in town, and half a dozen more are oil-field workers out of jobs this time of year. I asked around. No one said they'd seen a little girl about five or six wearing a red coat, but some aren't cop-friendly."

Cody found the possibilities easy to put together. "You think if we find the little girl, we find the two guys who tried to kidnap Thatcher Jones? Somehow the two things are related."

"I do, only Thatcher's not telling me everything he knows. I'm guessing he thinks he's somehow protecting her. Maybe he saw something or heard something."

Cody was interested suddenly. "You think he's that kind of kid? The kind who'd risk his life for a little girl he doesn't even know?"

"I know he is." Brigman turned off the paved road onto Cody's place.

"You got a regular crime spree going on, Sheriff." Cody made a habit of not keeping up with anything happening around him. He wasn't even sure who owned the land on either side of his. One place had been up for sale the last time he heard, and the other farm was in the middle of a court fight over which one of the dead owner's stepchildren should inherit.

By the time Dan bumped his way over the unkept road past the gate, Cody thought of suggesting going back to the hospital. Something else must be broken. Harry should have skipped the vacation in Hawaii and spent the money on shocks for his truck.

Dan didn't seem to notice; he just kept talking. "At least knowing Thatcher is safe will be a load off my mind. The sheriff in the next county over can worry about the fire. I've given him as many names and descriptions of people that I could remember. Don't see much else I can do to help."

Cody looked up and saw Tess standing on his front porch. She was tall and had that healthy, all-American look going on. Funny how she appeared to belong there. She wore a blue park ranger shirt and trousers that fit like a man's, but he didn't care. Poor girl probably didn't have a butt, but she made up for it with well-rounded breasts.

If she knew he was even thinking about her body parts, she'd probably karate chop him into tomorrow. Park rangers might not wear weapons on their hip, but Cody had no doubt she could take care of herself. After all, weren't they trained to fight off bears?

She smiled as she helped him out of the truck, but whispered that they needed to talk.

He kissed her cheek. "About what, honey?"

While the sheriff was checking on Thatcher, she whispered back, "About our marriage." Her smile was so sweet he knew it was poison. "I don't believe in divorce, Ranger Winslow, so I guess I'll have to make myself a widow."

He tried to smile, but he wasn't sure she was kidding.

She helped him into a chair and pulled up a stool for his leg. "I thought the banker simply trusted me, but thanks to the sheriff, I've figured out he thought we were married. Wonder how he got that idea?"

Cody might as well confess. "I may have told one of the nurses we were. I thought it would be funny if they thought we were a couple."

She smiled that sweet smile that frightened him more than the sound of a shotgun being racked on a dark night. It seemed to hint that she'd murder him as soon as they were alone.

Cody fought down a laugh. He hadn't had so much fun in years. He'd better stay on full alert.

Hell, he'd better get well fast because he had a feeling she'd come at him full out when she got the chance.

Within an hour the sheriff had Cody settled in, with his Colt next to his pillow and a rifle just under the bed. Tess had tried to fuss over him, but Cody kept pushing her away. He didn't need any help, and he didn't want to get used to accepting any or he might miss her when she was gone.

Plus, he didn't trust this sweet act she was putting on. He had no doubt she was still mad at him.

But mad or not, she'd be gone when this assignment was over. When he was healthy, most women barely seemed to put up with him. Now, hurt and probably half-crazy, Tess would disappear soon enough.

He'd teased her about them having a date, but there wasn't much chance of that. Not when she saw who he really was. Broken, angry and too hard to care about anything.

Top that off with the fact that she knew he lied about their relationship, and his chances of getting that kiss on the porch he'd told her he wanted weren't good.

The kid he was supposed to be watching wasn't too happy either.

"This is not necessary, Sheriff," Thatcher complained as he sat up from his makeshift bed on the couch. "Just leave me with a rifle, and I'll shoot the guy's other ear off if he dares show up here. I don't need two strangers watching over me."

"It's just a precaution, Thatcher." Dan put one hand on Thatcher's chest and pushed him gently back on his pillows. "You're lucky you've got a Texas Ranger looking out for you, because they don't miss a thing."

Thatcher frowned. "He must not be too observant. He's been here an hour, limping all over the house and hasn't even noticed his kitchen changed colors."

Cody looked over at the kitchen. He'd thought the sun reflecting off all the snow outside just made the place look bright. But the walls weren't white, they *were* yellow.

It took some effort, but he swiveled enough to see Tess reorganizing his supply cabinet. "You taking over my life, Tess?" He had a faint memory of asking that question once before.

"Yep," she answered simply. "But at least I'm honest about it."

"I like the mess." He tried growling at her.

"You'll have the same mess, it'll just be in alphabetical order," she growled back at him.

Cody heard the kid behind him whisper to the sheriff, "You know, I think I'll hang around. This might be interesting. He's a wounded bear. She's bound to poke him with a stick at some point if her organizing bothers him half as much as it does me, and it's not even my stuff. I might learn something here, Sheriff. Plus, I got a bull snake in the box by the door. Hell, I don't need a TV. I have a feeling this reality show is about to start."

Cody closed down his anger. He had no intention of being the sideshow for the kid. Besides, he had an assignment. It came first.

He glanced over at Tess. She was smiling at him again. He'd like to wipe that smile off her face, and it suddenly occurred to Cody that kissing her senseless might just be the way to do it.

CHAPTER TWENTY-FOUR

LAUREN STARED OUT the back window of the lake house. The sun was burning away morning fog, but she could still see thin, low clouds shifting just above the water as if waiting for the lake to freeze so winter's breath could settle.

There was something haunting about the scene, like unclaimed souls gathering, huddling, mourning the passing of night even though they no longer needed the darkness or one another's warmth.

Deep down she realized that she'd packed her loneliness and brought it home with her from Dallas. She was finished believing in dreams. Nothing in her life was working out as planned. Somehow she'd started driving her car of goals and hopes without a steering wheel. She'd lost herself in life's confusion and didn't know how to get back on a path forward.

Lucas didn't want her around. He'd dropped her off first last night. Tim was so angry he might toss their friendship out with the trash left from their affair.

In a nutshell, her love life was rushing through the rapids, and every now and then she bashed her head on a passing rock. Polly, her college roommate, found a guy around every corner. Lauren had known two who mattered to her, and somehow they both managed to end up angry with her. She was the plague where relationships were concerned.

Maybe she should be like her father. Live alone and go to bed without even doing the dishes. He seemed perfectly happy. After running them off last night, he must have taken the singer home, returned to the lake, then gone right to bed. He'd even locked his door so she couldn't wake him up and talk him into helping clean up.

When he'd left early this morning, she'd heard him whistling as he went out the door.

Pop didn't seem to mind being alone. Maybe she'd follow his lead. Only she didn't have a career to fill her days. She felt like she had about as much substance as paper clouds floating on icy water.

She drifted over to the long windows that faced the lake and watched the water, always shifting, moving.

For a few moments, she thought the figure standing at the bottom of the deck steps was just a shadow, but then she saw the Stetson in his hand. Someone was out there. Standing still. Waiting.

She knew his build. She'd seen him both dressed in western clothes and in a pricey suit. This shadow of a man by whom she'd measured every other guy she'd dated.

Whether she was mad at Lucas Reyes or not didn't matter. He couldn't just stand out there.

Last night, after the three of them had talked and argued over coffee, Lucas had brought her home, then turned toward Tim's place. Lauren hadn't talked to either of them later, but she guessed they'd spent a few more hours arguing or, if Tim had a vote, drinking.

The two men had been friends once, in high school and in college for a while, but they were polar opposites. Tim drifted, daydreamed. Lucas was, and would probably always be, a man on a mission.

Pulling on her pop's thick sweater, she stepped out onto the deck and walked slowly toward Lucas.

He didn't move.

She could hear her own footsteps and knew he must know she was there, but Lucas didn't look up. Damp, cold air hung over them like a curtain about to fall.

"If you've come to kiss me again, forget it. That was just a spur-of-the-moment thing when you were saddling up the other night. If you'd wanted to kiss me, you should have done it last night when you came to dinner."

He showed no sign of being aware of her coming closer.

"Why did you come over last night anyway, Lucas? Not to see me. Not to talk to me." She moved closer, letting her bottled up anger out for once. "Why are you here now?"

"Why'd you invite Tim last night?" he shot back as he raised his face to her. Eyes dark as coal stared at her.

Lauren crossed her arms, determined not to let him intimidate her. Typical lawyer, answering a question with a question.

She saw herself as more of a mouse than a fighter, but Lucas had finally made her furious. Their entire relationship, or maybe lack of one, was ups and downs, and she wanted off the roller coaster.

In the edges of her logical mind, she knew he was the reason she couldn't move on with her life. When she'd been fifteen, she'd worshipped him, and he'd stepped away again and again. Well, no more. This time she wouldn't let him in.

"What does it matter why I invited Tim?" What was the point in arguing with him? It didn't matter if they fought or kissed, he'd disappear when it was over, and she'd be mixed up even more than she was right now.

A clean cut and he'd be out of her life.

Let him say whatever he came to say and be gone.

He took one step up to the deck and was suddenly eye level with her. The anger in his eyes shocked her. His jaw was clenched so hard it could have been made of granite.

"I wanted to ask you one thing." He took another step, and she watched his hands ball into fists. "Why'd you sleep with Tim? Answer me!"

Lauren stood her ground. "Why do you care?"

"I don't." He lowered his voice, but rage still salted his words. "Not anymore."

"Good." Lauren was surprised that she could still feel her heart crack. She'd thought it was already broken. "Get off my property. What I do, who I sleep with is none of your business. This cross-examination stops now."

As she whirled toward the house, he grabbed her arm and closed the distance between them. His fingers dug into her, even through the sweater. She clenched her teeth, refusing to cry out.

Just before she drew back to fight, she felt his heart pounding against her own. Like it had that night almost ten years ago when he'd saved her life. She might have died in a fall if he hadn't been there watching over her. She'd been fifteen, and he'd been almost eighteen. It had started then, this attraction, this obsession.

Anger left her. This was Lucas. The boy who made her believe in love. The man who came to her in her dreams. The one who shattered her world every time he walked away.

"Say what you came to say, Lucas, but turn loose of my arm first." Like lightning striking an already dead tree, she realized the obsession was hers. The attraction his.

He opened his grip so fast she wondered if he'd even been aware that he was holding her.

"You can't hurt me anymore, Lucas." She stumbled backward a step. "I've given up on all relationships, including Tim's *friends with benefits* bargain."

He stared at her. In the glow of the foggy light, she saw the anger go out of his dark eyes. The polished lawyer won out over the angry man.

He took a step back and leaned against the railing. "Do you love him, Lauren?"

"Who?"

"O'Grady." Frustration threatened his front. "Or are there so many other lovers you can't remember their names?"

"No, but what is between us has nothing to do with Tim."

"He told me you've been lovers since college days. I'd say that he's definitely standing between us, if there is or ever was an us."

Any way she explained Tim would make her sound cold. Technically, they had slept together just before she graduated. Her pop was in the hospital fighting for his life, and she'd turned to her best friend for comfort. "We're not lovers. It's not like that. It'll never be like that. He's my best friend. I'll never be with him the way he wants it to be, but I don't want to hurt him."

Lucas slumped as if suddenly exhausted. "You were with him that night at the Two Step when you saw me. After kissing me like you did, you went home with him, didn't you?"

She didn't answer. Tim had been drunk; she'd had to take him home. She'd stayed at his place that night because she was worried about him. "I don't have to answer your questions, Lucas."

He moved farther away, accepting defeat. "I searched for you for half the night after we met in the bar. I even woke your dad up. He told me you'd gone to Lubbock with Tim. Only I went by Tim's house. His car was there, and I knew you were, too."

He was just stating facts, finishing up an argument he'd already lost. "I drove all the way back to Houston when I realized that a kiss that blew my mind was just foreplay for someone else. I thought no one could kiss me like you did and walk away. I thought you'd call and tell me I was wrong, you weren't with Tim."

"Pop never told me you came by. I didn't know." All her excuses sounded weak. How could she tell Lucas that she'd never once kissed Tim like she'd kissed him that night? That part of her unopened heart still waited for him.

"What we had in high school was real, Lauren. I thought it was. I thought we'd find our way back to each other one day, when the time was right. At first you were too young, then I got in a hurry to graduate, then we were in different worlds for a while."

She had to defend herself. "You pushed me away. You left when my dad was in the hospital.

Tim offered comfort when I hurt and you were nowhere around."

"I had to make it into law school. I didn't want to be like my dad, working for the man who owns the land, living in a house that comes with the job and will never be in his name."

He shook his head. "You needed to finish school and then your dad was hurt, and I knew you had to be home. And now there's Tim. He loves you, you know. He told me you two were together and were just having a lovers' quarrel. He said if I even thought of asking you out that I was too late. He's bought a ring. I saw it last night."

She shook her head. "No. I can't take it."

"Why not?"

She couldn't answer. How could she tell Lucas that she couldn't wear another's ring? If she said a part of her still loved Lucas and had since she was fifteen, she'd sound like a romantic idiot. Besides, she obviously made Tim miserable, so why would he want to marry her and make it a permanent condition? He was stuck in this black hole with them, no one winning, everyone losing.

She stood three feet away, but they might as well have been an ocean apart. She asked the same question she'd asked before. "What are you doing here, Lucas?"

He shot an answer without hesitation. "I want

it finished between us. I want it over so I can get on with my life."

"Me, too."

They both waited as if one had to come up with a way that they could part with the least amount of fallout. She thought of suggesting they shake hands and say goodbye, but she doubted that would solve anything.

Finally, he said, "You really don't love O'Grady?"

This she knew the answer to. "No. I've broken it off with him again and again, but he thinks it's temporary. I don't want to hurt him. I'm lonely, he's my best friend, but I can't marry him for those reasons."

"You have to let him go."

"No." The thought of losing her best friend hurt deep inside.

"Then we've nothing else to say." Lucas turned and seemed to vanish into the last of the morning fog. Lauren stood in the silence and wondered if he'd been there at all.

She walked back into the house.

For the first time in months, Lauren opened her laptop and began to write a story about ghosts haunting a house on a cliff near an ocean. None of the spirits could move on to heaven or hell because they all refused to turn loose of one another.

As the hours passed, the story grew dark

with flashbacks of murders and betrayals. An Englishwoman bought the old house on the cliff and began to unravel the lies and crimes of each spirit. One by one the ghosts disappeared, and the dark house began to fill with light.

At four o'clock when she read the first two chapters of her book, she smiled. The story was so dark it scared her, but it was good.

She felt she was truly writing as she saved it under the file name Imprisoned Lives.

For the first time in years, she had a direction. She was growing, changing. She'd move on with her life.

Something was happening, deep inside her. She grew, not by inches but by miles, and she felt it. The shifting from a girl to a woman.

And Lauren knew she'd never go back to before.

CHAPTER TWENTY-FIVE

DAN WALKED THROUGH the trailer park just before dawn on Saturday morning. He'd put in another late night shift, another night without seeing Brandi. It frustrated him that she was so close and he couldn't be with her. Their time was short. In days she'd be gone. He'd be alone again.

After Thanksgiving she'd be moving on to New Mexico to another engagement. She'd be out of his world, out of the state, out of his life. Maybe they'd try to keep in touch, but the absence of her would be painful.

Dan forced himself to concentrate on his job as he walked through the poorly kept RV park that seemed to have exploded in size lately. He could smell trouble in the still air. The faint odor of marijuana blended with the stench of rotting food and spilled beer.

In the summer there were usually families staying in the mobile homes. Cowboys working roundup often rented some of the trailers in the spring and fall. Oil-field workers building rigs might stay here during the week before heading back home on Friday after work. A few folks on vacation stopped over for a cheap place to hook up with water and electricity before they rolled on down the road south toward the coast or north to the cool of Colorado.

But in winter, the homes on wheels were in poorer condition. Drifters stayed here when they couldn't sleep outside. A hundred a month and free water and electricity if you weren't too particular about it running regularly. The place was occupied mostly by men trying to earn enough to get back home. Dan rarely saw a family after school started.

That's why Thatcher telling him about a little girl here surprised him.

Dan suspected a few of the strangers sold drugs to make ends meet, but he'd never been able to catch them. Locals didn't buy, at least not in their own town, but crews doing construction jobs did, and he thought some of the drug business came from neighboring counties. People tended to drive outside where their family lived to commit a crime.

As sheriff, he did the best he could to fight even petty crime with Deputy Weathers's help. The two of them had to cover almost a thousand square miles counting land, water and canyons. And having a stakeout in a town this size would be impossible. So he walked at dawn and dusk, hoping to get lucky.

Dan had put on an old black coat and a cap before he left the office. In the shadows, he might not be noticed.

He circled one last time. Nothing. The sun would be up soon. With the light, he'd be recognized, even out of uniform. Dan had given up sleeping with Brandi tonight for not even one clue.

Of course, sleeping with her was almost impossible. The Franklin sisters guarded their place like Pinkertons. He'd called her a few times when he'd been driving. Once when he went over to the Nowhere Club to see if there was any news. Another time when he borrowed a friend's car and drove out to check on Thatcher. The kid was bored and calling in requests for books and food.

It was the weekend now, so the construction crew working across from the jail was nowhere to be found. If Dan had to, he'd interview every one of them to find out if anyone had seen two men enter or leave the courthouse on Thursday morning. Between him and Weathers, they'd gotten statements from all but four men who worked Friday. Come Monday, he planned to get the rest.

Dan unlocked the office door and went inside, just as a foggy sunrise lifted the night. He'd change clothes and still have an hour to be alone before anyone came in.

If anyone came in. Some Saturdays were so quiet he went home at noon and fished the rest of the day.

His cell buzzed, and he smiled when he saw Brandi's number.

"Morning, beautiful," he answered.

She laughed softly. "I thought you might be up. Without you to keep me awake last night, I went to bed early and now, a first in my life, I woke up early."

"Want to meet for breakfast?"

"I'm at a bed and breakfast, Dan. I think it's a requirement that I eat here."

"All right, meet me for coffee over at the diner. Consider it an appetizer for the grand breakfast that's to come."

"I'm on my way." The phone went dead.

"Goodbye, darlin'," he said to no one on the other end, then laughed. "You're a fast woman, Brandi."

It might be the weekend, but he didn't plan on being off duty unless Brandi had discovered a way they could be totally alone. What would be the point?

When he walked over to the diner, Brandi pretended to be surprised to see him and invited him to join her for coffee. Sissie was still half-asleep and didn't seem that interested in her first two customers of the day. If she thought their meeting was strange, she didn't comment.

He sat across from the singer and whispered as soon as the waitress was out of hearing distance. "Move your feet over here. I'll warm them up."

She did, and his hand slid up her pant leg to feel her calf. The memory of how she'd propped her foot on his knee while he'd slipped her socks off returned. The thought of every detail of how she'd looked as she'd undressed made him hungry to get her alone. The need to have this sexy lady against him made Dan feel drunk on her nearness.

"We've got way too many clothes on, Sheriff."

He tightened his grip on her leg and saw her eyes fire with need.

"You'll leave a bruise," she said low.

"Do you want me to ease up?"

"No," she said. "I'll take all you got and wake you up for more."

"I know." He moved his hand over her sock. "I remember."

"I look forward to seeing all of you. With all those clothes on, I can't see that tattoo you have on your . . ."

Sissie brought their coffee and stayed around to refill all the napkin holders. Their private moment was gone. He told Brandi about the investigation on the fire, and she told him she had a theory that whoever set the fire wasn't interested in her, or Sorrel, but only the bar. This was coming into the holiday season. Lots of relatives home for Thanksgiving and Christmas. Maybe the club was taking away business from other bars?

"A Texas Ranger suggested the same theory." Dan didn't buy into the idea. The only place around for thirty miles was the Two Step Saloon. Ike Perez had lost interest in the bar lately and turned it over to one of his sons. Word was the younger Perez was drinking up most of the profits.

"It's just an idea," Brandi said as Sissie walked back into the kitchen, "but if I was setting a fire I wanted to burn a while before it was noticed, I'd set it at the back of the club."

"What about your van?"

"I've thought about that. It was just in the way. Whoever was pouring the gas probably was drunk. He just got mad at my van for being in the way."

Dan smiled. "You interested in law enforcement?"

"I'm interested in one man who wears a badge."

For a moment neither of them said a word. The silence was so loud he swore he could hear her thoughts. She wanted to go somewhere, anywhere, where they could be alone. For the first time in his memory, he wished his daughter were in Dallas.

"I want to touch you," Brandi whispered.

"Where?" He grinned.

"All over."

He spotted Sissie heading their way with the check. The sheriff stood and straightened, hoping he looked very official. "If you don't mind, Miss Malone, there are a few more mug shots I'd like to show you. When you have a few minutes, I hope you'll stop my office."

Brandi stood. "Anything I can do to help."

As he stepped to the front counter to pay, Dan thought he saw something red blowing across the street, almost like a piece of cloth rolling in the wind and disappearing behind the diner.

He dropped a few bills and gave a quick sign to Brandi, silently telling her to stay put. Then Dan darted behind the counter and through the kitchen. As he quietly opened the back door, he glanced up and saw the cook staring at him, but obviously not interested enough to ask a question.

A moment later Dan was in the alley behind the diner. What he'd actually caught a glimpse of was a small girl, now moving toward the gas station half a block away. She was wrapped in a filthy old red coat several sizes too big. It almost touched the ground in front of her as she hobbled on.

Dan moved silently to intersect her.

She didn't look back, but he could see her limping, forcing her body to move. The child was hurt.

He closed the distance between them with each step. At the curb, she stumbled and fell into a mound of snow someone had scraped off the gas station lot.

He heard her whimper in pain as she fought to stand.

Dan moved closer, and she saw him. Before he could help her up, she cried out and jerked away. In an instant Dan saw the terror in her big, dark eyes. She was more afraid of him than she was of the pain. Like a wounded animal, she backed away, scooting through the snow on her bottom. Pushing herself over frozen rocks.

He didn't know what to do. He wanted, needed to help her, but if he grabbed her she looked like she might shatter with fear. Even with her coat on, he could see bruises on her wrists and neck. This had to be the girl Thatcher kept talking about. The one he wanted the sheriff to help, but how?

If he grabbed her arm and she jerked, she might break a bone.

Suddenly, someone brushed past his shoulder and knelt in front of the child.

Brandi.

"Come here, sweetie," she whispered, as only a mother could. "I'm not going to let anyone hurt you."

Dan watched in surprise as the tiny little girl climbed into Brandi's waiting embrace. Her dirty, birdlike arms wrapped around the singer's neck and held on for dear life.

"It's all right, baby. You're safe now," Brandi

whispered as she rocked the child. "No one is going to hurt you. I won't let them."

He didn't move as she picked the child up and slowly walked toward the front of the diner. Dan followed as Brandi hummed and the little girl held on tightly to her.

"Don't you worry, sweetie. I'm going to take you somewhere warm, and we'll have something to eat." Brandi's voice was as smooth as silk. "If you like, we could ask your mother to join us."

The child shook her head. "I don't know where she is."

Brandi hugged her close. "We'll find her. How about we have pancakes while we wait. I know how to make a smiling face on the pancake."

Dan followed, trying to get a grip on what had just happened. In a low voice, he said, "I'll get the nurse from the clinic and meet you at the B and B."

Brandi looked up at him and nodded. He couldn't miss the tears running down her face as she whispered to the little girl. "You're safe now, baby. No one is going to hurt you. I promise. I'll carry you all the way to my place, and we'll get warm."

As Brandi walked down the still-sleeping street, Dan ran to his car and headed toward the clinic. He drove, hitting the number for the clinic and swearing while he waited for an answer. After several rings, the nurse practitioner picked up. Sheran the clinic only until noon on Saturday, so she always came in early to have everything ready.

When he explained why he needed her, she said she'd be waiting on the porch. When he pulled up a few minutes later, she was taping a note to the door.

An hour later, after the child had been examined, bathed, doctored and fed a few bites, she fell asleep with her head on Brandi's lap and her thin hand wrapped tightly around two of Brandi's fingers.

Dan forced himself to leave them and stepped into the hallway with the nurse. The little girl who'd been so afraid of him had trusted Brandi immediately, and the singer had a way with the child that seemed magic.

As soon as Dan closed the hallway door, the nurse began her report without waiting for him to ask questions. "The child was beaten. I've seen belt marks like that across a child's back before. Only these go down her legs, as well. Some cut so deep they broke skin, and they're now infected. As near as I can tell from the dried blood, the wounds have had no care. They haven't even been washed. Another day or two and we'd have real damage here."

"Did she say anything?"

"Not a word." The hardened nurse was fighting back anger and tears. "She's showing signs of being starved. No one, Sheriff, is looking after this kid. No one who has an ounce of human being left in them." She lifted her cell. "I took pictures. I'm betting you'll need them."

"Have any idea why she was out in the cold?"

The nurse nodded. "We found scraps from the diner trash in her pocket."

"I'll call family services. They'll send someone to get her."

The nurse shook her head. "She won't let go of that lady in there. Let the child rest and heal a little before you make the call. Right now, she's been hurt so badly I'm afraid she's more animal than human. If you pull her away from the one person she trusts, I'm not sure what might happen."

Dan dealt with a load of shit sometimes in his job, but this . . . this made him furious. "I'll give it time. If there is a parent or anyone who cares about her, they'll drop by my office or call 911."

The nurse shook her head. "I'm betting no one will be looking for her."

The words Thatcher had told him one of the kidnappers said echoed in his head. The guy bragged that they took turns beating the kid for letting Thatcher follow her home. The kidnapper Thatcher had called Shorty had sounded disappointed when he'd told Thatcher that she wouldn't even scream by the time it was his turn to beat her.

Crimes were piling up in Dan's county, but right now, this one was his top priority. If he found the man who tried to kidnap Thatcher, he'd also have at least one of the men who'd beaten the child.

He looked back in Brandi's room and saw the woman he thought of as wild. She was tenderly moving her hand over the child's hair as she hummed a gospel tune, and he knew that if he even thought of taking the girl away, he'd be fighting her as well as the kid.

There was far more to Brandi Malone than a wild side, and Dan found himself wanting to get to know her from all sides.

CHAPTER TWENTY-SIX

WHEN THATCHER SAW the sheriff's number, he answered his phone on the first ring.

"We got her," Brigman shouted. "The little girl in the red coat. She's at the B and B. She's safe."

"Thank God." Thatcher pinched his nose to force back tears. "Is she all right? I've been worried. If they could get to me in the jail, no telling what they did to her."

"She will be. They must have beaten her the day they saw you talking to her. She could barely walk when I saw her, but I had the nurse treat her cuts and she's resting now. She's in good hands." Dan let his words sink in before he asked Thatcher, "Did she talk to you? We can't get her to say a word."

"Not much, Sheriff. She told me that she missed her mommy and her dolls. When I asked, she said the man she's with says he's her daddy, but she doesn't think he is. She said her mommy always said she didn't have a daddy."

"Why?" Brigman shot the question.

"That's what I asked. She said it was because when he took her away, her mommy was crying."

"Did she tell you her name?" Dan needed a direction, a clue.

Thatcher shook his head, then remembered he

was on the phone. "Nope. I asked twice, too. Said she wasn't supposed to tell people her name or that she was from Oklahoma. That's all I know, Sheriff."

"You did good, Thatcher. I've got a lead." Dan changed the subject. "How are things where you are?"

"Pretty crazy. I've never seen married people yell so much. They act like they've never had a conversation before. Cody's in a hell of a bad mood, and she don't take no lip."

Dan laughed. "Wait until you're in their place one day, son. The first year of marriage isn't always easy, but it's interesting."

Thatcher snorted, then groaned when he bumped his elbow on the couch's arm. "I think the Civil War was quieter than this place. It might be because they're both rangers and used to being bossy as hell. The last fight was because he wouldn't sit down and rest. Cody's got a leg in a cast, broken ribs and who knows what else, but he hasn't stopped marching around like a handicapped sentry on duty. The fight this morning was over her alphabetizing the canned goods. He yells about her running his life, but from what I see he hasn't been doing much since he was shot up three years ago. And Tess is one of those women who is always busy. Gives me the feeling I'll be swept under the rug with the rest of the dirt if I don't keep moving. When she's not telling Cody what to do, she's doing something to make the man furious."

"True love doesn't always run smooth, Thatcher. My wife and I fought our whole first year of marriage. Only problem was, we never stopped."

"Smooth, hell. If Kristi ever calls me back, I'm going to break up with her. I don't think my ears could take this kind of true love. Sheriff, I don't want to be ungrateful, but do you think you could come get me? I'd rather take my chances with Slim and Shorty than stay around here."

"I don't hear any yelling now, Thatcher. Are you sure you're not exaggerating?"

"Maybe a little, but not much. They went in the bedroom to fight it out. She said she was going to organize his drawers and he said, 'Over my dead body.' I haven't heard anything for a while, so I'm guessing one of them killed the other one. I'm so bored I've started talking to the bull snake in the box by the door."

Dan laughed. "Hang in there, kid. I'm working on getting you out of there. While I've got you on the line, I want you to think about every detail when you took that little girl home. Describe the trailer she was standing in front of. What color was it? Any markings? Any cars in front? Any sounds you heard? I know you left out details because you thought you were protecting her, but she's safe now. I need to catch these guys and to do that I need the whole story."

"All right. Anything I can do to help. I only got a peek at the men in the trailer. Lowlifes huddled around a table covered with stacks of bills. I wanted to tell you, but they said they'd take it out on the kid if I told anyone." He gulped back a dozen swearwords trying to come out all at once. "Sounds like they did anyway."

Thatcher talked to the sheriff, retracing every moment from the time he offered the tiny girl a ride until he took back the cans. He answered every question. He didn't think he needed to talk about what happened in the truck stop. Luther had gone over that several times, and everything the old guy said was pretty much true. Thatcher had decked him for talking about his family that way. Which was the truth, but only relatives were allowed to talk that way about his kin.

"Thanks, kid," the sheriff said. Both knew how hard it was for a boy from the Breaks to talk to the law. Children who grew up out there were taught from birth to turn a blind eye to questionable behavior, only Thatcher trusted Brigman; he'd always been straight with him.

"Were either of the men who attacked you in the jail at that trailer?" Dan asked.

"I don't know. I only got a glimpse. Five or six men, all dressed in work clothes." He paused, then rushed on. "I almost forgot. There was a dead hanging plant in the window. All brown and twisted. It was the first thing I saw when I looked in. Everything and everyone was seen through the spaces between the deformed leaves."

The sheriff asked several more questions, but Thatcher couldn't think of anything else.

When he hung up, Thatcher called Tim O'Grady. "Hemingway" sounded like he'd been asleep, or hung over. But then, Tim usually sounded that way. The writer struck him as an old drunk in a young man's body.

"What do you need, Thatcher?" he grumbled when he answered. "You're not in any trouble again. If you are, I can't help you. The sheriff won't tell me where you are." Tim talked faster as anger boiled. "Like I'm going to give away state secrets or something. He did say you're all right, so why are you calling?"

Thatcher thought of hanging up, but he was desperate. "No, I'm fine. I'm under protective custody. And believe me, it's no picnic."

"Welcome to life, kid." Tim wasn't a man anyone would go to if they needed a shoulder to cry on. Too many chips on them. "I just broke up with Lauren again. Hell of a week, ain't it, Thatcher."

"I didn't think you two were together." The words were out before he realized that probably wasn't the right thing to say.

"Apparently neither does she. She's calling our great love affair a friendship. I guess it all depends on the wording." Tim coughed and added, "Why are you calling me? I'm sure it's not to ask for advice, because you never take it. Didn't Lauren and I tell you to stay out of trouble, make good grades—"

"I know the lecture by heart," Thatcher interrupted. "Save your words, you might need them for the next book you're supposed to be working on."

Thatcher figured that he'd better ask for his favor fast before Tim remembered how mad he was at him. "This hideout they've got me in is great, but there's no TV and I'm out of books. You know how you're always talking about how everyone should read the top hundred books of all time? Well, I'm ready to get started. Could you pack me up a bag full and deliver them to the sheriff's office? Just put my name on the sack so Pearly won't think they're for her. Brigman will see I get them."

"The greatest books of all time are not all westerns, Thatcher." Tim calmed. Books were his favorite topic, outranked only by talking about *his* novels.

"I'll read whatever you send." He thought about adding to leave out Tim's kind of horror books, but he guessed there were not many on the top hundred list.

"I tell you what," Tim said. "I'll loan you a dozen. Read those, and I'll give you the next dozen."

"Great. Don't forget. Put them in a paper sack, write my name on it and deliver them to the sheriff."

"No problem. I heard you the first time. I've nothing to do. I have no girl. And I'm suffering from writer's block again."

"Tim, if you don't mind me saying, you get one of those blocks so often you might start building a house with them. You'd have a three bedroom in no time."

"Just what I need, another critic. I'm a published author, you know."

"Yeah, I know and so do probably thirty or forty other people." The words were out before Thatcher remembered he'd just asked for a favor. "Just kidding. I think your books are great. The last one scared me so bad I swore off reading for a week."

"Really?" Tim sounded suddenly interested in the conversation. "I'll pack a copy of the first five chapters of my new one in the sack."

"That'd be super. Thanks, Tim." He hung up before O'Grady had time to tell him the entire plot of the new book again.

Tess walked out of the bedroom with a huge box of clothes. She'd switched out of her uniform and was wearing her T-shirt and those yoga pants she looked so good in.

"Where's the ranger?" Thatcher asked, figuring she'd finally killed him.

Tess smiled like she'd solved the formula for world peace.

"Strangest thing." She sat on the other end of the couch like they were friends now.

Thatcher pulled his blanket up and tried to act normal, but he wasn't used to a woman sitting on the end of his bed. "Tell me what's strange about Cody." Thatcher was sure he could add to the list, like the ranger didn't sleep at night and he sometimes stared out the window as if he was seeing something in the shadows.

Personally, he could think of a few others, like the ranger had a death wish and was hell-bent on making everyone around him miserable.

It suddenly occurred to Thatcher that maybe Brigman put him here with these two so prison wouldn't look so bad if he ever had to go.

Tess seemed to be organizing her thoughts the same why she did everything else. "I was working, ignoring him with my back turned. He'd stretched out on the bed and was staring at the ceiling telling me that it wasn't my fault if I haven't got a rounded bottom. He knew a few movie stars that were that way and others were flat chested, but that hadn't stopped them. Then he talked about how it was wrong how men sometimes judge women by their bodies. He claimed those things don't matter."

She patted Thatcher's blanket, and he started sweating. His leg was under the quilt, and she was getting too friendly for a lady ten years older than him.

Thank goodness she jumped up about then and started pacing. His close call was over. He'd always dated Kristi. He'd never been out in the field. He didn't even know where it was. What if he turned out to be irresistible now he wasn't spoken for?

"I was warm from working," she said as she paced, "so I pulled off my uniform and kept working." She pointed at Thatcher. "You said it was all right to wear this. You said I looked good in these."

Thatcher was thinking of retracting his opinion. Now the park ranger thought he was flirting with her. It would hurt his ego, but maybe he'd better tell her he didn't even know how to flirt. He'd only been to second base with Kristi, and to tell the truth it didn't seem all that exciting.

"When I straightened from emptying the bottom drawer, I looked over at him and thought he had a stroke. His mouth was gaping and his eyes were wide open, like he hadn't blinked in hours."

"So what'd you do?"

"I just turned back around and went on working."

Thatcher nodded as if he understood what she was talking about.

"Cody mumbled something about being a

complete idiot. I don't know if he's asleep or passed out. This job might have been too much for him just out of the hospital. I decided to just let him sleep."

Thatcher smiled. He knew what was wrong with Cody, and the ranger was right; he was an idiot, at least when it came to women. Thatcher knew the signs. A guy was walking along with a girl thinking they were friends, then all at once he noticed she was a woman. She was different from him, and from that moment nothing was ever quite the same.

Thatcher would have thought Cody would have noticed it earlier, but maybe he was a slow learner, or maybe he forgot what his bride looked like when he tumbled into the canyon.

"You got any advice, kid?"

"Yeah," Thatcher said. "In two hours, wake him up with a kiss. Not a little kiss but a full out, ride 'em cowboy kiss. He's got Sleeping Beauty Fever. It's rare but happens after a hospital stay. Tim O'Grady told me about it." If this plan backfired, he wanted Tim to share the blame. "You've got to wake up the nerves in the body all over again. Hold him down while you do so he don't hurt himself jumping around on that broken leg."

She looked skeptical.

"What's the worst thing that can happen? He'll yell at you. He's already doing that. You want him to go back to being the nice guy he might have been. You got to do a Sleeping Beauty treatment on him."

Tess gave in. "I'll try, but I want it on the record that I think you're full of bull."

"Yeah." He tried to look innocent. "Just me and the snake over there."

CHAPTER TWENTY-SEVEN

BY MIDAFTERNOON DAN found himself missing the singer. No, correction, he was missing his lover. How strange to have Brandi in his life and to think about her that way. He also realized she thought of him in the same way. It made him feel more alive, like he'd been walking through a world in black and white and suddenly discovered there was color. She'd somehow filled in the gaps between every other thought.

What they'd done, meeting and deciding to sleep together before they spent hours talking, was foreign to him, but it felt right. All of it, from the first surprise kiss before they'd even had lunch to waking up with her in his arms.

He had a job to do. Crimes were popping up like bindweed. Yet her memory drifted in his thoughts like smoke, and he wouldn't push it away. He didn't even try.

He'd searched for the little girl's mother and waited around the office, hoping someone would report that she'd disappeared. Nothing. Whoever the child belonged to was not looking for her or worried about her.

Once, out of boredom, he typed Brandi Malone into his computer. A dozen sites came up about where she'd performed over the past year, and her reviews were unbelievably good. One critic wrote she was a bright, rising star in the songwriting world and on stage. There was even a short article about why someone with her talent would insist on performing in small, out of the way places when she'd easily pack a venue in Nashville.

Dan found nothing personal about her. Brandi was a ghost behind the singer.

Then Dan remembered that she'd mentioned her father named her after the queen of England, and her mother always insisted they have tea at bedtime.

Hesitantly, he typed in Elizabeth Malone. A dozen people with that name came up. One by one he eliminated all but one name. An Elizabeth A. Malone in Wyoming.

Three simple links. One, Elizabeth A. Malone graduated from high school in 1999. She'd been valedictorian, and the article commented that she had not shown up at graduation.

Dan smiled at Brandi's high-school picture. She'd been a smart, wild child. That didn't surprise him.

Second article was an obituary from 2006 about a Jonathon Day Malone who died at sixty-one, leaving his ranch in the hands of his four children. Two sons and two daughters. One named Doris Malone Black, the other Elizabeth Malone.

Dan studied the screen. Brandi had inherited a ranch, and it had to be big if the paper did an article about the Malone spread in the same edition they carried the obit. She'd either never married or had gone back to her maiden name after a divorce. If he were guessing, he'd say never married. Brandi didn't seem the type to want or need a ring.

The third article was also an obit. Short, no long paragraphs. One Evelynn Day Malone, age nine, passed away at St. Jude Children's Hospital after a long fight with leukemia. The only relative listed was Elizabeth A. Malone. No grandparents. No aunts and uncles. No father.

Dan leaned back in his chair and let his logical mind put what wasn't said together. No husband or father in the picture. No family had been with Brandi when her child died; if they had, she would have listed them. And she must have loved her father if she named her child after him.

Brandi, his beautiful, wild Brandi had lost a child a little over a year ago. She wasn't living the wild life, running free—she was simply running.

He closed his eyes and remembered how she'd looked holding the little girl he'd found. This woman who always smiled when she saw him, who sang like an angel, who was his definition of sexy, was far more complicated than he'd thought.

Maybe it wasn't him, but her who needed this no-holds-barred, crazy encounter they were trying to have. She hadn't mentioned anything about her life back in Wyoming, and Dan could come to only one conclusion. She didn't want him to know.

He could pretend he knew nothing about her if that's how she wanted it, but the woman who'd said she'd be moving on soon was slowly seeping into his soul.

Thirty minutes later, he walked into the kitchen of the Franklin B and B and found Brandi sitting alone by the window with a pot of tea in front of her. The winter scene outside framed her like a fine painting. Her hands were wrapped about a cup, but she wasn't drinking. She was silently crying.

He forgot about the *only in private* rule and almost knocked a dining chair over to get to her. Gently, he pulled her to her feet and wrapped his arms around her. She came to him easy like a trusted friend or a longtime lover.

For a while, they just held on to each other. She felt so right with her head resting on his shoulder and her arms wrapped about his neck so tightly he could almost believe she didn't ever want to let go.

"You all right, pretty lady?" He kissed her cheek.

"I'd like to file a crime in progress report,

Officer," she whispered. "I'm planning to murder whoever hurt that child upstairs. I'm going to kill them slowly, then follow them into hell and kill them again."

He pushed her dark curls away from her face. "I know how you feel. I've been out all day collecting information. I'll find them. They are not locals, or Thatcher would have seen them around. I'm guessing they are working one of the construction sites, if they are working at all." He kissed her forehead and breathed her in as if she were the air he needed to survive.

"How is our little fighter upstairs?" he whispered in her ear, wishing he had other words to say.

"The nurse came by about one. We tried to get her to eat, but she'd only take a small bite. She's sleeping now. I think the medicine on her wounds has eased her pain enough to make sleep possible. Both the sisters are sitting with her. Rose was singing to her when I came down for tea. I think the child understands when I'm talking to her, but she hasn't said a word."

He held her loosely in the circle of his arms when she backed away. "What's wrong?"

Shaking her head, she tried to get closer. "Hugging you with your uniform on is like cuddling with a porcupine."

"Sorry, I'll take it off next time we're alone, I promise. Where's all the other guests staying here?" he whispered as he finally took the time to look around. He hadn't planned to touch her at all on this visit, but now he had, he couldn't seem to let go.

"They're all gone. The groom left early. He got a call from his bride. She said she's changed her mind about the marriage, but can she keep the ring. The couple studying the canyon said they'd come back in spring. Now the roads are clear, the others decided to move on. The sisters tell me there will be more guests coming the day after Thanksgiving, but it should be quiet for a while."

He didn't say what he was thinking. He knew she could read his mind by now. For one night they'd made love, and he'd held her in his sleep. One night, yet he felt changed inside.

She smiled up at him and took his hand. Without a word, they walked silently to a door at the back of the kitchen.

"The sisters showed me this room they keep for a professor who visits his son in town a few times a year. No one ever uses it but him." She pulled Dan into a shadowy study and didn't bother to turn on the lights.

The walls were lined with bookshelves except for one bay window.

Dan knew the guest at the B and B that she was talking about. Yancy Grey's father. The sisters had both loved him when they were teenagers. Dan wouldn't be surprised if they still did.

He must be very fond of them, too, because he always stayed with them, even though Yancy had plenty of room at his newly remodeled place.

Love stories ran long and deep in this town, but Dan knew he'd never have a lifetime with Brandi. She'd told him from the first that she'd be moving on. He'd said all he wanted was a good time, but he was starting to realize that when she left he'd miss her. Maybe what he really needed was far more than a few wild nights, or even weeks.

She closed the door to the hideaway study. Reaching around him, she turned the silver key left in the lock. "We're alone for a moment, and we're locked in."

He didn't waste time talking. Dan pushed her against a bookshelf and kissed her in a rush.

"Slow down." Her words tickled across his lips before she pulled away. Lifting her cell from her back pocket, she sat it on the shelf. "I told the sisters to text me if our patient wakes. Until then, I'm all yours." She winked. "Do with me what you like."

Dan's kiss turned tender as his hand moved under her sweater and spread out along her bare skin. The wool was soft and her skin warm beneath it.

The kiss grew hot, but he couldn't get close enough to her. Not here where both knew they might be discovered or overheard.

Finally, he ended the kiss and whispered, "This

is torture, not being able to undress you. I want to feel all of you next to all of me."

"I know. You're reading my mind."

He buried his face in her hair and simply breathed. A minute later she was fighting to unbutton his shirt.

With effort, he put his hands on her shoulders and pushed her gently away. "We can't do this. I'm afraid I'll go too far and when the text comes in, you'll be running up the stairs half-naked."

She laughed. "But I don't want to leave until we have to. I want to be alone with you for whatever time we can steal. I need to be near you. One time sleeping with you will never be enough."

He led her to a tiny bay window with a bench barely big enough for two. Dusty lace curtains let in the light but hid them from view. "How about we talk?"

He sat and pulled her beside him with her long legs draping over his knees. They were close; that would have to be enough for now.

"Tell me about what you were like as a kid," he said as he held her in his arms. Enough for now, he told himself.

She laughed. "This sounds like a first date. Don't you think we're a little late for that?"

"If we're going to steal a few minutes, let's make it a happy time." He moved his hand along her leg. "Talk to me, Brandi, about anything."

"All right. I was raised on a small ranch in

Wyoming. You can't get any happier than that. My father was good man, but distant. After my mother died when I was fourteen, he became very strict. My brothers were already grown, but my sister and I rebelled. I ran away with a band, and she married young."

"That's not a happy memory, Brandi. Try again."

"I'll try." She looked like she was concentrating so hard it made him laugh, and he kissed her on the nose.

She brightened. "I used to have a pig named Pepper."

"Pepper?"

She nodded. "My brother said every time he saw the pig he wanted to say *pass the salt and pepper.*"

Dan laughed. "What happened to Pepper?"

"I don't know. I was five at the time. My dad said he ran off and got married, but my brother claimed he went to freezer camp. That fall I got my first horse and forgot all about the pig."

"So you were a cowgirl?"

"Not really. As my dad bought more and more land, it became a business, and our home became a headquarters with a dozen houses around it. My sister and her husband still live on the place. He's the ranch foreman now." She looked at him with her winter green eyes and whispered, "I don't want to talk anymore, Dan."

She shifted and sat facing him, her long legs folded on either side of him.

"What are you doing, Brandi?"

"I'm going to drive you wild with my clothes on."

And she did.

CHAPTER TWENTY-EIGHT

TESS HAD NO faith in Thatcher's diagnosis of Cody having Sleeping Beauty Fever. But she wasn't sure. That was the problem with homeschooled kids who went away to college and lived alone: their bullshit radar was broken.

She couldn't tell when she was being conned, even by a beat-up teenager. She didn't understand men either, and at twenty-seven years old she should definitely understand men. It was like she was raised on Mars and at mating age been tossed back to Earth.

Once in college a guy told her on the third date that he loved her. She liked him, too, and thought it was all right to talk about getting married. He ran off so fast he left his car parked in front of the dorm for three days.

The other park rangers were all in their forties or fifties and treated her like a little sister.

She hated that, too. She knew her job. She was an equal, not someone who needed to be given the easy jobs, the boring jobs. If the other park rangers found out she was protecting a fugitive, they'd probably storm the ranch to save her.

Tess walked into the bedroom and stared down at Cody Winslow. Thatcher was right about one thing: what did she have to lose? If Thatcher's diagnosis and treatment were stupid, Cody would just yell at her. He'd been doing that already. Plus, it wasn't that big a deal; she'd already kissed him a few times.

She moved to the side of him that wasn't bandaged and carefully slid in next to him. Nothing new, right? They'd shared a pillow before.

For a moment, she simply studied him in the afternoon light streaming through the dirty window.

Begin new list. Clean windows.

Tess mentally slapped herself. *Get back to the problem at hand. Curing Cody.*

He had a week's growth or more of whiskers, and his sandy hair needed a cut, but in a rugged way he was handsome. There was a tiny scar at the corner of his lip that almost made him look like he was smiling.

Her fingers gently brushed his hair off his forehead. That night when she'd found him in the canyon, she'd thought his hair was mud brown. When she'd checked his ribs, he'd asked her if he could touch *her* sometime, just to check for broken ribs, of course. She'd said yes, knowing it was a joke.

Even when they were yelling at each other, Cody was never cruel; in fact, she'd caught him smiling at her when she shot back. Maybe she could try to convince Thatcher that she and Cody were simply talking to each other at full volume.

She looked down, seeing the man this time and not the wounded Texas Ranger. He was lean, broad shouldered. When his eyes were closed, she didn't see the anger, the pain he carried. Sleeping, he looked younger.

Without thinking about it, she moved above him and lightly rested the upper half of her body on his.

Then she kissed him. Soft at first, until he jerked a bit. Then she deepened the kiss and he responded.

Deeper. *Wake him up,* she thought. *Fully and completely awake.*

She felt his arm slide around her waist as he began to taste her. His chest rose and fell, moving against her breast as if adding pleasure to an already delicious kiss.

Then, he took control and began teaching her exactly how he liked to kiss. She was lost in the excitement of it all. The feel of him, the smell of his skin, the pounding of his heart. Thatcher had been wrong. She was the one who'd been asleep, and Cody was waking every cell in her body.

His hand spread out along her back and across her bottom. He broke the kiss long enough to whisper in her ear. "I was wrong, Tess, you are perfectly built." He patted her hip. "You feel so good close to me." He kissed his way back to her mouth. "I could get used to you, honey."

She knew she was blushing, but she didn't want to stop. "Me, too," was all she all she had time to say before his mouth covered hers.

When he finally broke for air, his fingertips brushed over her cheek. "My whiskers are hurting you. I didn't mean to do that. I'll shave next time. Hell, Tess, I'll shave twice a day if you'll keep coming this close."

Just before he kissed her again, he whispered, "We should have done this before, honey."

She put her hands on either side of his head and pushed herself up. The T-shirt was stretched to its limit. "Are you okay? You know how to whisper? I never would have guessed."

She felt his laughter. "You were just too far away before. If you'll stay this close, I'll never yell again. Kiss me, Tess. I could get used to waking up like this."

She did, a quick kiss, then she slipped away, feeling a little unsteady. She'd expected a change, but she wasn't sure she could handle this man any better than she handled the one yelling before.

"I wanted to tell you it's time for your shift to watch Thatcher. I have to take a shower." She needed to get some amount of control back. This was a stakeout and a make-out session. If she kissed him much longer, she'd not only forget about Thatcher, she'd forget her own name.

He didn't say a word when she marched to the bathroom, but she could feel his eyes on her.

When she closed the bathroom door, she leaned against it and breathed deeply for a few moments. How could a man who seemed so hard and unyielding make her heart pound? If she'd met him before he'd been shot, would she have liked him, or loved him? Would he have even noticed her? Probably not, she reasoned. She had the world's record for being invisible to the opposite sex.

Or she did. Not any longer. At full volume or whispering, Cody definitely noticed her.

The kiss cure definitely worked, but could she deal with this new Cody? One way or the other she'd have to figure it out for herself. She was not going to ask Thatcher.

She didn't believe the one man for one woman theory about people looking for the right person. She'd always thought she'd find some man who was compatible, they'd have the same goals, maybe worked together, and she'd marry him and settle down.

Tess had a feeling there would be no settling down with Cody, but she knew she would never settle for less than the man one door away. She'd had a taste of what passion was between two people, and Tess added that to her list of must-haves.

When she finally came out twenty minutes later, Cody and Thatcher were playing poker with beans. Neither looked up at her.

"I hope it's all right if I borrow one of your shirts. I only brought two uniforms in the few minutes the sheriff let me have to pack." Her hair hung wet past her shoulders, and his shirt hung like a short dress. She'd packed in such a hurry she had no hair dryer. She did have her flannel pajamas, but it seemed wrong to put them on before dinner. So, she was back in the yoga pants until she had time to wash both uniforms.

Moving close to the fireplace, she began combing out her massive tangles. One luxury she always allowed herself was conditioner, and she'd forgotten that, too. She knew she wasn't properly dressed, but no one was around, and Cody seemed to be ignoring her. Which was exactly what she was trying to do.

If she looked up and met his gaze, she'd start thinking about what had happened in the bedroom.

At least he'd stopped yelling at her. Now and then he said something to Thatcher that had obviously been meant for her to hear.

Tess grinned. Maybe he was as afraid to look at her as she was to look at him. Maybe he thought she'd be able to read his mind.

Pulling her hair back in a ponytail, she decided to start supper. They hadn't really discussed who did what duties, but she guessed since Cody operated on crutches she'd be in charge of meals.

Which was fine. After all, her mother was a

cookbook expert. Cody's freezer was full of steaks, ground meat and ice cream. She thought a meat loaf and baked potatoes sounded good. An hour later, she'd made cornbread and a salad and delivered their plates.

Thatcher bragged on the meal and had his plate half empty by the time she sat down. Cody looked at her as if he'd never seen her before. Finally, after the silence stretched too long, he said, "You're a good cook."

"Thanks." She sat cross-legged in the chair by the fire. "You want the first shift or the last tonight?"

For a moment he seemed confused, almost as if he'd forgotten why they were both here.

"I'll take the first. I feel like I slept all afternoon."

It was odd having him no longer yelling. She was beginning to think something was wrong with him. Maybe too many meds, or maybe she woke him up too fast or too much.

Standing, she said, "I'll do the dishes and get both your medicine."

"None for me," Cody said.

"Me neither," Thatcher echoed.

Tess ignored the kid. Thatcher's wounds had scabbed over. "Cody, the hospital sent you home with four bottles."

"I'm off meds. I had thought to have a little whiskey if I needed medicating, but since we're on the job, I think I'll just handle the pain. It's not that bad. I've already been distracted once today and forgot all about it for a while."

She didn't want him to remind her that she'd been the distraction. "Fine. I'll relieve you at 2 a.m."

Instead of continuing their conversation, she decided to step outside for a moment. While she was growing up, her family always watched the sunset outdoors if it was above freezing. For her parents, it was like a show put on just for them every night.

Tugging on Cody's boots, she walked out on the porch. The sun had been out all day; it couldn't still be that cold.

The scene before her was beautiful and so calm. Miles of flatland covered in snow. She could hear the call of an owl far off to the north. The sun made the snow sparkle like a field of diamonds. People thought the country was quiet, but it was not. It was full of sounds; they just blended in with the night like a soft melody playing and shifting through the shadows.

Hugging herself to stay warm, she smiled. Whenever she got out alone, away from towns and people and cars, she always felt she was going home. Her base wasn't a house, but nature. She'd been raised in the open, and her heart always settled when she returned.

This place. This little run-down ranch felt

welcoming. Not because of the house, but because of the stillness. The pure air. The sounds of the earth. Her parents had loved always waking up to new horizons, but Tess had longed to belong. Maybe someday, if she saved and waited, she'd find just the right porch to watch the sunsets for the rest of her life.

She wondered why it couldn't be as peaceful inside houses as it was outside. Maybe it was in some homes, but not here. Cody had come home angry this morning. He must have been hurting, but it was more than that. He'd accepted the assignment, so Thatcher wasn't the problem. It was as if he wanted her gone or thought she wouldn't be any help at all. All his anger had been directed at her. Until now. Now he was ignoring her.

First he'd said he didn't like the kitchen. Apparently his mother left the paint there, hoping he'd fix up the place. Then he claimed he couldn't find anything because she'd moved it all. He even complained about the soup she'd made, saying it didn't have enough salt.

The only time he hadn't yelled at her was when she kissed him to wake him up, and since then he didn't talk to her. Men were strange creatures. They never seemed to let logic interfere with their actions. Maybe avoiding men would be wise. She didn't seem to have the knack of handling them.

Cody bumped his way out the door. She didn't bother to turn. "It's too cold out here for you." He almost spit the words.

"I'm fine."

Tess squeezed her eyes closed. This wasn't working out like she planned. Nothing ever did. Her mother was right; she tried too hard, cared too much, did too much before people even asked for her help. She could see herself as a little old lady, running fund-raisers and charity garage sales for every cause, then going home alone every night to her dozen cats.

She could hear the tapping of Cody's crutches moving up behind her, but she didn't want to start another argument. He was handsome, a hero for what he'd done, but he was a hard man to understand. The wounded Texas Ranger didn't want her in his house. Couldn't he see how much help she was? Did he really think, beat-up and on one good leg, that he could take care of the kid?

She gripped the icy railing on the porch, welcoming the freezing pain. *Just get through this,* she almost said aloud, then get out and get on with her life. The kisses they'd shared hadn't meant anything.

She needed to just do her job and then leave. Eventually she'd forget the way he yelled at her, the way he'd kissed her with such passion, the way her emotions rolled through her body when he was near. He was just a man, an almost friend, a coworker, nothing more. This time she wouldn't make more of things.

Cody reminded her of something her father said once. He'd claimed that some men were born out of their time. Cody would have survived 150 years ago in the Wild West just fine. It was civilization he seemed to have a problem with.

It was strange, she thought, that it was that kind of man who got to her. Not the polished ones, but one who seemed as out of place with the opposite sex as she was.

But he was not the man she thought he was that night she'd helped him. Or even the man she'd seen in the hospital. The one who'd called her honey and asked for a kiss. Or the man who'd kissed her with such passion when she woke him. That man had vanished like the others and been replaced by a stubborn, brooding, bullheaded—

He interrupted her silent rant with a light touch on her shoulder.

For a few minutes neither moved. It was like one soft touch was all he could allow himself, and one touch was all she'd accept.

They simply stood watching as the sun touched the frozen earth and began to spread out the day's last light over the snow on the horizon.

He cleared his throat. "I didn't mean to make you mad when I came home and found things changed. I could blame it on the pain or the fact that the sheriff shouldn't have put you out here in danger, but it's more than that." His words were measured, planned. "I can't decide if I'm just too ornery to live around people or I've stayed alone so long I've become that way, but having you around has made me think about a few things."

"I meant to help." She wondered if Cody was considering the danger of being on guard or the danger of having to put up with him. "I'm sorry I get in your way. It was not my intent."

His hand gripped her shoulder and turned her to face him.

For a moment, he stared at her as if he wasn't sure who she was. "Don't apologize, Tess. Don't ever apologize to me. None of this was your fault."

She felt her anger at this hard man melt away. He must be hurting and cold, but he'd stepped outside to be with her. To set things right between them. "No, you're right," she said. "I should have asked before I painted your kitchen, but the cabinets did need organizing. I don't see how you could ever find anything in there. You had two cans of motor oil next to the beans." Suddenly she was rattling and didn't know how to stop. "I get nervous sometimes and have to keep busy. I didn't mean to make you mad."

"I know that," he admitted. "Before you found me that night, it had been weeks since I'd talked to anyone." One crutch tumbled to the porch when he brushed her shoulder as if he worried that he'd gripped too hard. "Can we start over?"

"From where? From when you fell and were hurt? From the hospital? From . . ."

He lowered his lips to almost touching hers. "From right here."

His kiss was tender, hesitant and familiar.

Tess closed her eyes and accepted his apology.

When he pulled away, he stared at her as if seeing her, really seeing her for the first time. "I'm not used to being around people, honey. If you'll give me some time, I swear I'll make an effort to get back to being human. Only you have to let me this close to you because I have a feeling you're all the medicine I'm going to need."

She grinned, knowing he was trying. "When this assignment is over, no matter how much you yell at me or don't want me around, I'm holding you to your promise for a date."

He looked surprised. "I thought I'd blown any chance of that, but if you're still willing, I'd like to take you out. Only no uniforms."

She thought of telling him that her other clothes weren't much different. It crossed her mind that she could change, reinvent herself for a date, but that wasn't her style.

Picking up his crutch, she held it out. "You need to get inside and off that leg."

Mothering again, she thought as she bit the tip of her tongue.

He growled, but it didn't frighten her as much as it had before.

"You running my life again, Tess?" His words held no anger.

"Of course. Someone has to, Cody." She smiled at him, hoping to take the edge off her comment.

He leaned on her as they moved to the door, his hand a caress along her side. "I'm counting the hours till we get rid of this kid." The tips of his fingers brushed the side of her breast, letting her know his thoughts.

He'd leaned to kiss her again, when they heard Thatcher yell, "I heard that, Ranger, and the feeling is mutual. If I didn't have two idiots trying to kill me, I'd be out of this place like lightning over grease."

Tess held the door for Cody as she fought down a giggle.

"Maybe we should think about having a dozen or so kids so you can get over this need you have to collect the wounded," he whispered as he passed.

"We'll discuss it when you're out of the cast."

"We'll discuss what?" Thatcher yelled.

They both answered, "Nothing."

Cody didn't argue when she pointed to the chair across from Thatcher.

She thought her ranger looked a bit pale, but she didn't comment. If she was going to date a bear, she needed to limit the number of times she poked him.

Long after dark, when she fussed over Cody's covers on his half bed beside the door and asked Thatcher a dozen times if he needed anything, Cody told her to go to bed.

"I'll wake you for the next shift." His voice was gruff, an order, nothing more, but his eyes watched her every move.

She vanished into the bedroom. A few minutes later, in her flannel pajamas, she crawled into Cody's bed and wished he was sleeping with her. They'd only kissed twice on the porch. A few fiery kisses, that was all. This time she wouldn't make the mistake of thinking it meant more. He'd been joking from the first that they should get married. It didn't mean anything.

For a moment this afternoon he'd stood in the cold, looking like he had something more he wanted to say, but the words wouldn't come.

She fought the urge to help him, suggest topics, rattle on about nothing until he got his thoughts in order. But she hadn't. She was in uncharted territory with this man, and she had a feeling he felt the same way with her.

Cody was different than any of the men who'd asked her out or looked at her with need in their eyes.

He was different because she wanted him.

CHAPTER TWENTY-NINE

LAUREN WALKED INTO the diner a little after dawn and saw Lucas sitting at a table alone.

Strange how things worked out. They'd ended what was between them, and it somehow freed her to believe they might be just friends for a change.

Lauren smiled at the cracks in the old linoleum as she crossed the diner. She didn't miss the bald spots on the counter where some waitress had wiped the color off. At twenty-five, her life was starting to be that way. No longer perfect, but still workable. There were places on her heart that were worn, scrubbed raw by tears.

A grin suddenly spread across her face. Better worn than unused. Hope was always around the corner.

On a whim, Lauren had invited her roommate from college to spend Thanksgiving with her. Polly had texted that she wasn't flying home, and the drive from Amarillo would take her only a few hours.

Thanksgiving at the Brigman lake house was sometimes no more than takeout and football, but Polly would enjoy it.

Plus, Tim had always been drawn to Polly more like a moth to fire than a bee to honey. No matter how many times he saw her, he never seemed to mind getting burned. Polly had broken his heart half a dozen times. Lauren didn't want Polly to go that far again, but she wouldn't mind if Tim's old lover took his mind off their "breakup."

Tim deserved someone who could love him completely, and she'd made up her mind she'd rather be alone than in an almost-enough relationship. Polly would flirt with Tim, so he'd get over Lauren faster. Knowing Polly, Tim and she would probably end up in bed together, and Polly would be so much better than Lauren ever was. Tim would count himself lucky.

When she walked up, Lucas stood. "Okay if I sit down?"

He nodded but didn't meet her eyes.

Several people in the café watched. Lauren fought the urge to announce, "Just having coffee, nothing else."

Lucas waited for her to slide into the booth, then moved to the other side.

She didn't miss the confusion in his lawyer eyes, as if he was silently saying, *we've talked out this and the case is closed.*

Dressed in the worn clothes of a working cowboy, he didn't look much like the lawyer she'd seen less than a week ago. Being this close to him was a walk down memory lane. They were in high school again, and she thought he was perfect.

Only today, memory lane was only a short sidewalk.

She didn't start the conversation. She was too busy wondering what she would say to the eighteen-year-old Lucas if she could go back in time. Maybe everyone wondered that when the time and the love had passed. Would they go back and say one thing that would alter history?

Lauren climbed out of her melancholy thoughts.

"Do you have any news from Thatcher? I talked to Pop this morning, and he says the Little Red Riding Hood is doing better, but she still doesn't say a word."

"That's some good news," Lucas said, as if he thought he was expected to answer.

Lauren just waited.

He folded his hands atop the table and finally said, "I called Thatcher this morning. He claims he's well. Said none of his cuts are dripping, so he might as well stop complaining. He wants to go home."

"Pop's not going to let that happen until he finds the two guys who attacked him."

Lucas shook his head. "It doesn't make sense. How hard could a one-eared druggie be to find in a town this size?"

A noise at the front distracted both of them. Tim had banged his way inside and managed to knock over the coatrack.

Lucas moved to help, but Lauren motioned

him back. "No," she whispered. "He hates it when people help him or even look like they notice he limps."

Lucas shook his head. "He's not limping, Lauren, he's drunk."

She watched with everyone else as Tim straightened and carefully walked toward the back booth without the usual limp he had when he thought no one was looking. Lucas was right; he had been drinking. The goofy smile on his face always gave him away.

"Why does he drink?" Lucas whispered. "Trying to get over you, maybe?"

Lauren shrugged. "He started in college and just never stopped. I don't think it's me. He hasn't seemed to need a reason for years."

Lucas stood. He walked straight to Tim and put his arm around his friend's shoulders. "Join us for coffee."

Tim looked surprised to see him and went along, even though the last time they'd talked hadn't been friendly.

Lucas shoved him into the booth across from Lauren and pulled up a chair at the end of the table. "We need your help, Tim," he said, as he held up two fingers to the waitress.

Tim straightened, obviously believing no one in the room knew he was drunk. "I'm at your service. I'm considering switching to writing crime novels. My hometown appears to be a hot spot of activity, and I might as well use my skills to help."

Sissie clunked down two coffees in front of Tim and looked at the other two people at the table. "Can I get you anything?"

"Two more coffees," Lucas said. "And a round of apple turnovers if Dorothy still makes them."

"She does." Sissie pointed with her thumb. "How about I bring the whole pot of coffee over here? I got better things to do than walk the length of this place." She winked as if she thought she was funny. "If you want better service, you might think of parking closer to the counter."

"Noted." Lucas frowned at her.

The waitress darted off so quickly Lauren thought she vanished.

Lucas grumbled, but Tim didn't seem to get what they were talking about. He simply stared at Lauren with a kind of sick-puppy-dog look.

"We still broken up, L?" His voice was steady, but his eyes looked like fog had settled in them for the winter.

"Yes." She smiled at her best friend.

Tim grinned back. "That's nice. Do tell the next guy you're frigid, would you, L?"

"Of course, but it's winter. Maybe the next guy won't notice."

Tim downed half the cup of steaming coffee. The fog seemed to clear a little, but reality obviously still drifted only at the edges of his mind.

"Polly is coming in to spend the weekend with us. Be nice to her, will you, Tim?"

He shrugged. "I'm always nice to her." The coffee was sobering him a bit. "No," he said with only a slight flavoring of bitterness in his voice. "Maybe I won't be nice this time. Being nice doesn't seem to be getting me anywhere in life."

Lauren couldn't speak. Tim had never been so cold, so honest before, and it hurt her to know that she'd hurt him.

Lucas interrupted. "Now that's settled between the two of you, we need to help out the sheriff whether he wants it or not before this mess with Thatcher drags on into Thanksgiving. One man cannot worry about a little girl, guard Thatcher and solve a crime at the same time."

"I agree. As a crime writer, I know a few things. We need to expedite the conclusion."

Lauren remained silent. Pop was not going to like them interfering, but if she didn't go along with Tim and Lucas, there was no telling what mess they might step into.

CHAPTER THIRTY

"YOU AWAKE, RANGER?" Thatcher whispered. "Something's wrong outside. It's too quiet."

"I'm awake and I agree. I heard a car turn off the road about five minutes ago." Cody's voice was stone-cold alert.

Thatcher had no doubt Cody already had his rifle pointed at the door.

"I thought I heard it, too. From the sounds, they circled around and parked behind the corrals. I'm guessing they're coming ins on foot through the barn." Thatcher had grown up listening to the sounds of the night. "You think we're about to be attacked, Ranger?" He couldn't keep the excitement from his voice.

"I know we are. Slip on my boots and grab my coat." Cody moved from his bed to the far wall, where he could see every window. The slight tapping of one crutch was the only sound.

Thatcher did exactly as he was told. The coat was way too big, but the boots almost fit him.

"I need you to follow orders." The ranger wasn't asking, he was telling. "Stay low. I want you to crawl to the bedroom. There's a .22 behind the door, and it's loaded. It won't be much help in a fight, but it will sound an alarm if you're in trouble. Can you do all that?"

"I can." Thatcher's nerves were popcorning out of his skin. He was about to be involved in a shoot-out. Holy cow!

Cody's voice was low and steady. "Next, wake Tess. Say exactly this or she won't go. Tell her to get you out the bathroom window on the far side of the house, and the two of you run for my pickup parked in the back shed. You got that?"

Thatcher thought of arguing, but the ranger didn't sound like he wanted a discussion.

As Thatcher moved, Cody kept up his low orders. "When you hear the first shot, start the truck and press full throttle when you put it in Drive. You'll fly out the back of the shed and be halfway to the road before they'll have time to glance in your direction."

"I can stay and help fight," Thatcher whispered back. "I'm one hell of a shot, Ranger."

"No. You're who they are after. I can't run with this leg, so I'll keep them busy here. You get your ass and Tess out of range as fast as possible, then call the sheriff. He'll find a way to get to me."

"Tess isn't going to like leaving you," Thatcher whispered as he began to crawl across the floor toward the bedroom door.

"Tell her it's standard procedure. One stands guard. One protects the witness."

"I could double back?" Thatcher was at the closed bedroom door. "Once I get her to safety, of course."

333

"Not necessary," Cody said so calmly Thatcher believed him.

Thatcher disappeared into the bedroom. The rifle was exactly where Cody said it would be. The weapon felt good in his hand. He couldn't see himself firing it in a gunfight, but a few shots might send anyone within hearing distance running.

With a quick shake of her arm, he woke Tess and told her what was happening. "It may be nothing outside but a stray coyote," Thatcher lied. "The ranger just wants us to take precautions. If a shot is fired, we'll be out and safe before a round is fired in answer."

Tess nodded and slipped on her boots as she grabbed her cell. She didn't look too official in her flannel pajamas with elk footprints in the designs, but at least she'd be able to move fast. Without a coat, she slipped out the bathroom window and followed him across the silent night.

"It's probably nothing," he whispered.

"I know," she said.

Both kept low, folded at the waist. They moved with their feet making a swishing noise as they brushed across the earth, one that sounded more like tall grass in the wind than footsteps. They ran even with each other so their shadows blended.

Fifty feet from the back of the house was a two-car garage, built tall to handle large pickups. Of course, it wasn't locked. They slipped through the small door, which faced away from the main house, and climbed into a huge Dodge made for rough roads. Thatcher took the wheel and passed her the rifle.

He was so excited he felt like he might just jump out of his own skin and take off running with only muscles and bones. Tess, on the other hand, was calm. She checked the rifle to make sure it was loaded.

All was silent inside the garage. It was dark except for the sliver of moonlight shining from the slightly open door. The truck faced away from the house, and the garage door was still down. They could see nothing. Hear nothing.

The men coming after Thatcher could be sneaking up to the house right now. There might be more than two this time. There might be five or six or even more.

"We need to go back and help the ranger," he whispered.

"No," Tess answered. "These were his orders. My job is to protect you, and the best way to do that is to get you away safely." She sounded like she was quoting from a rule book, not doing what she wanted to do. "If you hear a shot, your orders are to turn on the truck and go right through the back of this garage. We've no time to back up. That might give someone time to fire at us."

"Yes, ma'am," Thatcher answered, wondering when he'd joined the service. But, in the past, any time he thought he was in danger, his plan was always to run. So this plan went along with his own. Now he might be doing it in a truck that looked like it was powerful enough to cross the Alps. Not that he'd ever seen the Alps. Hell, at the rate his life was going, he might not even see daylight.

She was silent for a moment, then answered, "It's Miss. I'm not married."

Thatcher tried to make out her face in the darkness. Was she confessing something or just trying to distract him from mentally writing his will? "The sheriff told me you were. You're married to the ranger."

"No, it's just a joke Cody started the night I found him in the canyon. I heard he even told the nurse I was his wife. I guess he just wanted kin around."

Thatcher thought about it in the silence. "No, ma'am. I've seen the way he looks at you. I've heard the way you two fight. You're married."

She didn't say anything, so he added, "If we all die in this fight tonight, I'm telling someone with my last breath to bury you two side by side because you two are the most married couple I ever met."

"Suit yourself." She sounded as if she was about to laugh.

Thatcher grinned. Funny how unimportant the truth was when you thought you might have minutes to live. He didn't think about Kristi or anyone else; they'd all be all right with or without him. But his mother did cross his mind.

If she could see him now with her eyes that matched his, maybe she'd send a little luck in his direction. She used to sing to him, and he kind of had a memory of her holding him in her arms and dancing around the cabin with him.

The rapid pop of gunfire cracked the silence.

Thatcher clicked the engine on, pushed the accelerator to the floor and raced right through the back wall. Board and paint cans flew in the night sky in every direction as he shot across the open land toward the main road.

Thatcher yelled like a bronc rider in full flight.

Tess raised the rifle as if she knew what she was doing and leaned out the window.

Halfway to the road, the rubble from the collapsing garage silenced and they heard the pop-pop of gunfire, but no one followed them. The fight was still on at the house, and the ranger was returning fire.

Tess lowered the rifle to the floor and pulled her cell out of her pocket.

They were bouncing around in the cab of the truck, but she managed to get the sheriff.

To Thatcher's surprise, she gave the facts in bullet points. When she ended the call, she told him to pull over next to one of the highway construction sites and turn off the lights. The huge road equipment would hide the pickup.

Thatcher did as ordered. The big truck tires ate up the gravel at the site. When they were fully hidden behind the machines, Thatcher cut the engine.

The sudden silence weighed on them both. They were too far to hear the shots. Not close enough to see the lights of town.

"I have to get you somewhere safe as soon as the sheriff passes," she whispered. "Then I have to go back and check on Cody."

"Don't worry about me." He could cross the field and be back in town in twenty minutes, maybe less. Thatcher knew every part of this land. He'd grown up here, hunted snakes for thirty miles around. He could vanish easily. Right now, he wasn't worried about himself; he was worried about a little five-year-old girl.

A car raced toward them.

Thatcher blinked his lights once. If the car was coming from town at this time of night, it was the sheriff.

The cruiser barely braked in time to pull up next to them. The sheriff swung out of his car as Tess jumped from the cab of the truck. They were whispering so low Thatcher could hear only parts. More men were coming to help. The highway department was setting up roadblocks in every direction from the Wild Horse Springs. If the men didn't slip away on foot, they'd have them in custody within the hour.

If the men stayed and fought, Cody would hold them at bay until dawn, then the sheriff would move in. Once the bad guys knew they were surrounded, they'd give up.

Thatcher knew he couldn't help Cody. If he tried to slip in at night, the ranger was likely to shoot him by mistake. But if one of the men did manage to get away, only one person besides himself was in danger.

He couldn't take a chance of her being hurt. Not when it was all his fault. If he hadn't followed her home, got her in trouble, she wouldn't have been beaten.

He slowly picked up the rifle on the floor of the truck and slipped it next to his leg. He opened the driver's door of the pickup and melted into the night without Tess or Brigman noticing.

A moment later he was darting across a rocky field scattered with mesquite trees.

He had to get to the little girl first.

CHAPTER THIRTY-ONE

BRIGMAN HAD BEEN ready when the call came into the office. Ready for anything. Within minutes he was headed toward the Wild Horse Springs, knowing he'd find Thatcher and Ranger Adams somewhere en route toward him.

The only thing he hadn't planned was that his daughter and Lucas Reyes would be in the office looking over records when trouble called.

They'd found little, except that a man fitting the description of the kidnapper Thatcher called Shorty had been involved in two previous fights. The first one had been at the Two Step Saloon, where two men had been sent to the hospital with knife wounds, but neither was sober enough to ID their attacker. A month later, at the Nowhere Club out on county road, a short, chubby guy named Yuma was involved in another knifing, and this time the club owner could identify him and was willing to testify.

Yuma Fleming had sworn he'd get even with the club owner. He was probably out on bail awaiting trial by now. As soon as this crisis was over, Dan planned to look into the possibility of Yuma being responsible for the fire at the club.

If he happened to have only one ear, the sheriff

340

might be lucky enough to wrap up an entire crime spree.

But one crisis at a time.

If it was the same short guy, there was a good chance that the man arrested with him might be the other kidnapper. Maybe the skinny guy was even the leader of the gang. Thatcher would ID them both as soon as they found him, then Dan could bring them in. He wouldn't be surprised if Shorty and Slim were involved in several other petty crimes in town.

Tim O'Grady had been in earlier looking up divorce cases all over the area that involved custody over a five- to seven-year-old girl. When he couldn't find any that fit, he also searched missing persons. Three in Oklahoma matched the child's age, and he'd had Dan email for more information.

When Tess's call came in, Lauren called Deputy Weathers and the other county offices. She'd grown up in the sheriff's office. She knew what to do. Dan was proud of her.

Dan left the office with one plan. Get to Cody before he was killed and be sure Thatcher stayed out of danger.

When he got to Tess Adams, he was surprised she was relatively calm, considering her husband was taking fire, but then, she was a professional. They went over the options while Weathers and the sheriff a county over joined them.

"Take Thatcher back to town and let me know when you've got him somewhere safe."

"Will do." Tess stepped back into the pickup. "Only problem is, Thatcher is gone."

Dan did something he rarely did: he swore.

"What do I do, Sheriff?"

"Don't worry about it. The kid will take care of himself." Hell, Dan thought, the kid probably figured out he'd be better off alone. "I'd appreciate it if you'd go back to my office and help my daughter handle calls. If he checks in, tell him to stay safe until I call him."

"I'd like to—"

Dan didn't let her finish. "You're not going back to the ranch. When you took on the assignment, you stepped under my command. That's an order, and that is the way Cody would want it."

Tess nodded. "I'll be at the office. You'll let—"

"I'll let you know as soon as we get there. The truth straight out. You've earned that, Ranger Adams." He figured she deserved to be kept in the loop. She'd done her job. She'd got Thatcher out. "Cody's facing a bunch of druggies and small-time crooks. They're no match for him, even banged up."

"I know." She made an effort to smile. "One ranger, one riot."

"Right." Dan nodded, remembering the story of the time a ranger stepped off a train over a hundred years ago. He'd come to help out a town that was being run over by outlaws. Someone asked why the state only sent a single ranger, and the ranger answered, "You only got one riot."

Dan stood in the darkness and watched her drive away. She was a strong woman, one who would fit as a ranger's mate. When this was all over, he'd remind Cody how lucky he was to have Tess.

As soon as her lights disappeared, they loaded up and headed to the ranch.

Two cars packed with lawmen and weapons drove onto the property, using only the moon for light. Two highway patrol cars stopped at the fence line. A half mile out, Dan and Deputy Weathers cut their engines and moved closer on foot.

The sound of gunfire echoed in the air. Every time a shot was fired, one came in answer. Cody was still alive. He'd be saving ammunition but always answering fire.

In an hour it would be light. The men surrounding him would rush him before that. Once he could see them clearly, they'd lose the advantage.

Dan put it all in order in his mind. What he would do if he were in the house. Keep moving. Keep firing. Wait.

Only Cody was hurt. Moving around couldn't be easy. If the men firing at him were smart, they'd wait until Cody shot from one side of the house and rush the other side.

But these guys didn't seem long on brains, plus they might not know Cody was hurt. Even if they were watching the house, Cody probably hadn't ventured outside.

Dan stopped, knelt behind some sagebrush and pulled out his phone. He texted Tess. Did Cody leave the house?

She answered back. He stepped out on the porch this afternoon.

A sick feeling landed in the pit of the sheriff's gut. The game had just changed. They knew Cody was hurt. They'd rush him before dawn.

Weathers moved up beside Dan. "From the sounds, I'm guessing there are eight, maybe more, men shooting at the house. Only one firing back."

"They're going to rush him." It wasn't a question. Dan knew the answer.

"Correct," Weathers answered. "Before dawn, if there's one man with a brain among them. When they do, the ranger can get two, maybe three, but he'll take fire from all around."

When the sheriff didn't say anything, Weathers whispered, "I got an idea, Sheriff. It's crazy, but it might work."

CHAPTER THIRTY-TWO

CODY ALWAYS THOUGHT he'd crack up if he had to listen to gunfire at night again. The hell he'd lived through that night in the mud of the Rio Grande kept replaying in his head. He'd taken one bullet in the shoulder when the fight had started. He ignored the pain. His partner had been shot in the chest, and suddenly the rangers were being hunted.

In the darkness, Cody had lifted his buddy over his good shoulder and moved through the knee-deep water. He heard shouts and screams, but he kept moving. Two rangers were behind him. Another hundred feet, and they'd make cover.

He heard the shot that hit its mark, then a body splashing in the water. A scream. More fire. Cody blocked it out and kept moving until he finally laid his friend on home soil. He'd leaned close, trying to detect a heartbeat or breathing. Nothing. The man he'd carried for half a mile was dead.

Then another bullet hit Cody. As he fell, another and another jerked him to one side, and then he tumbled. After that the pain washed away all thought but trying to keep breathing. Even when he was kicked, he didn't react. He had to play dead if he had any chance of staying alive.

Drug dealers were moving among the bodies talking, laughing. Men with no country. Men wanted on both sides of the border.

Cody shook himself back to the present. He didn't want to relive that night again. That nightmare already haunted every dream he'd had for three years.

Tonight he was in the house where he grew up. His parents' house. His home. Tonight he was protecting his property, his life. He was doing a job, the job he'd been born to do.

Anger built as he searched the night, hoping to see something, someone move. He could hear the horses in the barn screaming, stomping, trying to break out of their stalls and run.

Hell, he wanted to run, but he couldn't, he wouldn't. The longer he kept up this blind shooting, the more time Tess and Thatcher had to get away.

Part of him reasoned that in the end, if he died tonight, it didn't matter. He hadn't been living anyway. Not for years. Not since that night on the border. First there had been operations and rehab, then rage blocked all else. Anger at his bad luck had settled in, and slowly he'd forgotten how to be alive.

Maybe God figured since he wasn't using his life, he might as well give it up.

But lately something had changed. Tess Adams had taken over running his life as a project, and she'd be mad if those idiots outside shot up her project. Hell, she'd probably repaint the whole house, if there was anything left of it after tonight. Half the windows were already shot out, and he'd heard the garage tumble.

As he waited for the next shot to give him a direction to shoot at, he smiled. She sure did have a nice body. Not little and petite but big, just the right size for a man his size. He could put up with her talking all day if she'd push that rounded bottom up against him at night. And those breasts. They showed off pretty in that thin T-shirt.

She'd probably lecture him if she had any hint of what he was thinking right now, but dreaming of her body kept him wide-awake.

He didn't plan on mentioning how he'd enjoyed the brush of her breasts against him. They'd be a handful he'd enjoy holding. When she'd walked out of the bathroom in his shirt, he'd given up thinking altogether and started daydreaming about taking that shirt back.

Unless she uglied up in old age, he doubted he'd ever be able to form more than a few sentences in front of her.

He couldn't carry on a conversation with her now, not after they'd kissed in the bedroom. He knew if he even tried to talk, he'd say something to make her mad, but that didn't keep him from loving every inch of her.

Speaking of her clothes, he planned to burn her pajamas after they got married. He'd buy her a dozen nightgowns if she wanted them, or she could wear nothing. He wouldn't complain.

As he searched the night, the memory of kissing her on the porch drifted in his mind. Tess came to him so easy. She'd given back just as hot a kiss as he'd given her, and he knew when they finally did get together alone it would be the same way. They'd make love until they were both too exhausted to move.

Then they'd do it again the next night and the next night and the rest of the nights of their lives. Maybe some folks needed years to know they'd found the right one, but for Cody he knew he'd found the only one. And the kick of all was that he knew she felt the same way.

It might have taken a tumble off the canyon wall to meet her, but he wasn't giving her up.

A bullet shattered the glass of the window five feet away.

Cody frowned. All he had to do was stay alive while eight or so men outside were trying to kill him. As he raised his weapon, he decided he'd better marry Tess on their first date because he didn't plan to kiss her good-night on any porch and walk away.

Stay alive. If she needed him half as much as he needed her, he had to live.

No problem. He had too much to look forward to. He didn't have time to die.

With the next shot, he fired in the direction the bullet had come from and heard a yell.

Seven men or so left.

CHAPTER THIRTY-THREE

SHERIFF DAN BRIGMAN stood alone on the west side of the house. He could hear the creek twenty feet away and the night owl in a cottonwood a hundred yards beyond that, but from the direction of the barn and homestead, there was only silence. The firing had stopped. Something must be up. The outlaws might be taking positions, about to attack the ranger inside. Or Cody could have finally frightened them away.

Deputy Weathers and a highway patrolman were on the east side, moving as close to the house as they dared. Two more deputies from the next county were on the north side with their cruisers parked back in the trees, and a highway patrolman had driven his vehicle up on the south side. Six men, all with a weapon in both hands, stood ready.

Six men facing an unknown number.

Dan wanted this night to end without any lives lost, but the chances of that happening didn't look good.

When two shots came close together from the east, all the lawmen circling the house began to fire. Ten shots in the air, rapid-fire from both weapons.

The air seemed to echo violence for a moment, then the silence was deafening.

Deputy Weathers had said the six of them had to be an army. It was like they were facing down a grizzly. They had to make a lot of noise and become a bear to frighten a bear.

Weathers's big, booming voice carried across the prairie. "We got you surrounded! Drop your weapons and come out with your hands in plain sight or when we fire again, we won't be firing toward heaven."

For a few heartbeats even the wind was still. From somewhere near the barn the sound of a rifle hitting the dirt clanked in the silence. Then another and another.

Slowly, men stepped away from the shadows and into the moonlight. Two sets of car lights crossed the grassland. The lawmen, still holding their weapons, moved slowly forward.

Weathers's plan had worked. The attack on Cody's ranch was over.

The only question remaining: was Ranger Cody Winslow alive or dead?

CHAPTER THIRTY-FOUR

TESS TOOK THE call at the sheriff's office. Her voice was steady, but her hands were shaking. For once it didn't matter that she was out of uniform or wore funny pjs. All that mattered was hearing from the sheriff that Cody was all right.

The whole roomful of people in the office were silent as she listened.

"Yes, Sheriff," she said. "Yes, I'll tell them."

Then, she smiled and raised her head. "It's over," she shouted to Lauren and the dozen others in the room. "Cody's safe."

Tears bubbled in her eyes as she said the words. *He's safe.* Her Cody was safe.

Everyone was dancing around and hugging, but Tess stood perfectly still. Her man was out of danger. He'd made it through another gunfight.

"You still there, Tess?" The sheriff's voice sounded from the other end of the call.

"I'm here," she whispered, afraid somehow there was bad news to come.

"Send an ambulance out. Two of the gang who attacked Cody were shot. The highway patrolmen will stay with them until the ambulance gets here. Weathers and I are bringing the rest in."

"What about Cody?"

"He'll have to wait till I get them locked up.

There is no room in the car for a man his size with a cast on one leg."

Tess started walking toward the door. "Tell him I'm on my way to pick him up." She didn't wait for an answer. She dropped the phone in her pocket and took off running.

Ten minutes later they were still loading outlaws in the cars when she pulled up. A few of the tough guys were late on their dose of drugs and were already beginning to whine and shake. The two who had been shot were tied down to makeshift stretchers. From the way they were cussing, neither was in any danger of dying.

Tess parked the truck by the front porch and jumped out. The sun was just starting to light the sky, but it was still more dark than light. She moved between the men, looking for Cody. A tall man with a bandaged shoulder and a cast on his leg shouldn't be hard to spot.

She'd been away from him only a few hours, but she ached to see him. This hard man who cared about her had somehow stomped his way into her heart.

"He's in the barn," Deputy Weathers yelled when he saw Tess. "Sheriff's already told him to sit down and wait for you, but the ranger's not listening."

"I'm not surprised." With Cody she knew exactly what she was getting if she took him on. Hard-headed, quick to fire up, mule-headed and a hero.

Tess ran to the open barn door. It took her a few minutes to find him leaning against a stall gate, one arm over a crutch and the other over the neck of his black horse. His head was down, almost touching the horse's mane.

"You shouldn't be on your feet," Tess snapped.

He looked up at her as if he wasn't sure she was real. "There's three bullet holes in the barn door. I could have shot Midnight or one of the others."

She moved closer, realizing what he must have gone through the past few hours. "But you didn't. She's fine."

He turned, pivoting on his cast, and reached for her.

Tess stepped into his arms. For a while, she just held on to him as tightly as she could. She'd almost lost him. Her one chance at loving someone almost ended before it began. This man who yelled and cussed and acted like he didn't care about anything in the world had just risked his life to save her. He'd stayed behind to fight and made her go. In doing so, he may have not only saved her life, but Thatcher's, as well.

She pulled away enough to see his face. "Don't ever push me away again, Cody. I mean it. I won't stand for it."

She'd expected him to argue, but he smiled. "I don't plan to, honey."

He kissed her cheek, then gripped her chin and

pulled her mouth to his. Tenderly, like he was testing, he tasted her bottom lip, then tugged her mouth open for a full kiss. When she responded, the kiss grew hot and she felt herself melting against him. Somehow the time they'd been apart had stripped away all the conversations and questions that weren't important.

They were together, and they both wanted it that way.

Without breaking the kiss, he tugged at the collar of her pajama top, popping off the first button. His fingers shoved the material away from her neck and shoulder as he kissed a path down her throat. "You taste so good," he whispered. "I'm so hungry for you, honey. Do you mind?"

She laughed. "No, I don't mind at all."

She closed her eyes, loving the way he held her. She might not be a woman men chased after or made fools of themselves over, but she'd found one man who couldn't resist her, and considering he was Cody Winslow, one was enough.

He'd just brushed his hand over her hip when they heard the deputy sheriff calling his name.

Cody bit gently into the flesh of her collarbone. "Marking my place," he whispered, then moved away. "I'm not sure I'll ever get enough of you." He laced his free hand in hers, silently telling her that he didn't plan on going anywhere without her.

Tess followed, but didn't talk. She'd just been hit by a tidal wave. She'd never known passion like this, and all she could think of was that she wanted more.

She smiled, realizing she was this one man's obsession.

Cody never let go of her hand as he talked to Deputy Weathers and agreed to meet him back at the office.

A few minutes later, Tess helped Cody into the passenger seat of his truck. She rushed around to the driver's side.

The minute they were alone, Cody said, "I see you and Thatcher wrecked my new truck." His voice was rough now.

"I did. Do you mind?"

"Not at all. Run the thing off the canyon if you want to, just make sure you're not in it. We might as well get something straight right now, Ranger Adams. I don't care much about anything else on the planet except you. I made up my mind in the middle of the gunfight that that's the way it's going to be. So paint my kitchen, don't salt my soup and organize to your heart's content. Just don't ever leave me."

She drove, eyes on the road, hands gripping the wheel and tears dripping down her face. His words might not be poetry, but she knew they came from his heart.

They rode in silence for a few minutes, then she began to plan. "We'll have to wait for the sheriff to process all the guys through to the jail.

Then, knowing Sheriff Brigman, he'll want you to fill out a report. A step-by-step of when and how everything happened. We may be tied up at the office for several hours."

"Pull over," Cody ordered.

She saw the construction site with all the heavy equipment shining in the morning light. "Oh, this is where the sheriff met me. Are you all right? Are you sick? Maybe I should call back and get the ambulance to stop and take you in to be checked. You could have pulled something." She frowned at him. "I wouldn't put it past you to forget about mentioning to anyone that you're bleeding somewhere."

She stopped the truck and turned to him. "I want you to tell me what's wrong."

His face was red, but he didn't look sick.

"I'm fine, Tess, but I'm not waiting around until we're finished with the sheriff." He moved over, stretching his broken leg out straight. "Turn around and face me." He almost smiled. "What we're about to do won't hurt one bit. I just want to touch you. I've been thinking about it all night while the bullets were flying and the demons were creeping up on me. The thought of you kept me on alert and sane, and now there is something I'm going to do before I live another minute."

She shifted out from behind the wheel and turned around, resting her hip against his good leg. For the first time in her life, she found she liked someone telling her what to do.

"Pull your hair free." He lowered his voice. "This won't take long, but it's got to be just as it was in my thoughts."

She smiled and did what he suggested.

"Now unbutton that top all the way. And I'm not looking for broken ribs or bullet holes. All I want to look at is you, honey."

Her fingers fumbled as she moved down the buttons, but she didn't say a word. She only watched him. His eyes grew darker, his breathing faster.

When a two-inch opening of skin showed, she stopped and waited. He was studying her as if memorizing every part of her.

Finally, he raised his hand and dug his fingers into her hair. In an impatient jerk, he pulled her to him and kissed her quick and hard on her mouth already slightly bruised from his last kiss. "I can't get enough of the taste of you."

The next kiss was slower. He took his time until she moaned with pleasure, and she felt his smile against her lips. "You like that, do you?"

"Very much," she whispered back against his lips.

When he straightened her back in front of him, he said, "I don't ever want to hurt you, Tess. Not by something I say or do. Do you understand?"

She nodded, hesitant to say a word.

"Say the word," he ordered.

"Yes," she answered. "I understand."

"Close your eyes, honey, and don't open them until I tell you, too."

She smiled, realizing she had nothing to fear from this man.

Slowly, she felt him push the front of her shirt open, sliding the fabric off her shoulders. His hands started at her throat and moved slowly down until he covered her breasts tenderly, then she felt a kiss on each. As he caressed her, he whispered, "I'm going to make love to every part of your body when we finally find time, but while we're in the sheriff's office, I want you to remember the way I'm touching you right now. I may yell sometimes or not know the right words to say, but I'll always touch you this way."

She felt the caring in his touch.

"Raise your head, Tess."

She did what he asked.

When his lips touched hers, he gripped one breast tightly in his hand. Her cry of pleasure was caught in his mouth.

One long powerful kiss, and then he pulled away.

"More," he whispered against her ear.

She nodded and raised her head, but his mouth kissed between her breasts, then pulled away.

She sat, eyes still closed, as he buttoned up her pajama shirt. "You're the woman I've always looked for and never thought I'd find, Tess." His hand brushed along her side, which was now covered in flannel. "But I'm not a man who wants to play games. I want you in my life and in my bed."

She didn't move.

His hand slid beneath her shirt and spread out over her middle. "If you don't want this, if you don't crave my touch, we can stop now. Because if we go any further, I plan on loving you full out. So look at me and tell me only the truth."

Slowly, she opened her eyes and for the first time saw the uncertainty in his gaze. She didn't know the right words to say any more than he did. "I feel the same, Cody. I'll take all you've got and beg for more."

"And you'll love me," he said, as if testing her. "Only me."

"I will."

"Then you'll marry me."

"I will."

Cody pulled her against him and kissed her, then this hard, broken ranger laughed and pushed her back in the driver's seat. "Let's get this last report over with so we can get on with the rest of our lives."

She put the truck in gear and drove. For once she could think of nothing to say.

Cody broke the silence first. "We're going to burn those pj's when we get home."

She thought of arguing, but after thinking about it decided he might have a good idea.

CHAPTER THIRTY-FIVE

DAN HAD THE six prisoners locked away. The tall skinny guy turned out to be the most talkative. He claimed they were all threatened, that if they didn't go out and help get Thatcher, that the boss would crush them like ants. He said no one was going to kill the kid, they just wanted to talk to him about not testifying to anything he might have seen in the trailer.

Dan took their statements, but didn't believe a word of it. If they only wanted to talk, why did they all bring guns?

Thatcher hadn't checked in. Dan wasn't even sure the kid had his phone with him. He wouldn't be too hard to find. The sheriff knew all the places he hung out, but it bothered him that Thatcher hadn't called, if for no other reason than to check on Cody.

Another piece of the puzzle also bothered him. When he walked in his office, he went straight to his daughter. "Notice something not right about the gang we just arrested?"

"Yep. They all have two ears. Any chance one of the two who went to the hospital was missing an ear?"

"Nope. I counted."

She smiled at him. "Pop, Shorty One-Ear is

still out there. And if he's free, Thatcher is still in danger."

"Right." Dan looked around the room as if just noticing something was missing. "Where are your old and new boyfriends?"

"They both went home. Would you mind if I just gave up dating? It's too much effort. I could move back home and take care of you in your old age."

Before he could comment, his cell rang.

Brandi's name popped up as the caller.

He picked up on the second ring. "What's up, beautiful?"

Dan didn't miss the raised eyebrow his daughter gave him. Maybe it was time to explain the facts of life to her. Her pop wasn't a monk.

Brandi sounded like she was gulping down screams. "Dan, can you come quick? We can't find the little girl. She's disappeared."

"I'm on my way." He dropped the phone in his vest pocket and started shouting orders.

"Weathers, can you handle the jail? I've got an emergency."

"Got it," the deputy answered.

"Cody, can you stay around a little longer? We have another problem I may need your help with."

The ranger frowned, but nodded once and sat back down at the desk he'd been taking statements at for over three hours.

"I'll stay, too," Tess offered. "I'll go over and order lunch for everyone, then I'll call the hospital and keep you informed on the other two prisoners." She bounced up. "Oh, I can also search the files for each inmate's record."

Cody growled at her. "You running the office now, Tess?"

"Somebody needs to," she snapped back.

Dan didn't miss the way she patted his shoulder at the same time. "All right, Tess, you do all that, but go home first and get your uniform on."

"Will do," she said. "I can be changed and be back in time to pick up the order from the diner."

As Dan hurried out of the office, he heard Cody ask Lauren what time the justice of the peace came in.

He didn't have time to wonder why. He had to get to Brandi. The little girl was probably hiding in one of the dozen bedrooms in the old bed and breakfast. It wouldn't take long to find her, but he was worried about Brandi. She'd been so upset, like losing the child was bringing back all her pain from losing her daughter a little over a year ago.

He thought about his daughter and knew if he lost Lauren he'd probably never get over it. Loss like that doesn't pass; you just have to get through the pain. One of Brandi's songs played through his head. Her music was her way of coping. Her way of learning to breathe again.

When he headed up the steps, Brandi opened the door. Her beautiful eyes were full of tears. "We've searched everywhere. She's gone. Someone took her."

Dan put his arm around her and calmly asked for details. The Franklin sisters seemed even more upset than Brandi. No one had ever disappeared from their house.

They all went up to Brandi's room. The window leading out onto the roof was unlatched. One of the blankets on the bed was missing.

Fear moved over him. They started at the basement and searched every room, every cupboard, every drawer big enough to hold a child.

Nothing.

When Dan called in the report twenty minutes later, a terrible feeling washed over him. Someone had stolen the girl, and this time they'd make sure no one would ever find her.

Thatcher was the only one who'd seen the men in the trailer that day. Maybe he'd recognize one. But whoever took the child would either be out of the county by now, or hiding, waiting to get to Thatcher next.

In all his years as a sheriff, he'd never felt so helpless. There was always something he could do, but not this time. He had no leads. He didn't know what to tell the office to do even after he made the call.

"Pop?" Lauren said from the other end of the phone call. "Pop, what do we do?"

He was out of answers. Weathers had his hands full with the jail. Cody was too banged up to go hunting. Pearly was too old. Lauren was too young. Dan had to say something. "Call everyone you know and trust. We're going to have a manhunt that will cover this whole county, and we're going to find that little girl."

"Organize a manhunt," Lauren said, as if there was a manual for that.

"I can do that!" Dan heard Tess Adams yell. "Park rangers do that all the time when people are lost. We start at the site they were last known to be and spread out."

Dan tried to remember to breathe. "What do you need, Tess?"

"A map of the county. After Lauren calls, people will start coming in. I'll have a planned search organized."

Dan had been switched to speaker. "Lauren, pull the one off the wall in the courtroom. It should be big enough. I'll be there in ten minutes, and I want volunteers already signing up."

He hung up, took the time to carefully search for any clues in the bedroom and on the roof. It wouldn't have been impossible for the child to slip out the window, but there were no little footprints in the snow still on the roof. Only big ones. Probably a size twelve at least. A man's footprints.

Someone had carried the little girl out of the upstairs bedroom. She must have been wrapped in a blanket, and it had to have been before dawn because surely someone would have seen them otherwise.

He checked the area around the house. The walks had been cleared days ago, and no cars had driven into any of the slots out back. He found fresh footprints in the alley, but they disappeared at the street.

The only good news was that whoever took the child appeared to be moving away from the trailer park. With that direction, they would have had to cross either in front of the county offices or directly behind.

WHEN DAN STEPPED into his office, fifty volunteers waited for him. A few were using walkers and had to be given other duties, but most were ready and willing to work.

He went over each rule: stay within sight of each other; if you see fresh footprints, be careful about destroying any evidence. On and on he went through rules he'd only read in books and never had to put into practice.

They had no name to call the child and no picture to use, so the search would be silent.

"We're looking for two persons," Dan said as he stood in the middle of a crowd that had grown to a hundred. "One little girl, thin, brown hair, about five, and one short man, about five-four, with one ear missing."

When he stepped down, Tess took over. She was amazing. Every team had its area marked off on a map. The people in wheelchairs or walkers were photocopying extra maps and phone-number lists to call. Each team had a cell phone and a bottle of water. The ranchers were given instructions by phone to search everywhere on their ranches. A hundred cowhands were already in the saddle, moving across their camps and reporting back to headquarters.

Cody had called in every lawman he could find. Roads were closed in every direction until every vehicle was inspected.

Tim showed up looking hungover, but sober. He quickly informed everyone he had experience and would handle overall coordination of resources.

Dan stood in his office in front of everyone and hugged Brandi when she rushed in, announcing she was helping with the search.

"We'll find her," he whispered.

Then, he did something he thought he'd never do in public. He kissed Brandi right on the mouth in front of everyone. Then, without a word, he put on his hat and headed out to do his job.

CHAPTER THIRTY-SIX

THATCHER CLIMBED IN through the window and carefully set down his bundle. "We'll be safe here," he whispered.

He turned and locked the window. "You'd think the sheriff would be more careful about locks."

The little girl pushed the blanket away and stood smiling at him. "That was fun, That." She giggled at using his nickname twice. "Is this your house?"

"No. It belongs a friend of mine. He won't mind if we use it. You want to pop some popcorn and watch a movie?"

She nodded and followed him to the kitchen. "My mommy always let me have candy and popcorn together."

"Great. You look for the candy, and I'll pop the corn." He pointed to the big brown recliner. "You might find a jar over there."

Thatcher decided he'd get her settled with some cartoons and snacks, and then he'd call the sheriff. He'd lost his cell phone somewhere in the night when he'd been running, and the sheriff had his hands full of other problems right now. Brigman probably hadn't even noticed he was gone.

Thirty minutes later he tried to call the sheriff's office. Busy. He tried again and again. Every commercial, he'd use the landline on the lake house to dial the sheriff's office, and it was always busy.

Finally he left a message on Brigman's cell. "Sheriff, it's Thatcher. Me and the girl are safe. She's eaten all those little Baby Ruths you keep hidden beside the chair. Call me when you have time."

The little girl fell asleep on the couch, but Thatcher stayed on guard. He'd used his belt to make a sling for the little .22, and carried it on his back under Cody's big coat so she wouldn't see it. Now he pulled it out and rested the rifle over his legs.

Only, what were the chances Shorty would find him here? For the first time since he'd seen the drug guys counting money in the trailer, Thatcher felt safe.

CHAPTER THIRTY-SEVEN

AN HOUR INTO the manhunt, Lauren noticed Lucas pulling Tim O'Grady aside.

"I got an idea where to look. Want to go along with me?" he asked.

"I just sent notice out over half the state. I think I'll stay around and see what happens." Tim looked bothered that Lucas even asked.

"I'll go." Lauren had been close enough to overhear. She'd been answering phones all morning. She needed to break free for a while.

"Yeah, Lucas, take L with you," Tim said. "She's not needed around here."

Lucas looked at Lauren, silently pleading with her not to go. Both of them knew it would only irritate Tim.

"I'm going," she repeated, knowing he'd have to tell his plan to everyone around if he argued with her.

"Fine." He headed out without glancing back to see if she was following.

Some friend, she thought. She couldn't believe she'd spent years longing and wishing they were together.

Lauren hurried past the army of senior citizens taking calls. When she passed Miss Bees, she picked up the old golf club the former Phys Ed teacher used as a cane. "Mind if I borrow this?"

Miss Bees shook her head. "Bring it back and don't dent it. I'm down to three clubs."

"Promise." Lauren gripped what might serve as a weapon and ran to follow Lucas.

She expected Lucas to head for his dad's pickup or his fancy sports car, but he passed them both and headed straight for the town triangle. Folks had given up even imagining it as a town square. With Crossroads' luck, people would drive for miles to see the bandstand that never got finished sitting in the town triangle.

Lauren had to almost run to keep up with him.

"I talked to the foreman of this project half an hour ago," Lucas said as he hurried across the street. "He said several of his men were missing this morning. We found three in jail and another two passed out in their trucks. He told me about one guy, a chubby dude who always wore hats, even indoors. The short worker had dropped by to pick up his check a few days ago. Said he was moving on. The foreman might not have remembered him so clearly, except that the guy took time to tell him how he hated this town and everyone in it."

Lauren was interested. Short guy. Always wore a hat. It could be who they were looking for. Or not.

"Only the foreman says his old car is still parked out in the lot behind where they're building the grandstand or whatever it's going to be. The foreman asked me if I'd tell the sheriff to tow it, since the chubby guy doesn't work for him anymore. He complained that the car was probably worthless, and he'd have to pay for the towing."

"Someone's already checked every car in town," Lauren reported. "I heard Tess announce it."

"I know, but I plan to check this one again." He looked down at her. "You can go back if you want."

"No, I'll go. You might need backup."

They crossed through a wire fence into where all the workers' cars and trucks were parked along with extra lumber and equipment. Lauren thought all these sites made the town look ugly, but maybe soon the building of the new houses and the baseball courts and the town square would be finished, and Crossroads would shine.

As they began to move from car to car, looking in all the windows and checking the trunks to see if any were unlocked, Tim joined them. "I got to thinking," he said as he rushed up. "If you guys do find something, I want to be in on it."

Lucas looked happy to see him. "The workers said they'd search their own land, but I could tell the foreman didn't want to let any of his men off long enough to do the job right."

Lauren spotted an old car that looked like it had

been planted in one spot since the snow started. No tracks showed, coming or going.

All three moved closer in silence. Tim checked one side, looking in every window. Lucas checked the other. She moved to the trunk and froze. It wasn't completely closed.

They stood staring. Lucas reached down and slowly opened the trunk. Tim leaned back ready to fight.

As the sun melted into the trunk, a sleeping, chubby little man raised his head. He was dirty and obviously drugged up, and missing one ear.

Lauren raised her golf club. "You're under arrest."

Lucas and Tim didn't give him time to object. They each grabbed an arm and pulled him out. He fought and squealed like a pig all the way back to the office, but Lauren kept threatening him with the club, and her friends held him tight between them.

Pop was just stepping out of his car. He just stood staring, like they were a parade passing by. Finally, Tim yelled for help and Dan pulled out his handcuffs. By then most of the fight had gone out of the little man, and he cooperated.

Dan passed Shorty over to Cody to book and stood on his desk. "The hunt is officially over. Thatcher and the little girl are safe and warm. I want to think every one of you for your help."

Everyone shouted and hugged, then Ranger

Tess organized them all again to make sure everyone was notified that the hunt was over.

Lauren hugged her father, but he only used one arm. His other hand was holding on to the singer.

"Where is he?" Lauren whispered.

"Follow us home." He winked at his daughter, and for the first time in days, she no longer saw exhaustion in his eyes.

She gathered Tim and Lucas and did just that. By the time she walked in the door, Brandi had the little girl in her lap hugging her, and Thatcher was filling Pop in on details.

"I figured Shorty wouldn't be at a gunfight. He's a knife man. If most of the bums headed out to get me, it just made sense that Shorty would stay behind to find the kid. But, can you believe it, the town actually kept a secret. No one told Shorty where the little girl was. I was planning to leave her there, but she cried, saying she wanted to come with me." He smiled. "I have that effect on women of all ages."

Lauren shook her head, then broke down and kissed him just because he really was a hero.

Thatcher rubbed off her kiss. "Don't be doing that, Lauren. Near as I can see, you already got two boyfriends, and I don't aim to be the third."

"Thanks for letting me down easy," she said.

Thatcher straightened. "Yep, you're too old, Lauren, and Hailey's too young."

Everyone but him froze like an ice age passed by and missed him. "What's wrong?"

Dan's words broke the silence. "Who is Hailey?"

"I am," the little girl whispered. "That—" she pointed at Thatcher "—said if I talk, I can go back home."

Dan leaned down and smiled at her. "That's true."

Tim moved closer. "You're Hailey Davidson from Norman, Oklahoma, aren't you? Your mommy's been looking for you for four months. I read the report. Her ex took you just to get back at her for leaving him."

"He wasn't my real dad," Hailey whispered. "Mom says I don't have one."

Brandi lifted her up. "But you got a mommy, Hailey, and she loves you very much."

While everyone got organized, the singer simply rocked the child in her arms and sang to her softly.

Lauren swore she heard Brandi say, "Thank you, dear one, for letting me hold you for a while."

It was almost midnight when a patrol car led the way down to the Brigman home on the lake. Lauren stood in the shadows halfway up the hill, not wanting to be too close, unable to stay completely away.

She watched as a woman climbed out of the car

and ran to Brandi, who was still holding the little girl. Lauren couldn't hear the words, but she could see the joy. The mother hugged Brandi and Pop, then moved away, kissing on a child she'd thought she lost.

"You all right?" Lucas asked from the shadows behind Lauren as they watched the mother wave goodbye.

"I'm fine. You didn't have to stay with me."

"I know. I wanted to." He offered his hand. She took it, and they walked together back down the incline. "Thatcher would have wanted to see it, too, but the sheriff said to let him sleep."

"He lives a busy life." She laughed. "Pop says Thatcher's aging him double time. He'll be glad when the kid goes to college."

"You want to come out to the house tomorrow? Mom's starting the baking. We could help make tamales, then go for a ride. The weather's warming."

"Lucas, you don't have to invite me. Polly will be in tomorrow. We could stay around here."

Lucas stopped. "Polly can come, too. I've already invited Tim. Maybe it's time we all remembered we're friends."

She thought about it. Her world was shifting again. She was changing, growing. "All right. Friends. I'll bring Polly."

They walked on until they reached the deck. "Where's your dad going?" Lucas asked.

She looked out front and saw Pop walking toward his Jeep with his arm around the singer. "Oh, he's taking Brandi Malone home. She doesn't have a car. Pop's nice like that. It's part of his duty."

Lucas grinned. "Yeah, right."

They stood in the shadows, watching as Pop opened her side of the Jeep, then leaned in and kissed her before closing her door.

Lucas whispered, "Your pop takes his job very seriously. How about, in the line of duty, of course, you kiss me good-night?"

"Why not?" She moved into the arms of an old friend.

Her kiss was playful, leaving two friends feeling good, wanting more, but she pulled away. "Good night, Lucas."

"Good night, *mi cielo*."

Lauren shrugged and walked inside. Who knew, maybe one day she might be his sky, but for right now, she needed to find herself first.

CHAPTER THIRTY-EIGHT

DAN SAT ON the corner of the bed and watched Brandi tug off her beautiful blue boots.

"I love those boots," he said.

"Maybe I'll leave you one to remember me." She smiled as she circled around. "I can't believe we're alone for the whole night."

"What's left of it. It was almost two when I checked in, and we have to be out by ten."

"I don't care." She moved up, shoving her leg between his knees so her body could rest against him. "You're all mine, Sheriff."

She wrapped her arms around him and kissed him.

When he tugged her away, he said, "Put your foot on my knee, and I'll pull off those long socks."

She followed orders, and he took his time.

"I think I fell for you that first day when I helped you on with your boot. There was something about touching you. It felt so right."

While he was removing her socks, he decided to help her take everything off.

She spread out on top of the covers, beautiful and bare. He drank her in like fine wine, loving every ounce.

Neither of them talked. It seemed they'd been

talking for days and only had moments to touch. Now they made love like longtime lovers did, slow and easy, cherishing every part.

Then they cuddled close and slept until dawn. He woke her slowly, making her body hungry for him even before she turned loose of her dreams.

This time the loving came in a hurry. Both wanted more, as if they knew they were running out of time. When it ended, he caught her crying.

"What's wrong?"

"I'm just going to miss you, Dan."

He sat up. "Then stay."

"I can't. I have another gig in New Mexico."

"Then come back to me when it's finished."

She pulled the sheet over her and sat up beside him. "You knew from the first this was only going to be a wild love affair. No promises. No forever. We agreed. We'd walk away with a beautiful memory."

"I know I agreed. I even thought that was what I wanted, but it's not. I'm not a wild love affair kind of man. I'm a commitment, forever, kind of man. Don't leave me, Brandi. Saying I love you isn't half enough. I need you. I want you."

He climbed from the bed, knowing he was saying too much. She was right; they had agreed. A wild affair, nothing more. They'd both said they were not looking for love.

Brandi stood and began to dress. She'd cried

when the little girl left, but she'd said she was happy a mother found her child. She'd never told him, not once, that she wanted to stay or that she loved him. And now, he was making leaving so hard on her. On them both.

Dan dug his fingers through his hair. He was ruining what was between them. He should just enjoy the few days they had left. There would be years to miss her once she was gone.

Now wasn't the time to argue.

He moved behind her and gently pulled her against his chest. "Come back to bed, pretty lady. I didn't mean to make you mad or sad. How about we work on making you happy."

She turned in his arms and kissed him.

It took time, gently wooing, feather touches, but she finally warmed. Without a word he carried her back to bed. The loving this time was a sweet losing of himself in her arms.

This time, when she slept in his arms, he never stopped touching her, but she didn't wake. Finally, he drifted to sleep, breathing in the smell of her hair, feeling her warmth beside him. Hearing her little sighs of pleasure when he touched places where she loved to be touched.

Hours later when he woke to a maid knocking and yelling "Housekeeping!", Dan rolled over and found Brandi was gone.

He dressed and paid the bill, but he knew she

wasn't coming back. The clerk at the desk said she'd called a cab from the lobby.

He didn't try to call her cell. He didn't track down where she had the Franklin sisters ship her things. He didn't go looking for her.

Dan simply went back to Crossroads, Texas. Back to his life. Back to fishing and watching football and talking to his daughter when she had time between her friends and her new job in Lubbock.

A month went by. Almost Christmas now. No word from Brandi. No call. No text. No letter. Nothing had changed in his life except him.

She'd given him exactly what he'd wanted. A wild time with a beautiful lady. She'd given him a memory he'd carry with him to the grave.

Only she'd also given him a part of her that he'd miss every day until the last day left in this life. No one ever had or would love him like she did. Passionately. Freely.

Christmas passed, and Lauren came home and told him that her first collection of stories would be published in the spring.

Tim moved out of the lake house next door and went to New York with Polly. He said he needed to write in the city that never sleeps, and Polly just tagged along to party.

Dan worked. He fished. He watched football and reread a dozen books. He waited, but he didn't know for what.

No one consoled him. No one knew his heart had shattered.

Finally, one dark February morning, he came home for lunch and found Brandi sitting on the steps of his porch.

She stood when he walked up.

He fought the urge to run to her and swing her around, but he simply walked toward her slowly.

Dan wasn't sure his heart could take another hit.

"Why are you here?" he asked in his most official voice.

"I'm here to report a crime."

Her beautiful midnight curls were blowing around her face. Her cheeks were red from the cold, but he couldn't rush toward her. Not this time. She'd left him once, and once was all he could handle.

"What crime?"

She stared at him without smiling. "Someone stole my heart, and I want it back."

He took a step onto the porch. "Who?"

"You. I've tried my best to forget about it, but I can't. I never thought a man with honest eyes would steal. I drove two hundred miles out of my way to stop by and pick it back up."

"I'm not giving it back." He stood his ground.

"I'm not leaving without it."

"Fine. Come on in." He walked past her and

unlocked the door. Then he stormed in ahead of her, still doubting she'd follow.

For a few minutes he thought she wouldn't, then one tall, fancy blue boot almost hit him as it flew past him and slammed against the wall.

He turned. She was standing in the doorway. One boot still on. He'd tried all the words he knew to say to make her stay. He had none left.

Brandi took one step inside. "You helped me put a boot on once. You think you could help me take one off now?"

He knelt on one knee. She put her boot up, and his hand slid over her leg as he gently tugged it off.

"Turns out," she whispered as he tugged off the thick socks, "I'm not made for wild times either. If you're willing, we could start over. Maybe work on forever."

Dan stood. "I'm not giving back your heart, Brandi, but if you'll stay I'll give you mine."

"Fair enough, Sheriff."

Dan didn't bother to call in sick or tell Pearly where he was for the rest of the day. If she'd called and asked, he'd be tempted to say he was having a wild affair, and it looked like it might last the rest of his life.

LARGE PRINT
Thomas, Jodi.
Wild horse springs